SWIFT AND HAWK UNDERCOVER

LOGAN MACX

WALKER BOOKS

For Tally and Sharko

First published 2023 by Walker Books Ltd
87 Vauxhall Walk, London SE11 5HJ

2 4 6 8 10 9 7 5 3 1

Text © 2023 Edward Docx and Matthew Plampin
Cover illustration © 2023 Coke Navarro

The right of Edward Docx and Matthew Plampin to be identified as authors of this work has been asserted in accordance with the Copyright, Designs and Patents Act 1988

This book has been typeset in Roboto

Printed and bound by CPI Group (UK) Ltd, Croydon CR0 4YY

British Library Cataloguing in Publication Data:
a catalogue record for this book is available from the British Library

ISBN 978-1-4063-9494-8

www.walker.co.uk

MIX
Paper | Supporting responsible forestry
FSC® C171272

ec

CONTENTS

SWIFT AND HAWK TO THE RESCUE

*T*his was an emergency. Caleb Quinn and Zen Rafiq – codenamed Swift and Hawk – were strapped into the back of a specially converted Aston Martin, watching the British countryside race by at close to one hundred and seventy kilometres per hour. They were heading to a research facility in Cambridge, owned by the American robotics company SolTec. Some kind of cybersecurity breach had occurred, and their mission – Professor Clay had explained to them back in London – was "to stop an embarrassing mess from turning into a very public disaster".

Caleb and Zen both went to a specialist computing and technology school called the ARC Institute, which stood for AI, Robotics and Cybertech. A few months earlier, they'd been recruited into the Möbius Programme – a secretive organization run by Professor Clay, the ARC's deputy head teacher, that used the unique skills of the ARC's pupils to solve high-tech spy problems. Clay had personally taken them out of their morning classes and scrambled them into one of the ARC's prototype electric cars.

"Why are we helping SolTec, exactly?" Caleb had asked.

"It's a favour," Clay had replied. "Call for back-up if you need it. Mr Mitchell will get you there."

And it was Lance Mitchell who was now at the wheel of the car – weaving in and out of the regular motorway traffic with incredible precision, anticipating gaps and accelerating into empty lanes – all at heart-stopping speed. Mitch, as everyone called him, was the new head of security at the ARC Institute. Nearly two metres tall, white, with a square jaw and short dark hair, he'd been a US Navy SEAL and then a special agent with the CIA, before going freelance at the age of forty-seven.

The tyres squealed as the car flew across three lanes, racing down the hard shoulder. Caleb could not stop himself from wincing and grabbing at the dashboard. He glanced in the rear-view mirror; Zen was reading the briefing Clay had given them at the ARC, completely unconcerned.

"You know," he said, "I think it would be way better if this was a self-driving car."

Mitch grinned as he eased back into the middle lane between two lorries. "Welcome to old school ops, kid. Back in the day, we solved all our problems with gasoline and guns." He stood hard on the accelerator. "Let's give this baby some gas."

"It's an electric car, Mitch," Caleb said. "There is no gas."

"And your generation didn't solve any problems," said Zen from the back seat, without looking up. "You just made everything ten times worse."

Mitch shook his head. "You ARC kids … you're too smart for your own good."

He yanked at the wheel and dragged them down the outside of a luxury coach. The gap between it and the barrier was almost too tight – but they shot through before it could close any further.

"If this is how you handle our security," Caleb said, "I'd hate to see you on a reckless streak."

An even, synthesized voice spoke through the car's speakers. "Our journey would be seventeen minutes faster if we left at the next police ramp."

It was Sam, Caleb's artificial intelligence program. The name was short for Simulated Autonomous Medic; Sam had originally been coded by Caleb's dad, Patrick, as a medical AI, but Caleb had significantly upgraded and expanded him since his dad had passed away two years ago. Sam mostly interacted with the world via a special handset Caleb had made, which he'd called the Flex.

"This route leads through the back of a farm," Sam continued, "and then along some very minor roads. But we would avoid a considerable amount of congestion ahead."

"Let's do it," Caleb said. "We need all the time we can get."

Mitch was now tailgating a plumber's van with some intensity. "Please don't tell me that we're going to let that Alexa thing of yours give us directions."

"Be nice, Mitch," Caleb said. "Sam is a thousand times more sophisticated than Alexa and Siri put together."

"The ramp is five hundred metres ahead," the AI said. "Just off the hard shoulder."

The car cut through a gap in the traffic, picking up speed.

"Given the weight of this car and its occupants," Sam said, "we will need to hit the ramp at an angle of twenty degrees off-centre and a velocity of one hundred and twenty-seven kilometres per hour to clear the fence and land safely on the track on the far side."

"What?" Mitch exclaimed. "Who said anything about jumping a *fence*?"

"Come on, Mitch," said Zen, putting the Möbius briefing aside. "I thought we were doing this old school."

"You guys have no idea what it takes to pull off a car jump so that we don't roll and crash," said Mitch through gritted teeth. *"No idea."*

"You are quite heavy for your height and age, Mr Mitchell," said Sam. "We will need to accelerate if we are to clear the fence and make the track."

"I won't take that personally..." Mitch said. "OK, hold on. Here we go."

Caleb was pushed back in his seat as the car sped towards the small ramp of the police-only vantage point, off to the side of the hard shoulder. They soared into the air, flying over the low fence at the edge of the motorway. Caleb gripped the ceiling handle above his head – the car was surely going to crash into the field beyond. But then a farm track appeared, and half a second later they were bumping down again, bouncing forward, careening from side to side.

Mitch hit the accelerator and fought with the wheel, trying to bring the car under some kind of control without sliding into a nearby ditch.

"Nice!" Caleb cried.

"You've got some serious driving skills, Mitch!" said Zen.

"I'm getting too old for this," muttered the security chief. "Now what, Sam?"

"Proceed straight past those trees ahead," the AI replied. "Then follow the dirt track to the right – among the farm buildings that you will see in roughly thirty seconds' time."

The sleek black car shot by a coppice of trees and jolted over a cattle grid into a farmyard. Just as they rounded the corner of a barn, however, a tractor appeared, driving directly towards them with prongs lowered. Caleb ducked in his seat, certain they were going to be impaled. Somehow, though, Mitch was already executing a handbrake turn – sending them sliding through a towering heap of … horse manure.

For a moment, everything went dark – then the wipers came on, clearing wide crescents in the muck. Caleb looked out through the one-way glass. The farmer was gazing down from his tractor with pure astonishment at what must have looked to him like a cross between a stealth bomber and some of the fastest travelling horse dung in the world.

"Great route, Sam," said Mitch. "Really great."

"Is that sarcasm, Mr Mitchell? Should I engage my sarcasm-learning subroutine, Caleb?"

"Not right now," Caleb said. "We need some new directions."

The AI guided them out of the farmyard and along a series of narrow, twisty lanes. A couple of minutes later, they reached a main road heading into the centre of Cambridge. Mitch accelerated again, tearing through the last few kilometres before swerving deftly across a busy roundabout, to a chorus of angry horns. Shortly afterwards, the car was racing alongside a perimeter fence.

"I think this is the SolTec facility," said Zen, peering through her filth-splattered window.

"That is correct, Zen," said Sam. "The entry road is on the left. I am detecting a security gate. Should I—"

"Hack it, Sam," Caleb told him, gripping the dashboard as Mitch threw them into a screeching left-hand turn. "Get us in."

They whizzed along a short driveway as the gate slid open ahead. The gap was only just wide enough, but Mitch squeezed them through without slowing down. A large white-and-blue sign flashed by, saying **SOLTEC: ROBOTICS FOR TOMORROW**.

Caleb saw Zen roll her eyes. "Nice slogan," she said. "Totally original."

"More sarcasm there, Sam," Mitch said with a grin. "You're going to have to learn it someday. Might be the defining human characteristic."

The manure-plastered car skidded to a halt in front of the compound's main building, reflected in the dark, mirrored glass that covered its facade. A sandy-haired man with a goatee, rimless glasses and a shiny black

SolTec shirt was standing by the front entrance. He'd been talking into a smartphone but was now staring at them in utter mystification.

"I'm guessing he's the welcoming committee," said Caleb.

"Facial scans indicate that he is Dr Aidan Lennox," said Sam, "the director of this facility."

Mitch turned off the engine, straightened his black tie and adjusted the holster under his jacket. "Stay close, you two," he said. "Let me handle this."

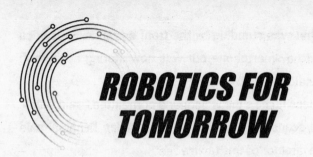

ROBOTICS FOR TOMORROW

*T*hey all got out of the car. The smell of manure was terrible; lumps of it were sliding off the bonnet and doors and plopping steamily onto the tarmac. Caleb had to admit – it wasn't quite the ice-cool super-spy entrance he'd been hoping for.

"Tell me you're not..." Dr Lennox began in an American accent, lowering his phone. "Tell me you're not the people Tilda Clay sent."

Mitch walked around the car. "Dr Lennox," he said, "I'm Lance Mitchell, head of security at the ARC Institute. And these two here are Caleb and Zen."

Lennox's disbelief was turning to anger. He looked over Zen, with her denim jacket and neon-blue trainers; and then Caleb, with his olive-green hoodie with orange piranhas swimming down the sleeves.

"OK," he said, "I knew there'd be kids – Clay's prodigies or whatever they are, from her special programme. But I thought there'd be a team of technicians as well. A whole truckload of equipment. You know – *professionals*." He glanced past them, towards the gate. "Are you honestly all that's coming?"

"Yep," said Caleb. "We're it."

He slid the Flex from his pocket and wrapped it around his wrist. Although it looked like an ordinary smartphone, this handset was loaded with extra features and capabilities – and it had a unique flex-tech shell, which meant it could be bent or stretched to almost any shape. Until recently, he'd operated it using a set of self-programmed apps, but an emergency upgrade to Sam meant that he could now do everything via the AI instead. He stepped away from the stinking car, taking in the compound. Across the car park, a crowd of thirty or so SolTec employees were talking to one another in low, nervous voices; they seemed to have just been evacuated from the buildings.

Mitch motioned for Caleb and Zen to stay put and walked over to Lennox; he was almost a head taller than the SolTec director.

"What d'you know about SolTec, Zen?" Caleb asked in a low voice.

Zen was a robotics specialist, as good with ultra-sophisticated hardware as Caleb was with software; her particular expertise was in building incredible insect-sized microbots.

"It's one of the world's major robotics companies," she said. "This is its main research and development centre. Most of it is underground." She refastened the band at the end of her black plait. "Try reading the briefing next time, Caleb."

"Sorry, Zen," he retorted, "but I was finding the experience of practically breaking the land speed record on the M11 just a *little* bit distracting – not to mention Sam's detour through that pile of—"

Zen nudged him in the ribs to shut him up, nodding towards where Mitch and Lennox were now talking. They moved closer to listen.

"Here's what we've been told," Mitch said matter-of-factly. "You've experienced a serious cybersecurity breach and your entire facility is in meltdown. Every in-house countermeasure has failed. The last thing SolTec needs is this mess going public and the UK authorities getting involved – so you called your old friend Tilda Clay to see if there might be another way of dealing with it."

"It's a virus, right?" Caleb chipped in. "Someone's got past your firewalls – released something really nasty into your system?"

Lennox pinched the bridge of his nose. "If you think," he began, "that I'm going to let a pair of kids and their ... their babysitter, who have just shown up in a car covered in horse dung, have full access to this facility, to our most confidential research, then you must be out of your—"

"Call Professor Clay," Mitch interrupted. He nodded at the phone in Lennox's hand. "She'll clarify the situation for you."

Lennox glared at him for a moment. Then he tapped the phone a couple of times, raised it to his ear and stalked off into the car park until he was out of earshot.

Caleb glanced over at Zen. "Think we can justify tapping this?" he murmured.

"One hundred per cent," she replied. "Can you find the signal, Sam?"

"Of course, Zen," the AI said. "Patching it through."

Lennox's voice came out of the Flex's speaker, just loud enough for Caleb and Zen to hear.

"Is this some kind of joke, Tilda? We're in the middle of a major crisis here. I ask for your top operatives and this is what you send me? How old are these two, anyway? Twelve? Thirteen?"

Mitch gave Caleb a sideways look, realizing at once what was going on. The ARC security chief put his hands in his pockets and sighed; then he leaned in closer, angling his head to listen.

Professor Clay came on the line. She sounded distinctly unimpressed. "I don't *joke*, Aiden. You told me that you had an urgent situation your own people couldn't handle. Caleb and Zen are extremely resourceful, with a combined skill set that is perfectly matched to your problem. They've proved themselves before now, believe me."

There was a short silence. Lennox paced in a circle, trying to absorb what he'd been told, while gazing up at the main building with increasing anxiety.

"Jeez," said Caleb. "He looks like he's expecting it to burst into flames."

Zen was watching the SolTec director closely. "This can't be good, Caleb."

"I need *complete secrecy*," Lennox hissed. "You know that, right? I can't have the – the local police or fire department or anyone else going into the facility. The SolTec board would have my head on a stick. There are things that—"

"You can trust the Möbius Programme, Aiden," Clay interrupted. "And remember – if we fix this, you owe me."

With that she hung up. Lennox frowned at his phone; then he put in it his pocket, turned back towards them and nodded. He was going to let them in.

"Nice one, Professor Clay," said Caleb softly. "Very clarifying."

A faint half-smile crossed Zen's face. "She can be pretty persuasive."

They were led quickly through the entrance of the main building into a wide, empty atrium with a silvery tree standing in its centre. Every surface had the smooth shine of polished glass. Massive screens were streaming films of sophisticated robots working in hospitals, chopping vegetables, or lifting girders on construction sites. The SolTec logo – a stylized copper sun – popped up repeatedly, along with the *Robotics for Tomorrow* slogan.

"Here's the deal," said Lennox, speaking directly to Caleb and Zen for the first time. "Tilda Clay is someone I have a lot of respect for. She speaks highly of you two, so I'm prepared to give you a shot. The clock's really ticking, OK?" He handed Mitch a security keycard. "This will get you into a couple of the restricted levels. That's where—"

Something changed in the atrium. Caleb looked around. The screens were freezing up; directly above them, a film of a robotic hand picking a daisy began to flicker backwards and forwards.

"What's going on, Sam?" Caleb whispered. "You getting anything?"

"I am, Caleb," the AI responded. "I'm afraid the fail-safes are giving out and a full system collapse is underway. There is a seventy-five per cent probability that SolTec has been infected by some kind of advanced multipartite malware. It is attempting a full takeover, probably by rewriting the codebase."

A familiar, determined look had appeared on Zen's face. "We need to get to the server farm," she said. "Right now."

Caleb turned to Lennox. "That'll be somewhere underground, won't it – at the base of the building?"

The director nodded, striding off towards a row of elevator doors. "The lowest level," he said. "Minus six."

Mitch hung back. "What can we expect down there, Dr Lennox? These two are my responsibility. I need to know exactly what we're getting ourselves into."

"It's a software breach, Mr Mitchell." Lennox hesitated. "There have been some … odd reports from those who were down in the labs. But we operate strict containment procedures in this facility. As long as you go directly to the server farms, there shouldn't be a problem."

"Don't worry, Mitch," said Caleb. "Sam and I have already taken a look at SolTec's operating system. And Zen knows basically everything there is to know about robotics. We've got this."

Lennox was blinking in alarm. "Who is *Sam*, precisely? And what do you mean by *taken a look*?"

Mitch ignored him. "OK, smart guy," he said to Caleb, touching the keycard against a security panel. "But I go first, you hear? Just in case."

A set of doors opened and Mitch stepped into a lift that was as immaculate as the lobby, with another screen filling its rear wall. Caleb and Zen followed him in – but Lennox stayed behind in the atrium.

"Aren't you coming, Dr Lennox?" Mitch asked.

"Ah, no," said the SolTec director, taking a small step backwards. "I believe I'll remain up here."

Caleb and Zen exchanged a glance.

"Don't you want to see what's going on?" said Mitch, a note of suspicion entering his voice.

"No, my duty lies with the staff. I want regular updates, though – a full account of everything you do."

"We really have to get moving," Zen said.

Mitch nodded and pressed the button for level minus six. "Probably for the best," he muttered as the doors closed with a slight *swoosh*. "I don't think Dr Lennox would've been a whole lot of use."

Caleb couldn't help grinning with excitement as the lift began to descend. He met Zen's eye again. She smiled back at him; she was clearly feeling it too. This was it. Swift and Hawk were back in action.

All of a sudden, the lift jerked to a halt. The screen went blank, the light panel overhead flickered and a low creak echoed through the shaft below them.

"We have stopped between levels minus three and minus four," Sam reported. "I don't think this lift will travel any further. The virus has jammed it somehow."

"It's deliberately blocking our path," Caleb said.

"To slow us down?" Zen asked. "To stop us getting to the server farm in time?"

"Yep." Caleb let out a low whistle. "Whoever wrote it really knows what they're doing."

"Hey, Mitch," said Zen, "can we get the doors open?"

"We can try." Mitch stepped up to the lift doors and began to force them apart. A tiny crack soon appeared, letting in the wail of an electronic alarm. Zen and Caleb went to help and together they widened the gap a little more.

Directly in front of them was the concrete wall of the lift shaft – but by their feet was an opening, perhaps fifty centimetres high, looking out at ceiling level into another large lobby. The room was bathed in the deep red glow of emergency lighting. Its smart modern furniture had been knocked out of place, as if by a crowd of fleeing people. Papers were scattered across the floor, along with a couple of discarded lab coats, a smashed tablet and a single box-fresh trainer.

"The virus will be continuing its takeover," Sam informed them. "We need to hurry."

"Let's find the stairs," Zen said. "Get to level minus six."

"All right." Mitch grunted as he pushed at the doors. "I'll climb down. Then you can—"

But Zen was already ducking through the opening, dangling briefly from the edge of the lift, then dropping into the lobby below.

"I said I go first," Mitch called after her.

"She does stuff like that," Caleb told him. "You'll get used to it."

They went after Zen. Mitch landed heavily, stumbling a little on the shiny floor.

"Where are we, Sam?" Caleb asked. "Can you pull up any plans of this place?"

"I have the basic schematics from SolTec's central archive," Sam answered. "This level is set aside for prototype testing. There are three stairwells that can be used to gain access to the server farm. The closest can be reached via the corridor directly ahead of you."

Zen was walking quickly towards this corridor when there was a movement to her left, behind an observation window. A horrible, grating whine started up – and just inside the corridor, a circular sawblade sliced through a sealed laboratory door in a dazzling spray of sparks.

Mitch drew his pistol at once, flicking off the safety catch with his thumb. "What the heck is *that*?"

The door crashed forward, cut off its hinges, and a construction robot like the ones in the films upstairs lumbered into view. It had no head to speak of, just three enormous arms bristling with industrial saws, drills and pile-drivers, and a set of short insectoid legs. It angled itself towards them, a cluster of LEDs at the top of its torso turning from yellow to red.

"It's scanning us," said Zen. "I think it's getting ready to—"

Abruptly, the robot charged at her, scuttling forward into the lobby. Zen dived to the side, just managing to avoid its path. The machine spun about as it passed, swiping at her with its circular saw and chopping a low black leather sofa neatly in half.

Mitch was levelling his pistol. "Zen!" he yelled. "Where do I shoot this thing?"

"Legs – go for the legs!"

The shots were deafening – five of them, fired so quickly the sounds blurred together. The robot pitched to the side, one of its legs blown clean off, servos straining as it tried to keep its balance.

Something zipped by close to Caleb's head, flashing in the red gloom like a tiny silver hummingbird.

"Beetlebat!" he cried.

Beetlebat was one of the many powerful miniature robots Zen had built back in the ARC tower, and her personal favourite. It looked like a metallic beetle with bat wings and a twisting mouse-like tail, and it had already helped them out of several hair-raising situations.

Across the lobby, Zen had jumped onto a sleek reception desk. She whistled one of Beetlebat's special commands – two short, high notes – and pointed at the stricken construction robot, providing a homing signal with a microdevice fitted on her forefinger. Beetlebat swept in, landed beside the robot's LED cluster and attached its mandibles to a protruding wire, which it then pulled loose as it flew upwards. The machine jolted to a complete stop and clanged down to the floor.

Zen's bot flew back to her shoulder. "Good work, girl," she said, as it folded in its wings. Then she hopped off the desk and looked over at Caleb. "Come on – we've got to get to the stairs."

"Agreed."

Caleb stepped around the fallen robot and they set off together into the corridor ahead.

Mitch was only a few paces behind, his pistol still at the ready. "Why did it attack us like that?" he asked. "Why did it try to…"

His voice trailed off as they advanced. There were observation windows on either side, facing into several different laboratories and testing zones. Every robot they could see was going haywire: thrashing around their enclosures, pounding against doors and walls, destroying anything within reach. All of the rooms were soundproofed – meaning that this mass robotic frenzy was eerily silent.

"OK," said Zen. "This is officially terrifying."

Mitch's mouth was hanging open. "What … what is going on here?"

"It's the virus," said Caleb. "This is what it was written to do. It's been replacing the code that handles the standard operating parameters for these robots. It's turning them into a load of killing machines." He watched something roughly L-shaped, striped with luminous yellow safety paint, bash away at one of the windows with the huge adjustable wrench it had for an arm. "Sooner or later, they're going to break out of there. And then they'll go for us just like that other one did."

Zen frowned. "Imagine doing this deliberately."

Mitch looked from Caleb to Zen. "So ... how do we stop it?"

"We have to get to the servers before the codebase is completely rewritten," Caleb told him. "Then we can isolate the virus. Perform a hard reset of the whole system. Force these things to crash."

Zen was nodding. "That should work."

"Why didn't SolTec try this?" Mitch asked.

"It's kind of a last resort," Zen explained. "It'll trash all the bots' software. Could do some permanent damage. But it's the only chance we've got left."

"Get Lennox on the line," said Mitch. "Let's see what he thinks."

"I'm afraid there is no signal," Sam told him. "We cannot contact the surface. This may be due to the virus. If it does manage to rewrite the codebase, SolTec's robots will effectively become autonomous. We will be locked out – unable to control or influence them. The machines will be guided only by their brutal new programming."

Caleb shook his head. "Killer robots on the rampage. Not what any of us expected when we got up this morning."

Mitch was cursing under his breath.

"There's a lot SolTec aren't telling us," Zen said, gesturing towards the windows. "These models are beyond anything they've made public. Way more advanced." Her lip curled. "I guess *Robotics for Tomorrow* was right after all."

Mitch fished a pencil flashlight from his pocket and attached it to his gun. "Hard reset it is," he said. "How long have we got, Sam?"

"It is difficult to be precise, Mr Mitchell," the AI replied, "but—"

"Call me Mitch."

"It is difficult to be precise, Mitch, but I would estimate that the original codebase will be gone in no more than four minutes and thirty-two seconds."

The Möbius team looked at one another. Then all at once they started to run.

SECRETS OF SOLTEC

*T*he stairwell was dark, its painted concrete steps glittering with broken glass. Mitch's torchlight cast harsh diagonal shadows across the walls as they raced down. After only one floor, however, their way was blocked by a heap of rubble.

"The wall's been blasted in," Mitch said. "Looks like some kind of high explosive."

"High *explosive*?" said Caleb. "But how—"

"We can get across this level," said Zen. "There'll be another stairwell on the other side."

They looked around the landing. The door to level minus five had been split apart by a length of twisted steel.

"I've got a *really* bad feeling about this," Caleb said, as they picked their way through the shards.

"I don't want to add to your alarm, Caleb," said Sam, "but there is something unusual about the schematics for this level. It has been designed for live-fire testing."

Caleb swallowed. "Wait, doesn't that mean..."

"Guns," said Mitch grimly. "It means guns."

The splintered door led them into a vast open space, like

an underground sports hall, but lit with red emergency lights and hazed with bitter smoke. There were heavy barricades at one end, reinforcing what looked like an observation room. The main floor was as big as a football pitch. It was dotted with obstacles – low walls, shallow pits, various ramps and slopes – and the burned-out wrecks of half a dozen armoured vehicles.

In a flat central area were two SolTec robots. Both were motionless, like they had powered down. One was the size of a minibus – a hulking humanoid torso bolted to some kind of tank. The other was more lightweight, built like an outsized greyhound, but with six multi-articulated legs that were folded up beneath it. They were made from the same shiny, dark green metal, with the SolTec sun emblazoned on their sides.

Almost as soon as Caleb noticed them the two robots came to life. The hound bot rose from its haunches, LEDs winking on, while the tank bot rotated on its chassis, sweeping a laser sight around the cavernous room. It located the Möbius team straight away. A panel on its shoulder slid back and a minigun clicked out, its long, cylindrical barrel already beginning to spin.

"RUN!" Mitch yelled.

Nearby, down a short slope, was an armour-plated barrier. They dived behind it at the last second, throwing themselves to the floor. The burst of minigun fire was unbelievably loud – a shrill, mechanical roar. Hundreds upon hundreds of bullets tore over them, shredding parts of the barrier and pounding the far walls to powder.

Eventually, it stopped, the terrible gun whirring down again.

"This is why that Lennox creep didn't want to let us in," said Zen angrily. "These are combat bots – automated soldiers. Which are *totally* illegal."

Caleb tried to rub the concrete dust from his eyes. "And if the virus completes its takeover, they'll basically be unstoppable."

"How many of them are there?" Mitch panted. "In the whole facility, I mean."

"The Flex's sensor readings suggest that eight models are operative at present," Sam told him. "There may be more in storage."

"Eight," Mitch repeated. "Good god."

No one said anything for a couple of seconds. They were all thinking the same thing: if just one of these combat bots got out onto the streets of Cambridge, an elaborate cyberattack would quickly turn into a massacre.

"Enemy combatants," announced a lifeless, synthesized voice. "Step forward with your hands raised. You will be treated in accordance with the Geneva Convention."

"Not sure I buy that," said Mitch.

"It's an automated message," Caleb whispered. "If we leave cover, they'll annihilate us."

The trundle of caterpillar tracks could be heard, along with the faint *tap-tap* of metallic feet. They were being flanked. Caleb racked his brain. He had to come up with something – fast. He reached for the Flex, detaching one of the half-dozen multi-purpose studs that were fitted into its shell. These could be used as trackers, or bugs for listening in – or powerful remote speakers.

"Sam," he said, "on my mark, run a *Terrorform* audio file through this stud at maximum volume. The Bulwark's railgun should do it."

"Very well, Caleb."

Terrorform was an open-world sci-fi video game that Caleb and Sam had made together – and the Bulwark's railgun was one of the most devastating weapons it contained. Caleb rolled the stud between his fingertips, shaping the mouldable flex-tech into a hard ball about the size of a pea. A thick cloud of dust was drifting through the chamber, blown loose by the minigun. He flicked the stud into it, sending the flex-tech ball bouncing off behind the combat bots.

Beside him, Zen had risen to a crouch. She'd tucked the jade necklace she always wore inside her T-shirt and was peering through a bullet hole in the barrier, towards the observation room.

"Someone's in there," she said.

Caleb stared at her. "Is it one of SolTec's people? Are they trapped?"

"No ... I don't think so," Zen replied. "I've got a feeling this is important. Think you could run that audio file now?"

"Do it, Sam," said Caleb.

A huge, zapping *thud* came from the other side of the live-fire zone – the report from a Bulwark's railgun, almost as loud as real life. Immediately, the two combat bots spun around and opened up with miniguns and micro-missiles. Massive chunks were blasted out of the floor and walls, releasing a fresh cascade of dust and debris.

"I'll catch you guys later," Zen yelled over the noise. "Don't do anything stupid."

She sprang forward, running around the end of the barrier. Without thinking, Caleb reached out to stop her, nearly rising to stand himself – but Mitch pulled him back.

Zen was heading for a large vent in the wall, just next to the observation room. It had been damaged, the grille hanging loose. As Caleb and Mitch watched, she slipped into it and disappeared.

"Wonderful," shouted Mitch, wincing with annoyance. "That kid is *impossible* to guard." He glanced at Caleb anxiously. "She can take care of herself, right?"

"Yeah," Caleb answered. "Better than anyone else I know."

"Then I guess we'll find her later. We have to get down to the server farm. These things have got to be stopped."

They looked along the barrier. An emergency exit could be seen about thirty metres away, in the opposite direction to the observation room.

"Is that a stairwell, Sam?"

"It is, Caleb. The Flex stud is still operational. Should I continue to run *Terrorform* audio files through it?"

"Play anything," Caleb told him. "Monsters. Explosions. Just keep it loud!"

A series of booms, bangs and strange alien howls began, followed by the thunderous, real-world sounds of the combat bots' weaponry. Caleb and Mitch ran for the exit, staying in cover as much as they could. The door was sealed with some kind of electronic lock. Mitch took aim with his pistol as they approached, firing four precise shots around the handle to destroy the mechanism, then kicking it with all his strength. It burst open and they ran out together onto another dark landing.

"How far, Sam?" Caleb asked.

"Ninety-eight metres. I estimate that the codebase will be completely rewritten in two point three two minutes. Caleb, we may be too late."

"At times like these, Sam," said Caleb as he started down the steps, "it's very important that we stay positive. Remind me to talk to you about optimism."

The door at the bottom of the stairwell was standing ajar, luckily; Caleb barged through, moving as fast as he could. Beyond was another open level, this time filled entirely with server stacks. It was like a maze with walls four metres high. There was no lighting at all, but countless LEDs were scattered along the server fronts, tracing out the shape of the rows. Sam lit up the Flex's screen, illuminating a strip of the grey concrete floor. Lines of various different colours had been painted on it, running off into the maze, to guide SolTec's engineers to certain areas.

"Where do we need to be?"

"The blue zone, Caleb. There is an access terminal in a booth at the end of stack 45-3C. Turn left. Twelve metres. Then turn right and head for the central avenue."

Caleb looked behind him. Mitch was a few steps back, the beam from his gun slicing through the darkness as he checked the huge room. Caleb ran on, skidding around a corner, sprinting for a stretch, then skidding again. He reached a small, glass-walled cubicle, inside which a single computer terminal had been built into a desk. Three screens were set up in front of it, the same warning message blinking on each: **SERVER INACCESSIBLE – PLEASE WAIT**.

"Caleb," said Sam, "we now have one minute until the codebase is entirely replaced." The AI simulated a hesitation; he lightened his tone. "But we are an effective team. We have worked well together in numerous high-stress situations. We can do this."

"Better," Caleb panted, rushing up to the terminal. He put the Flex on the desk. A second later, Sam got into the SolTec system, and dense lines of code began to stream across the three screens. "OK, let's search for all the usual malware signature patterns. Anything that's been registered."

"There is nothing obvious, Caleb. The virus is writing directly over the codebase. All behavioural inhibitors are gone. In thirty-eight seconds, there will be nothing left of the original system."

Caleb sat at the desk and flexed his fingers. "All right, Sam, dive deep. Get me whatever's left of SolTec's code. Let's fix this mess."

"On-screen now. We are down to the last two hundred and nine root directories. One hundred and ninety-six. One hundred and eighty-two."

"If we can't identify the virus, then let me try one of my own. See if we can counter-hack."

Mitch arrived at the entrance of the booth. "You on top of this?"

"Getting there," replied Caleb without looking around, his fingertips rattling against the terminal keyboard. "Although, I've got to say—"

A sudden, crunching impact made him leap clean out of his chair with a shout. To his left, a spurt of machine-gun fire had etched a dense spiderweb pattern across the reinforced safety glass. Through it, he could see an ominous black shape moving among the server stacks.

"Combat bot from upstairs," Mitch said. "Must have got wise to your little trick. Sit tight. I'll deal with it."

It was the smaller model, the six-legged greyhound, and it was closing in rapidly – running into the glass as hard as it could, like a self-propelled battering ram. There was a horrible crack, and a large section of the wall shifted, tilting inwards. Mitch leaned out of the booth and fired his pistol twice at close range, the muzzle flare lighting up the stacks that towered around them. This robot didn't have any weak spots, though, and his bullets zinged away uselessly.

"One hundred and four directories, Caleb," said Sam. "We're almost out of time."

Caleb forced himself to sit down again and ignore the bot that was now retreating among the stacks, lining itself up for another charge.

"We're not going to make it," Caleb said, typing furiously. "This virus is moving too fast."

"What do you advise?"

"I'm sending you a file. Put it in the very last directory. We're going to set a trap."

In five seconds flat, Caleb put together a fake command file, indistinguishable from the real thing, but with a new instruction added at the end. When this was done, he sent it over to Sam – just as the combat bot leaned back on its haunches, preparing to attack. The AI navigated the failing computer system with incredible speed, placing the fake file inside the final SolTec directory.

Caleb stayed completely still, his fingers suspended a centimetre above the keyboard.

The hound bot lowered its blunt, shovel-shaped head and surged forward.

All at once, the streaming numbers on the screens froze; the power was restored, strip lights snapping on throughout the server farm, and the charging robot jerked to a halt only metres from the booth, its curved metal feet scraping on the floor.

"The virus is contained, Caleb," said Sam. "I have executed a hard reset. What remains of the SolTec system is going into full shutdown. Your trap worked."

Caleb looked through the cracked window. The hound bot was folding in on itself, packing away its guns and its battering-ram head – deactivating.

Mitch switched off his torch, ejected an empty magazine

from his pistol, and held up his hand for a high five. "Caleb Quinn," he said, as their palms smacked together. "Tech wizard and all-round genius. What did you do?"

Caleb breathed out slowly; then he spun around on his chair. "I wrote in a fake command. The virus couldn't tell it apart from the rest of the directory. I ordered it to keep on repeating its previous action – replace a file, delete it, replace it, on an endless loop."

Mitched chuckled. "I'm just going to pretend I understood all of that," he said. "Come on, kid, let's get out of here. This is *way* beyond my pay grade."

Caleb retrieved the Flex and got up. "We've got to find out what's happened to Zen."

"Yeah," the security chief replied, holstering his gun. "That's top of the list."

They left the booth and started along the main aisle of the server farm.

"Caleb," said Sam, "I am getting a strange reading from the combat robots."

"Reading?" Caleb furrowed his brow. "What do you mean? They're deactivated, aren't they?"

"It seems to be a countdown." The AI paused, as if making a calculation. "Caleb, I think that you should run."

THE SABOTEUR

The ventilation shaft was just big enough for Zen to crawl down. After a couple of turns and short climbs, she was brought to the back of the observation room. Through a steel grille, she could see the figure she'd spotted earlier.

This person, a young man, was definitely *not* with SolTec. He wore close-fitting black clothes with a hood, face mask and gloves, and was standing at the broad windows with a smartphone in his hands. Zen realized that he was filming the combat bots as they blasted away uselessly at Caleb's *Terrorform* sound effects.

He was involved in the cyberattack – Zen was certain of it. Her hacking skills weren't as advanced as Caleb's, but she knew that actually breaking into the place you were targeting and introducing the virus directly into their systems made it much more difficult to trace where in the world the attack had come from. And of course – provided you escaped – it would be next to impossible for anyone to track you down afterwards. It was just *extremely* risky.

Zen eased off the grille and crept into the observation

room, trying to get as close as she could without being seen. Suddenly, however, the tank bot's minigun raked across the windows. Even heavy-duty bulletproof glass couldn't take this kind of punishment. The panes exploded inwards, along with a large part of their concrete frame. Zen and the saboteur spun about, crouching low and shielding their heads.

When Zen straightened up again a few moments later, the saboteur was facing her. He was barely more than a silhouette in the thick, choking dust. But there they stood – frozen for a second, staring at each other.

The saboteur turned abruptly and ran for an exit at the back of the room. Instinctively, Zen followed. She sprinted down a passageway until she came to the base of a narrow ladder. It had been fitted to the side of an unlit shaft that led into the facility above. Zen could hear the saboteur in the shadows overhead. Gripping the cold metal rungs, she began to climb.

A minute later, Zen emerged from a hatch onto a low roof, one storey up, around the back of the main SolTec building. A dusty, black-clad figure was away to the left, scaling a drainpipe. She took a breath and started after him.

Just as she reached the top of the drainpipe, the saboteur leaped off the far end of the building, windmilling his arms, towards a tall bank of scaffolding outside the SolTec perimeter fence. The gap was five metres wide at least, but he made it, grabbing onto a jutting pole and disappearing behind a curtain of plastic orange netting.

Zen was a dedicated athlete with a shelf-load of trophies back in her room at the ARC. She wasn't going to let this saboteur out-jump her. She bounced on her toes, shaking her arms to loosen them – and she began to run, giving it everything she had, looking hard at the scaffolding and where she might aim for, not allowing herself to think about the yawning three-storey drop that was getting nearer and nearer and nearer.

For a weird moment, once she'd jumped, time seemed to slow down completely. She couldn't hear or feel anything. All she could see were the poles and planks of the scaffolding, suspended ahead of her like an enormous grid …

… and then she struck against them with abrupt force, a bar bashing painfully across her chest, her legs flailing forward, her hands scrabbling frantically to clutch onto something. The left one found a piece of netting, the right a knuckle-shaped clamp holding two poles together – and she hauled herself up, gasping for air, almost laughing with relief and astonishment. That was easily the longest, most spectacular jump she'd ever done. She wished that her athletics friends back at the ARC had been there to see it.

A shout came from somewhere above – an indignant "Oi!" – aimed not at Zen but the person she was chasing. Through gaps in the scaffolding, she saw the saboteur run off onto an adjacent building.

Two scratched aluminium ladders brought her up to the same level – and past the same angry builder, whose clumsy attempt at capture she dodged without difficulty. Beside the scaffolding stretched a row of flat rooftops with low walls between each one. The saboteur was already six roofs away, vaulting over to the seventh.

Zen narrowed her eyes. She'd done some parkour before, mostly to train for other events. Older runners had told her it was all about *flow* – about reaching a point where your reactions became instinctive and near-instantaneous. As she ran forward, she tried to clear her mind – to focus only on the black-clad back ahead and closing the distance between them. She ran faster and faster, getting into the rhythm, taking the low walls in her stride.

The rooftops led onto a large department store. Now the two of them were flying along, Zen pursuing the saboteur over handrails and fire escapes, air vents and skylights. They swung down into a roof terrace café and hopped from table to table, scattering cutlery, glasses and plates of food, to the outraged cries of waiters and customers. The saboteur was good – he was *really* good. But suddenly he slipped on a plate and went down, vanishing among the white tablecloths.

An elderly lady rose from her chair, shouting amid the chaos. "What on *earth* do you think you are doing?"

Zen heard her angular-looking lunch companion say with some satisfaction, "I *told* you not to have the tiramisu, Agnes."

Momentarily, Zen faltered – she'd lost the saboteur. No, there he was, barely fifteen paces away – up again and launching himself off a dessert trolley, out of the café.

They were heading into an older part of Cambridge – the university colleges, Zen guessed, as she hurdled over an ornate balustrade and dashed along the ribbed roof of some kind of lecture hall. The saboteur had clearly planned his route in advance. He weaved around a turret-like tower and plunged out onto a steep slope of terracotta tiles, studded with attic windows and chimneys. As Zen went after him, she lifted her feet high so that they didn't catch the edges of the tiles and start a massive slide. A couple came loose anyway, rattling off to shatter on the ground. Only by maintaining her speed – and grabbing out, at one particularly urgent point, for an open window – did she avoid going with them.

Up ahead was something really ancient – a church with battlements and gargoyles and a dark, looming steeple. Without hesitation, the saboteur jumped over from the tiled roof to a semicircular ledge, no more than a metre wide. He did a tight forward roll as he landed, running on around the ledge until he was out of sight. Zen copied this move six seconds later – and then skidded to a stop, her flow broken, frowning in confusion.

The ledge led onto a narrow roof section above the church's left aisle. A row of pointed stone buttresses ran overhead, supporting the main roof. The saboteur was standing about halfway along, completely motionless, with nothing but a dead drop in front of him.

Zen stepped forward to demand who he was and what he'd been doing in the SolTec facility, but found that she was too breathless to speak. Her lungs were burning and her limbs were as heavy as lead. Suddenly, it was all she could do to remain upright.

The black-clad figure must have realized she was there, but he didn't turn around. His head began moving about like he was judging distances, waiting for a specific moment – sizing up another jump.

Zen was mystified. This church faced out onto a busy shopping street. There was literally nowhere for him to go. The saboteur started running nevertheless, quickly picking up speed.

"Wait!" Zen shouted.

As he leaped forward, however, he reached up for the final buttress – and his gloved hand seemed to *stick* to it, finding a hold where none existed. He swung around towards the front of the church, using the momentum to backflip out into the empty air.

Blinking in bewilderment, Zen hurried along the narrow roof – just as a blue double-decker bus eased around a junction in the street below and started to drive off. The saboteur was crouching on top of it. He looked back at her for the first time since they'd left SolTec, gave a mocking salute, and was gone.

Zen turned away, panting a curse. This made *no sense*. A few of his parkour moves had been dangerous, real knife-edge stuff, but that last one had actually been *impossible*. She looked up at the buttress. Something was there – a residue of some kind, where his hand had made contact with the stone. She took a deep, shuddering breath, then whistled a single low note and pointed with her forefinger.

Beetlebat had been clinging to Zen's jacket with its tiny hooked feet, pinned on like a badge. Now it released itself, fluttered up to the spot she'd flagged and began to scan it. Zen leaned against the church wall, took out her phone and opened the app that enabled her to access Beetlebat's sensor array. During their previous assignment for the Möbius Programme, she'd come by a couple of highly sophisticated microdrones, made by a sinister secret organization called Razor. After they got back to London, she'd worked hard to integrate some of their tech into Beetlebat. This had included a serious sensor upgrade.

"What have we have got here, girl?" she murmured to the little bot. "How did he *do* that?"

The results of the scan were baffling – chemical compounds so complex that the formulae ran to several lines on the phone's screen. Zen was attempting to figure them out when a huge, reverberating *thump* sounded somewhere across the city. Down on the streets, the crowds of mid-afternoon shoppers let out a great gasp of shock.

Zen rushed back to the semicircular ledge. Past the colleges and the department store, a gigantic cloud of black smoke was rising into the sky, like there had been a bombing or a missile strike.

SolTec. It had to be.

Numb with dread, Zen flicked the Beetlebat app off her screen and called Caleb's number.

"*Hawk!*" he yelled, the instant they were connected. "You're – you're all right! You got clear!"

Professor Clay's operatives were instructed to use their avian codenames on all Möbius Programme communications, for security reasons; Clay herself was "Goldfinch" and Mitch was "Buzzard".

"What do you mean?" Zen asked. "What's happened, Swift? Is Buzzard OK?"

"Yeah, we're both fine, but ... the whole place has gone up. It just freaking *exploded*. We think it was the combat bots – that they had some kind of built-in self-destruct mechanism, outside the rest of their programming. To stop them getting captured or something. We got to the virus in time, but now ... everything's been blown to bits."

Zen exhaled hard; she clenched her free hand into a fist to stop it from shaking. "The facility was definitely empty, wasn't it? No one was still inside?"

"As far as I can tell. It had been evacuated. There's just an ... *incredible* amount of damage." Caleb paused. "Where are you, anyway?"

"On top of a church. In the city centre, I think."

"I'm not even going to ask."

"It's a long story. I'll be with you in ten, Swift. Then we should go straight back to see Goldfinch." Zen looked out again at the black smoke. "Something very weird is going on."

DIGGING UP
THE DINOSAUR

Caleb could hear Professor Clay almost as soon as the lift doors opened. She was on the phone, it sounded like – and shouting furiously.

"I don't care, Aidan! You *lied* to me. You let me send two of my operatives into a life-threatening situation. Into *mortal* danger."

There was a pause as the other person on the line – Aidan Lennox – tried to explain. Caleb walked out of the lift and started along the corridor towards Clay's office, with Zen beside him and Mitch a couple of steps behind.

"No. No, I don't want to hear it. You said you'd been hacked. That it was a software breach. And now I'm looking at a … a *fireball*! I'm told my team only just managed to get out in time."

They reached the door. Caleb hesitated, unsure whether to wait until Clay had finished mauling Lennox, but Mitch leaned over him and knocked twice.

Professor Tilda Clay opened the door a few seconds later. Clay was a tall Black woman of about forty-five with an angular face and close-cropped greying hair. She was wearing dark trousers and a navy-blue top with a white horse stitched on the front. Her eyes went wide at the sight of them. Zen was bruised and still quite dusty, while Caleb and Mitch's clothes were covered in scorch marks and their eyebrows were singed.

Clay stepped back into her office to let them in, adjusting her hold on her phone; then she moved towards her desk, her silver-capped walking stick clacking on the floor tiles. Six weeks before, at the start of Swift and Hawk's previous mission for the Möbius Programme, she'd been shot in the head while helping them escape from a gang of dangerous mercenaries. Luckily, the bullet had only grazed her skull, not doing any serious damage – but she still wore a dressing on her left temple, and had to use the stick because of the occasional dizzy spell.

There was no sign of infirmity, however, in the way she was dealing with Lennox.

"An apology isn't enough, Aiden. I want *answers*. You need to give me a full explanation of what was going on in that facility – and why it's earned your company such dangerous enemies."

Caleb, Zen and Mitch stood waiting. The office occupied a corner of the ARC tower's thirty-fourth floor. The outward-facing walls were made entirely of glass, like most rooms in the ARC, providing a sweeping view of St Paul's Cathedral and the skyscrapers of the City of London. The autumn sky was low and overcast; lights were starting to come on along the streets and bridges far below, even though it was only a little after five o'clock in the afternoon.

To their left, among framed certificates and long rows of bookshelves, a muted TV was tuned to a streaming news channel. It was showing aerial footage of the SolTec facility, the buildings still burning ferociously. Dozens of fire engines were lined up around it, hoses trained on the flames, but to no visible effect. The caption along the bottom of the screen read **MYSTERY POWER SURGE CAUSES CAMBRIDGE BLAZE**.

"I don't *care* what the SolTec lawyers say. Listen, Aiden – if you won't tell me what's going on, I swear that I will use every tool at my disposal to—" Clay stopped talking abruptly; then she tossed the phone onto her desk in disgust. "He hung up. The little weasel."

"Yeah," said Caleb. "He didn't strike us as the nicest guy in the universe either."

Clay lowered herself carefully into her office chair. "Caleb and Zen," she said. "And Mr Mitchell too. Glad to see you're all in one piece." She looked them over again. "More or less."

"It was pretty touch-and-go out there, Professor," Mitch told her. "*Way* beyond mission parameters."

"What Mitch means," Caleb said, "is that it was totally and utterly *crazy*."

"A virus was reprogramming SolTec's robots," said Zen. "They were attacking on sight."

"There was this out-of-control construction bot," Caleb continued. "And then an automated tank thing with a *minigun*. And then—"

Clay held up her hand. "We'll do a full debrief in a minute or two. Take a seat. I've got a video call waiting here that I think you'll all want to join. The optics aren't ideal, but that can't be helped."

Caleb and Zen sat in a pair of comfy leather chairs in front of the desk while Mitch stayed over by the window. Clay tapped a key on a laptop and the TV switched from the SolTec footage to a video-conferencing app – with Caleb's mum, CIA Agent Harper Quinn, on the other end.

"Caleb!" Harper cried, breaking into a huge smile. "It's so good to see you. I miss you, honey. I can't believe I've been over here for three whole weeks already."

"Jeez, Mum," Caleb mumbled, blushing a little. "We Zoomed, like, two days ago. But yeah … I, uh, miss you too."

Harper was dressed in a grey suit with her red-brown hair tied back. She was sitting in a blank-looking cubicle, with nothing to reveal her location or even the time of day. Caleb knew that she was at CIA headquarters in Langley, where she'd been assigned to the investigation into what had become known as "The Spøkelsøy Incident".

That summer, after a number of top-level scientists – including Zen's father, Professor Elias Rafiq – had been mysteriously abducted, Caleb and Zen had followed a winding, dangerous trail to the island of Spøkelsøy off the Norwegian coast. Everyone had been rescued, and a pretty dark plan thwarted, but many disturbing questions had been left unanswered – particularly concerning Razor, the ominous, secretive organization that had ultimately been behind it all.

Harper Quinn was now part of the expert team that was sifting through the tech that hadn't been destroyed, interviewing and observing those who'd been held prisoner on the island, and trying to find anything, anything at all, that might give them some idea of what Razor might be planning next.

Harper was Caleb's only living parent, as his dad had died a couple of years earlier. Normally, they lived at Nine Elms, a short way up the Thames, but while she was in America he was staying at the ARC Institute, on the students' residential floor. He'd been given a room just down the corridor from Zen's – she boarded during the week as her family was based in Berlin, where her father worked at the Freie Universität. Right then, though, they were in Langley too, so Elias could help with the Spøkelsøy investigation and recover from his ordeal at the hands of Razor.

"I can see Lance Mitchell as well, over by the windows," said Harper. "And Zen is there too, of course."

"Hey, Agent Quinn," said Zen, with a small wave.

"I met with your folks an hour or so ago. Your dad's still pretty weak, but he's doing well. And we're hoping to send your mom and little sister home to Berlin by the end of the month."

"That's *really* great news," Zen said quietly. "I'm going to speak with my mum tomorrow, actually. I'm sure she'll tell me all about it then."

"Good." Harper paused, peering into her own screen. "OK, I've got to ask – what on earth happened to you guys? You look like you've been in a war zone."

"There was a minor operation today, Harper," Clay said, leaning back a little in her chair. "More of a favour, really, to an old colleague of mine. Someone I will *not* be helping again."

Harper's smile had frozen on her face. "I thought we had agreed, Tilda – no more of this Möbius stuff for a while. You know what Caleb and Zen went through over the summer. You were supposed to be giving them time to recuperate."

"Yes, I realize that." Clay pursed her lips; this was going to be as close as she ever came to an apology. "We were asked to assist with a cybersecurity breach at a robotics facility, and I'm afraid that Caleb and Zen are currently the best team we have for missions of that kind. It didn't go … quite as smoothly as I'd hoped, but everyone's safe and well, as you can see. And your guy went in with them. Kept them out of danger." She turned to Mitch. "Isn't that right, Mr Mitchell?"

Mitch and Harper were old friends, from his time in the CIA. He'd actually come to work at the ARC at her suggestion, to keep an eye on Caleb – and the activities of the Möbius Programme as well. Professor Clay hadn't objected. Mitch was extremely useful to have around, and she obviously thought it wise to maintain cordial relations with the CIA.

"Uh, sure," he replied, pulling his jacket sleeve down to cover a charred shirt cuff. "Nothing to worry about, Agent Quinn. It's all good."

Harper clearly knew that she wasn't getting the whole story, but she decided to let it go – for now, at least. She straightened her chair; Caleb could tell that she was shifting into work mode.

"Anyway," she said, "the point of this call is that I wanted to give you guys a quick update on the Spøkelsøy investigation. Our excavation crews have been working round-the-clock. The ruins of that island are a gold mine. There's tech in there that's going to take us years to figure out. I mean … we're talking *advanced*."

"What sort of thing?" Caleb asked. "The remains of those disc drones? Or Xavier Torrent's hard-light chamber?"

Harper shook her head. "That's classified, Caleb. But I can reveal that we've got some leads on that mercenary gang – the ones who escaped the island. And we think we're close to tracking down your old ARC schoolmate, Luuk Tezuka. We're liaising with Tsuru, his family's company. They've been conducting a search of their own."

"What about Erica Szabo, the mercenary leader that Razor captured?" Zen said. "Or Esperanza – any trace of her?"

Esperanza had been the Razor agent stationed on Spøkelsøy. Phenomenally dangerous, and equipped with some truly terrifying tech, she'd disappeared at a critical moment. The thought that she was still on the loose somewhere was a deeply unsettling one.

"Not yet, Zen," Harper answered. "But we'll keep looking."

Caleb and Zen glanced at each other. After Spøkelsøy, they'd both been given a thorough debriefing by the intelligence services – five solid days of questioning on every tiny aspect of their adventure. But since then, they'd been told next to nothing. It felt like they were being shut out of the investigation. Caleb knew his mum was just doing her job, but he couldn't help feeling a little annoyed.

"Sam is still picking up the Apex signal, Mum," he said. "Way fainter than it was, but it's there. Can you tell us anything about that? Like where it's coming from, maybe?"

Apex was the name of an advanced, extremely hostile AI they'd defeated on Spøkelsøy. It had been programmed by an unbalanced computer genius named Xavier Torrent – who'd been buried in rock when the island collapsed in on itself. Linked up to a superpowerful quantum computer and a complex network of microscopic nanobots that had been implanted in the abducted scientists, Apex had been central to Razor's nefarious scheme: mind control on a vast scale.

Harper was shaking her head again. "No answers there either, kiddo. The main thing is that it is no longer quantum-powered, which makes it considerably less dangerous. They can't get their nanotech to function without it. And they'd need a massive power supply as well to run a quantum system. But I'm guessing you already know all this." She looked hard into her camera. "How *is* Sam doing?"

Her meaning was clear. Until the summer, Sam had been confined entirely to *Terrorform*, the video game he'd made with Caleb – but a particularly deadly encounter during their last Möbius mission had given Caleb no choice but to let him out, releasing him onto the internet. This had led to some unexpected consequences, to say the least. It had actually been Sam who had destroyed the base at Spøkelsøy, by overloading a set of tidal generators. He'd done this for purely logical reasons, calculating that it was the only way to stop Torrent and Razor – but he'd also put all of their lives at grave risk. Afterwards, Caleb and his mum had agreed that some serious modifications would have to be made to Sam's program, to prevent anything like this from happening again. She asked for an update every time they spoke.

"He's … good," Caleb replied, a little warily. "I finished rewriting his volition protocols the other day. Everything's under control now. He was a massive help, in fact, on the…" He hesitated. "On the errand we just ran for Professor Clay."

The AI started talking through the Flex's speaker. "Thank you, Caleb. I do my best. Hello, Agent Quinn. I hope that Caleb's words have reassured you."

"Hey, Sam," said Harper. "They have, to an extent. But could you explain to me what your volition protocols actually are? Caleb throws these terms around like the rest of us will just automatically know what he's talking about."

"Yeah," said Mitch. "I noticed that too."

Caleb felt his ears growing hot. He stayed quiet.

"Certainly, Agent Quinn," said Sam. "My volition protocols influence both what I wish to do, and what I am able to do to realize those wishes. Caleb's recent alterations mean that I can still freely access information, analyse evidence and offer advice, and perform a range of minor actions inside the *Terrorform* game program. However, I am barred from making any administrator-level changes or doing anything that might affect the world outside the game without Caleb's direct permission."

Harper was listening closely. "That does all sound pretty sensible," she admitted.

"That's because it *is*," said Caleb defensively. "I promised you I'd take care of this, didn't I?"

"You did, honey. And it seems that you've been good to your word." Harper turned in her chair, nodding to someone out of frame. "Listen, everyone – I've got to run. Sorry I don't have any major breakthroughs to report yet. But that's how these investigations tend to go. Think of it like archaeology – digging up a dinosaur skeleton one tiny bone at a time."

"Whatever you say, Mum," Caleb murmured.

"I see that heavy rain is forecast this afternoon in Langley, Agent Quinn," Sam said. "I hope that you have an appropriate waterproof garment."

"I sure do, Sam," said Harper. "It's the first thing they teach you in spy school: always remember your raincoat." She leaned in closer to the screen. "OK, I'll be calling each of you separately as soon as I get the chance. Just to help me understand *exactly* what you've all been up to."

"Speak to you then, Harper," said Clay briskly, moving her laptop's cursor over the disconnect button. "Good luck with the dinosaur."

They all said goodbye and a second later the screen went blank.

"Why does it feel like we actually know *less* than we did before?" Caleb wondered.

Clay let out a short, sarcastic laugh. "That's the CIA for you."

"She did tell us about Luuk," Zen said. "You were worried about him, Caleb. Although with Tsuru involved, he was never going to stay missing for long."

Mitch crossed his arms. "Don't take it to heart, kid. Your mom will be passing on everything she can. These security restrictions tend to come from the top. She'll get in deep trouble if she says anything she's not supposed to say. Especially over comms."

Clay switched the TV back on to the news channel, with its footage of the SolTec fire. "Right. I think the best thing for us to do right now is work out what happened in Cambridge today. Before we go any further, though, there's something that we need – urgently." She sat up and pointed to a cabinet set against the back wall. "Bottom drawer."

Caleb walked over, expecting a slick gadget or some critical piece of intel – but inside the drawer was a Tupperware box filled with homemade biscuits.

"Double chocolate chip," Clay said. "My auntie Alice's recipe. Give a couple to Zen, for god's sake. She looks like she's about to keel over."

A minute later they were all munching away contentedly.

"That's better," said Clay, brushing a crumb off her top. "Now, you three – tell me everything."

PURPLE SLUDGE DISASTER ZONE

When the story of the SolTec mission was finished, Clay spun around in her chair and looked out of the window. Caleb could see that she was considering their report very carefully.

"OK," she said. "What are we dealing with here?"

"Whoever did this is dedicated," Caleb replied. "Like, *really* dedicated. Taking real risks. And ready to hurt people too."

"More than hurt," Mitch murmured.

Zen nodded. "I think they knew that the combat bots were down there – and that they'd go on the rampage along with the others."

"What about the self-destruct sequence?" Clay asked.

"It must have been a hidden sub-system inside the robots," Caleb said. "Nothing showed up on the Flex's sensors until it was too late. Looks like it was triggered when Sam and I halted the takeover of the codebase."

Mitch was studying the images on the TV closely. "I've seen this kind of fire before," he said. "Each of those robots must have been carrying a payload of white phosphorous. They'll be completely incinerated. I guess the idea is to stop the tech falling into the hands of an enemy army. That facility will burn for days."

"So these saboteurs wanted to damage SolTec," Clay said. "But what else?"

"They wanted to expose them," Zen answered. "That's why he was filming – the guy I chased. He wanted footage of the combat bots out of control. Destroying things. And maybe people too."

"Right," Caleb agreed. "So we should keep our eyes peeled. A video might be posted online. Something we can trace."

"I thought about this too, Caleb," said Sam, "and have been monitoring recent internet activity. But so far no video of the interior of the SolTec Cambridge facility has appeared."

Clay was looking over, a strange expression on her face; like most people, she didn't really know what to make of Sam yet. "Which global regions have you been … monitoring exactly?"

"All of them, Professor Clay," the AI replied. "But there is nothing to report. I will inform you if this changes."

"You do that," Clay said. "How about the virus itself? Any clues as to who might have written it?"

"We had a quick look on the drive back to London," Caleb told her. "It's supersophisticated, obviously. The work of a *serious* coder."

"Which means they knew how to cover their tracks as well," Zen added.

"A dead end, then," said Clay, her brow furrowing. "Think

I need another biscuit." She fished one from the box before offering it to the rest of them.

Mitch reached over eagerly. "I've gotta say, Prof," he told her, taking a bite, "these are delicious. What's that I can taste – spice, is it?"

"Cinnamon," Clay replied. "Auntie Alice puts it in everything."

"Cinnamon – I love cinnamon. You ever try it with bananas?"

"We've got the handprint, Professor," said Zen, a little impatiently. "The one the saboteur left on the church. That has to be our best lead. Beetlebat got a really good scan. It could be the key to the whole thing."

"Let's see it," Clay said.

Zen took out her phone, opened the Beetlebat app, swiped and tapped – and a dense, ultra-detailed image, clearly left by some kind of climbing glove, appeared on the TV. Numbers and symbols crowded around it, providing complex information regarding the print's chemical make-up. Everyone turned towards the screen and the office went quiet, save for the sound of biscuits being chewed and the soft purr of Clay's laptop.

"Well," said Clay, after a minute or so, "that all means precisely nothing to me. Anyone else care to explain what we're looking at here?"

"No chance." Mitch chuckled.

"Sam?" said Caleb.

"It appears to be a highly experimental compound,"

the AI replied. "One that defies all standard chemical classifications. I'm afraid that a more detailed analysis lies outside my present specializations."

"Luckily for us," Clay observed dryly, "we happen to be in the ARC tower. Finding an experimental chemist won't be a problem."

She put down her biscuit and started typing quickly on her laptop – and a video call opened in a window on the TV screen, next to the handprint.

They could see a lab, its white surfaces and orderly shelves of equipment all coated with a layer of purple slime. The camera jerked up and the top half of a face appeared in the immediate foreground – the hair wild and very slimy also, the brown eyes magnified and distorted by a pair of thick glasses.

"Professor Clay!" said a slightly nasal, rather alarmed voice. "Hang on, this is the Möbius channel – I mean *Goldfinch*, yes, Goldfinch, that's it – how are you? How can I help?"

"Afternoon, Crake," said Clay. "Everything all right up there?"

The camera swung about to a less gooey part of the lab. A lanky Black kid in a lab coat and a bright green T-shirt with a picture of a jellyfish on it was sitting down on a stool, trying to look composed and intellectual and not at all like he was in the middle of some kind of purple sludge disaster zone. Caleb recognized him as Art Lawrence, one of the year 10s, who always seemed to be winning prizes for complicated scientific stuff that no one else completely understood. He had no idea that Art – codenamed Crake, apparently – was in the Möbius Programme. Professor Clay kept membership details as secret as possible. But it did kind of make sense.

"Just putting in some extra hours in the lab," Art said, wiping some gunk off his knee. "You know how it is. I'm close to a big discovery, *really* close, and I just … can't leave. There's this one part I don't seem to be able to get right. It works in my calculations, Goldfinch, it works *perfectly*, yet the instant I introduce element Y to the test area, this reaction begins … this ridiculous and uncontrollable and really quite violent *expansion*. And there's nothing I can do about it." He raised a hand. "I know what you're going to say – I need to understand the relationship between the structure and performance of my electrocatalysts better. But it's not clear whether—"

"OK, Crake, OK," Clay broke in. "Take a breath. This is riveting, I'm sure, but I've got something I need you to look at. It's very time-sensitive. I'm sending it now."

Art blinked, his train of thought lost. He leaned forward on his stool to click a button – and then stared superhard at a point where Zen's Beetlebat scan had presumably just appeared. After a few seconds he moved off his stool, stumbling in his haste to get closer to the screen, until his face filled it almost entirely.

"What in the… How does that… Professor – Goldfinch – where did you get this?"

Clay extended her hand towards Zen and Caleb. "May

I introduce two of our newest Möbius operatives – this is Hawk, and sitting next to her there is Swift."

"Swift and Hawk!" Art exclaimed, backing away again to a normal distance. "I did already know that you two were in the programme, as a matter of fact. But how *amazing* to get a chance to talk to you. What you did on that island during the summer – my goodness…"

"I hope you haven't been spreading rumours, Crake," said Professor Clay. "Anything to do with the Möbius Programme is strictly confidential. Don't make me review your membership."

"Of course," Art said hurriedly. "Confidential. Of course. I haven't said anything, honest I haven't. All I've heard is that they travelled halfway across Europe on their own, saved a bunch of people and – and foiled an evil plot. A major win. Major, major."

Clay looked at him steadily for a few seconds, then continued. "Hawk came across this sample earlier today, during an operation in Cambridge. She can tell you the exact circumstances herself."

Zen gave Art a shorter version of the rooftop chase and the saboteur's acrobatic escape. Art soon forgot the scare Professor Clay had given him and listened to her with total fascination.

"That all figures," he said when she'd finished. "I mean, it's obviously some kind of adhesive. But the properties it has – this internal variation – it's entirely unique. Unlike anything else I've seen."

"I need you to run a full analysis," Clay told him. "We'd like a formula, if you can manage that – and anything you can tell us about who might have made it."

Art was shaking his head. "This is … this is someone *hardcore*, Goldfinch. There are, like, three labs in the entire world that might, just *might*, be able to pull something like this off. And even they wouldn't … I mean, I don't see how they'd be able to…"

"Just see what you can find out. You've got twenty-four hours." Clay closed the link before Art could say any more. "OK, I think we're done for now. Hopefully he'll give us something we can work with."

Caleb's mind was racing. "So what do we do next?" he asked. "Should we hack into SolTec ourselves, and try to find out—"

"What you both need to do," Clay interrupted, "is go back to your rooms and get some rest. And don't tell anyone where you were today. The mission remains top secret." She turned to Mitch. "What was their class told?"

"Caleb was at the dentist," Mitch replied. "Zen was at an athletics meet in Beckenham."

"The dentist?" said Caleb, his spirits falling a little. "What if anyone asks me about it?"

"Just say you were getting plaque removed," Mitch said, grinning. "Nobody really cares. Trust me, kid – a good cover story is a boring cover story."

"An effective agent always maintains their cover," Clay told him. "Remember that, Caleb. And Mr Mitchell is right – the more uninteresting it is, the better. You'd be amazed how many spies trip up just because they suddenly get the urge to tell people how exciting their lives are."

"So I'm plaque boy," Caleb muttered. *"Great."*

"Half-term starts the day after tomorrow," Clay continued, "as you are no doubt aware. Both of you are staying in the tower for the whole week, is that correct?"

"Yeah," Zen said. "Our parents are kind of … unavailable."

"We'll be here, Prof," said Caleb. "Ready to work on this mystery."

Spending a holiday at the ARC would normally be a rather bleak prospect – and not one that he, as a Londoner who only lived a few kilometres away, was used to at all. Now, though, things were looking very different. They had a new mission. He wouldn't want to be anywhere else.

Clay nodded. "Most of the other students and staff will be gone. That will give us a lot more space to operate." Her expression softened an almost undetectable amount. "You both did well today. You adapted to a rapidly evolving situation. I can't ask for more than that." She pushed the Tupperware box across her desk. "Here, take a couple of biscuits with you."

They were being dismissed. "But—" Caleb started to protest.

"Go to your rooms and rest," Clay repeated, turning back to her laptop. "Something tells me that this is just the beginning."

GOD MODE

Once he was in his room, Caleb changed his jeans and hoodie, clipped some of the really burned bits off his eyebrows, and attempted to read a few pages of *Animal Farm* by George Orwell, which he'd just started doing in English.

But it was no use. He couldn't concentrate at all. The afternoon's events kept replaying in his head with chilling clarity. The deafening screech of the minigun. The battering-ram charges of the hound bot. And that *explosion* – that blast so overwhelmingly massive it had felt like the world was being torn in half. He and Mitch had been crossing the lobby when the bots detonated. Every piece of glass in the facility had shattered simultaneously. White-hot flames had leaped up through the lift shafts, blowing apart the doors. They'd thrown themselves sprawling to the floor – then staggered to safety through the broken remains of the front entrance.

After a while, Caleb decided to fire up *Terrorform* – to clear his mind a bit, and maybe talk things through with Sam while he was playing. There was no surround-sound

VR set-up here, like he had at home – just the Flex, an audio headset and a controller. But it was enough.

Caleb had created *Terrorform* on a special barge lab, moored close to his house at Nine Elms, that had once belonged to his AI-expert dad, Patrick. It took place in a gigantic sci-fi sandbox that sprawled over an entire solar system. The game itself was part RPG, part intense shooter, part survival sim; you chose your character class, got your starting gear, and headed off to find adventure. This involved making alliances and enemies among the other players, fighting off *Terrorform*'s huge menagerie of monsters, and levelling up to gain more abilities and equipment. And if you died, that was it: all progress lost, back to the beginning.

The game had been Caleb's idea, his dream, but it was Sam who had made it possible. After his dad had died, Caleb had found the AI's program in one of the barge lab's back-up drives – almost as if it had been left there on purpose for him to discover. He'd adapted Sam to work with him on *Terrorform*, which up to then had been little more than a hobby. The AI's lightning-fast computational power – along with his ability to generate his own ideas, solutions and even opinions, using something in his program called the Talos Algorithm – had meant he could do the work of an entire games studio.

Together, Caleb and Sam had built something amazing: a deep, addictive, unpredictable game that now had a player base in the hundreds of thousands. The only hitch was that Caleb's dad had written a baseline into Sam's program that prevented him from being used to make money. This meant that *Terrorform* would always be free to play. No matter how good it was, or how popular, Caleb would never see a penny from it.

Caleb tapped the *Terrorform* icon and the game began to load. He turned on the Flex's projector, throwing a pin-sharp, two-metre-wide image up onto the bedroom wall. A silver face appeared in the bottom left corner, indicating Sam's presence. The AI acted as the game's overseer. He controlled its creatures and environmental effects, wrote patches and updates, and monitored the behaviour of its players; Caleb had been careful not to obstruct any of this when he'd rewritten the volition protocols.

"Hello, Caleb," Sam said. "Would you like to hear the daily player report?"

"Yeah, sure." Caleb sighed. "What have we got today?"

"Your tone of voice suggests that you are preoccupied. You may be undergoing a post-traumatic reaction to our experiences at SolTec. Would you like to take a short psychometric test?"

"Uh, no. No thanks. Maybe later." Caleb looked at the screen. "Tell me what's happening in the game."

A macro-scale, real-time map of the game's Cardano system appeared – part of a special "God mode" accessible only to Caleb and Sam. Caleb could see the eleven very different planets on and around which *Terrorform* was played, each one surrounded by moons, asteroid belts or space stations, and the glittering starships that moved between them. Sam reeled off a few statistics about new players. The game was still growing steadily – its settlements expanding and becoming more advanced, even on the most hostile planets. Everything was working really well.

"Forty-three new player clans have been declared since yesterday's report," the AI went on. "The largest has established a base on Comus, the eighth moon of Kolto. It already has exactly two hundred members."

"Whoa," said Caleb. "Two hundred members in a *day*? And two hundred *exactly*? That's insane. What's their name?"

"They have yet to register a name."

Now this was really strange. Terrorformers usually *loved* naming their clans. Sure, there was the occasional *PlayerClan1093* – but most were called things like *Dark Void* or *Star Striders* or *Warp Addicts*. Nobody had ever chosen not to enter a name at all.

"What are they doing right now? How many of them are online?"

"All of them. At present, they are constructing multiple buildings, and also seem to be clearing hostile creatures from a tunnel system beneath a mountain range. Caleb, this unnamed clan is playing the game with a focus I have not seen before. They are coordinating on a grand scale."

Caleb raised what was left of his eyebrows. He'd heard about this – large groups of players taking on an online game together, to test its systems and see what it could do. It hadn't happened to them yet, not really. He found that he liked the idea.

"We should go and say hello. Welcome them to *Terrorform*."

"That is a nice thought, Caleb. Perhaps you could suggest a name for their clan."

"Yeah," said Caleb, reaching for his controller. "Perhaps."

He logged in and selected his favourite avatar, the Navigator – *Terrorform*'s Explorer class, equipped with a suit of power armour, a jet pack and a powerful ion lance rifle. The suit had a new custom paint job: midnight blue with snarling wolf heads on each shoulder. He zoomed in on Kolto, a tundra planet at the system's outer edge, then clicked on Comus and rotated it until he found this new clan's settlement. It looked big, even from space: a square of bright dots in the middle of a mountain range, partly concealed by a spiral of white cloud.

A list of the moon's spawn points appeared, scattered across its surface. Caleb selected one a short distance from the camp – and suddenly he was inside his Navigator suit, standing on a small platform cut into a cliffside, looking down into a steep valley. Comus was entirely covered by barren, towering mountains, made from dark, marbled stone. Above, the night sky was half-filled by the huge silver-grey sphere of Kolto.

Further along the valley, rows of floodlights were illuminating a wide, dusty plateau. Activating the Navigator's long-range sensors, Caleb saw that this nameless clan was using dozens of Scrappers, *Terrorform*'s Engineer class, to carve out a large flat area amid the slopes. They were already building on top of it, laying out geodomes, refineries and research pods in astonishing numbers, connecting and combining them in all sorts of ingenious ways.

"They're properly settling in here, Sam," he said. "It's kind of … amazing, isn't it?"

"It is an ambitious project," Sam replied. "They seem to be constructing a *Terrorform* metropolis. Nothing quite like this has been attempted before."

Caleb was grinning. "This is *us*, Sam. This is possible because of our hard work. The game engine. The player freedom. All of it." He chuckled. "Let's take a closer look."

He activated his suit's jet pack, stepped from the platform and glided down through the valley towards the encampment. As he got nearer, he could see the Scrappers in more detail. Built like walking forklifts, they were slicing great chunks from the hillside with the laser cutters mounted on their arms, or using specialized holo-tools to warp in more structures. All of them were painted the same deep shade of red.

The boots of Caleb's Navigator thumped down on the raw, scoured rock. Every Scrapper stopped work immediately. The dust clouds drifted off, slowly dissipating, just as they'd been programmed to do.

Caleb opened an all-frequencies audio channel. "Hey, guys!" he said cheerfully. "This is incredible! I reckon you've already built the largest player-made settlement in the entire game. And you've done it in a single day!"

The fifty or so Scrappers turned towards him, deactivating their laser cutters and construction tools. They stayed completely silent.

"How do you all know each other? Did you plan it out in advance?"

Still nothing.

Caleb glanced up: his gamer tag, *CalQ_001*, was floating above his head, clearly identifying him. But not one tag could be seen among the red-armoured Scrappers. They must have switched them off in the game's options menu. He studied them a little more closely. Weirdly, *everything* about their appearance had been left on the default settings. No patterning. No insignia. Nothing.

"O-K," he said. "Getting a little awkward now. Guess I should introduce myself. I'm Caleb Quinn, and I created *Terrorform*, along with—"

There was a blast from across the plateau – and a bolt of searing white energy cracked against his avatar's shoulder, spinning it around. As the Navigator reeled, trying to regain its footing, Caleb glimpsed a flood of red forms pouring from an opening beyond the buildings. The energy bolt had come from one of them.

He fired his jet pack, rising into the air and wheeling about. "Wait," he said. "Wait a sec. I just want to..."

Red avatars already covered one end of the plateau. Caleb realized that they were emerging from tunnels in the mountainside – the ones Sam had said they were clearing of monsters. He could see all of the standard character

72

classes, from towering, heavily armed Bulwarks to the psi-adept, energy-bending Oracles. And to one side was a loose group of Navigators, like blood-red versions of himself, taking aim with their ion lances.

The next instant they began to fire, unleashing a barrage from the full range of *Terrorform* weapons, beams and bullets and shells lighting up the night sky around him. Caleb's Navigator was experience level forty, the highest you could go, with some awesome top-tier equipment – while the members of this red-armoured clan couldn't have been more than level three or four, and had only the most basic gear. But two hundred against one were not good odds. He'd also stopped fighting against other Terrorformers unless he absolutely had to. Something about it didn't feel right.

They were coming towards him now like a swarm of giant soldier ants. He turned away, boosting his jet pack to full power, and started back up towards the spawn point on the platform – a safe zone where he could log out and preserve his avatar. A few more shots hit home, his screen shaking to simulate the impact, but the power armour could take it. In his rear sensors, he could see a pack of red Navigators in hot pursuit, trying to match his speed and filling the air with ion bolts.

Caleb reached the green glyph of the spawn point in the nick of time. He punched the *X* button on his controller, then threw himself back in his chair as his avatar dematerialized into ribbons of multicoloured light and his view zoomed back out to God mode.

"All right, Sam," he said, taking off his headphones, "they are definitely *not* friendly."

"That is certain, Caleb. Would you like me to initiate a meteorite shower upon Comus? I estimate that I could destroy all of their buildings and ninety-two point five per cent of their avatars."

Caleb angled his head slightly; was that *enthusiasm* he could hear in the AI's voice? "Leave them for now," he said. "We should let them play however they want. But it is a bit suspicious. This isn't just a large-scale player co-op. Something else is going on here. These people are seriously organized."

Caleb found himself imagining a hangar somewhere, with rows of tables set out inside, covered with screens and keyboards; hundreds of people in matching T-shirts and baseball caps, playing *Terrorform* together; detailed directions and invasion plans being relayed over radio headsets.

"It could be a games company," he said. "I can think of a few who might pull a stunt like this. Crystal Kitten, maybe, or Heatwave – those guys love their pranks. And then there's Lodestar, of course."

Lodestar was a massive, long-established studio with over twelve thousand employees, and offices in New York, Budapest, Kyoto and many other places. It had released several broadly similar games to *Terrorform*, all of them enormously successful, and considered open-world sci-fi to be its territory. However, growing numbers of gamers were saying that *Terrorform* had an edge – a freshness and an unpredictability that Lodestar's triple-A blockbusters couldn't match. They'd made two attempts to buy Caleb out – to get him on staff and add *Terrorform* to their catalogue. He'd refused both times. If he took money for *Terrorform*, any money at all, Sam would immediately stop being able to work on it. And the absolute *last* thing he ever wanted to do was hand his game over to anyone else.

"That might explain it," Caleb said, warming to the idea. "We won't sell *Terrorform* to Lodestar, so they're trying to sabotage us. To unbalance the game or something."

"A reasonable theory, Caleb," said Sam. "But there are other possibilities as well. For example, a malevolent individual could be sending you a message of some kind – perhaps to indicate hostile intent."

Caleb thought for a moment. "You mean someone like Xavier Torrent, right?"

That summer, Torrent had used the Apex AI to steal parts of *Terrorform*, warping them with advanced hard-light tech to put Caleb through a nerve-shredding ordeal. It had taken all of his courage and ingenuity to survive.

"Yes, Caleb," Sam replied. "An adversary with access to similar technology would easily be able to exert these levels of control over the game world."

Caleb was shaking his head. "But there is no *similar technology* to what Torrent had on Spøkelsøy, Sam. The Apex AI, hooked up to a quantum computer – that was a one-off." He looked out of the window to where boats and barges were cruising underneath London Bridge, their lights gleaming in the dusk. "And Torrent's dead – buried underneath that caldera. Apex is like a ... a faint shadow of what it was. If that signal is accurate, it's so weak it wouldn't even be able to control one *Terrorform* avatar, let alone two hundred. It's probably not even operational."

The Flex buzzed on the desk. It was a message from Zen.

Want to check in on Crake? See if he's discovered anything yet?

Caleb's mind snapped back to their Möbius mission. Zen was obviously as keen as he was to find out what was going on. He switched off the Flex's projector, then picked the handset up and fired off a response.

Meet on the stairs in 2 mins.

"Keep an eye on these red-armoured jerks, Sam," he said, as he rose from his chair. "I've got a feeling they're just getting started."

MERLIN AND CRAKE

"**L**et's head up to the roof," said Zen, once they were both in the stairwell. "I reckon he's in one of the special project labs – you know, for experiments that need open-air access. That's what it looked like in the video call."

"Right," said Caleb. "Makes sense."

Zen glanced at him. "You OK?"

"That's the second time I've been asked that," Caleb said. "I'm totally fine. Something bizarre just happened in the game, that's all."

"I'll log on later," said Zen, as they started to climb the stairs. "We can check it out together."

"Thanks. That'd be cool. I'm … not really sure what it is yet."

They reached floor thirty-five. Beyond the stairwell doors was a small lobby, which led out onto a helicopter pad. On its far side were a few simple rectangular structures, a bit like converted shipping containers, with radar dishes and antennae on their roofs and large yellow numbers painted on their sides. It was almost completely dark by now, and feeling pretty cold. As they walked over, Caleb began to wish that he'd brought his coat.

They found Art inside number three. The lab seemed much smaller than it had in the video call. It was also immaculately clean, shining white under bright strip lights, with no trace of purple gunk anywhere to be seen. Art was standing in a corner, a tablet in his hands, totally absorbed.

"Hey, Crake," said Zen.

Art let out a wordless shout, jumping with surprise, the tablet nearly flying from his grasp. "Jeez, you guys almost gave me a heart attack!" he cried. "What are you doing, sneaking around like that?"

"Sorry," said Caleb. "We didn't mean to—"

Art was waving his hand about like he was swatting at an invisible fly; he took a couple of deep, steadying breaths. "Doesn't matter, doesn't matter. I'll get over it." He grinned. "Swift and Hawk. I almost can't believe you're really standing there. It's like … like I summoned you into being or something."

"What?" Caleb said.

"I think we can drop the codenames now," said Zen. "This is Caleb Quinn, and I'm—"

"Zen, yes, Zen Rafiq." Art nodded. "This is *fate*, you know, the two of you deciding to come up here. Do you believe in fate? Not a particularly popular notion here at the ARC, what with all the scientists and everything, but I find that sometimes things happen – coincidences and so on – for which there is simply no rational explanation."

"Art," said Zen flatly. "What are you talking about?"

The grin grew wider. "I'm talking about *progress*, Zen. Not a breakthrough, exactly, but definite, rock-solid progress. I've got a ton of work to do, an absolute *crap-load* of it, but that scan, that substance you showed me – that you found on your mission – it was intriguing. I mean, truly intriguing. I had to drop everything, everything at once, and have a proper look at it."

As he said this, Caleb spotted a couple of detailed print-outs of Zen's scan laid on a worktop. Notes and symbols had been scrawled over them – and a lot of question marks.

"What have you found out, Art?" he asked. "We're all ears."

Art was trying to remain calm, but he was moving constantly – changing his posture, crossing his arms and uncrossing them again, almost giggling now in his excitement. "The substance in that scan has a mutable, responsive structure. Its fundamental properties can change, change *completely*, with different stimuli." He turned to Zen. "This is how that guy you chased turned himself into Spider-Man. It's what you might call a *smart glue*. It adheres when pressure is applied – like when a hand presses against a surface – and then loses that adhesive quality instantaneously as the hand pulls away."

"It must have come from his glove," Zen said. "He must have been able to release this stuff when he needed it."

"Do you have a formula yet, Art?" Caleb said. "Could you … copy it?"

Before Art could answer someone outside shouted his

name and threw open the lab door. It was another year 10 called Astrid Yeoh. Originally from Hong Kong, she was slightly built with short, spiky hair, and wore a leather jacket covered with hand-painted orchids. Astrid was well known around the ARC for her eccentric flight tech, having made a range of experimental jet-bikes by connecting superefficient batteries to high-powered propulsive fans.

"Enough with the glue, Art," she said impatiently. "We didn't clean up this dump so you could stand around nattering with a pair of ... what are they, year eights?"

Caleb looked over at Zen. This was top-secret Möbius business. How much did Astrid know? What exactly had Art told her?

"Year eights!" Art scoffed. "Don't you know who these guys are, Astrid? This is *Swift and Hawk* – Caleb Quinn and Zen Rafiq. The kids who blew open that big case in the summer. The one that was picked up by the frickin' *CIA*."

"Huh," Astrid said, sounding very slightly impressed.

"It was Professor Clay who called me earlier. They needed me to examine a lead they'd picked up. Something really important, OK?"

"Hold on," said Zen. She turned to Astrid. "You're Möbius, right?"

Astrid met her eye. "Merlin," she said. "That's my codename. Although I can never remember when we're supposed to use them."

"Comms," said Art quietly. "We use them on all Möbius *comms*."

Astrid ignored him. "Me and Art have been doing Professor Clay's special assignments for more than a year now," she continued. "Nothing like the two of you, though. Seems you've outclassed us all."

An edge had crept into her voice; she was almost as famous for her burns and put-downs as for her flying machines.

Zen didn't react. "We just did what we had to do," she replied. "What any of us would have done. We had no idea what we were getting into."

"Heroic," said Astrid. She made to leave. "Listen, Art – I'm ready for another round of testing. *Outside* this time. You said you'd refined the solution after that last ... catastrophe. So let's get on with it, yeah?"

With that, she left the lab. As soon as she was gone, Art grabbed one of his scrawled-over printouts of the scan.

"Technically, Caleb," he said, lowering his voice a little, "the answer to your question is no. I don't have the complete formula. Ascertaining the precise atomic composition of a substance isn't really possible without a physical sample."

"I couldn't reach it without falling off the front of the church," Zen said. "And I didn't want to risk Beetlebat getting stuck to the wall."

"But," Art continued, raising a forefinger, "due to the incredible detail of that scan you took, Zen, I've been able to come up with this." He pointed to a string of letters and symbols written along the top of the printout, which he'd underlined heavily in red ink. "I've had to fill in a couple of gaps using standard compounds found in polyvinyl acetates and so on, which is definitely *not* right … but it should be enough to track other instances of this substance." He adjusted his glasses, a perplexed look crossing his face. "Now all I have to do is figure out where it came from."

"We might be able to help you there," said Caleb.

Art stared at him for a moment. "How? Don't tell me you're interested in the molecular chemistry of transferrable adhesives?"

"Whoa!" Caleb held up his hands. "No, I meant help you locate the origin of this substance, so you can … you can…"

Art snapped his fingers. "Of course – you're talking about your AI! I've heard about this. The one in *Terrorform*." He leaned in closer. "I'm a *humongous* fan, by the way. Level-twenty-two Oracle. I set up a forward base on Fraxis Prime yesterday – *loving* the slime jungle, all that wonderful acidic goo, it's like…" He just managed to stop himself and return to the business at hand. "What are you thinking?"

"If we give him – the AI, that is – access to this formula," Caleb said, "he can search for it online. On the dark web. And other places too. Way quicker than any human could."

Art passed him the sheet at once. Caleb slid the Flex from his pocket and held it over the formula.

"Got it, Sam?"

"I have, Caleb," the AI replied. "You were correct, Art. Your partial formula does provide a sufficient indication of the substance's uniqueness. I believe we can work with this."

Art's eyes had opened as wide as they could go. "Unbelievable," he murmured, peering down at the silver face in the corner of the Flex's screen. "That is … that really is extraordinary."

"I am also pleased that you enjoy our game," Sam added.

"You're *pleased*," Art repeated, smiling in amazement. "How fascinating. I mean, I – I do enjoy it, er … Sam. It's epic. In every sense of the word."

"Thanks for letting us have this, Art," said Caleb. "We'll let you know as soon as we find anything."

"No, no, thank *you*," Art replied, dragging his attention away from the Flex. "You're actually doing me a massive favour. I've *got* to finish off this joint project with Astrid. We're working on an aerial fire-suppression system – for spraying retardant foam on burning buildings. It's not Möbius or anything, but we've been stuck for a while now and she's getting quite … *annoyed* with me."

"Really?" Zen deadpanned. "Couldn't tell."

They said goodbye and started back around the helipad. Astrid had just brought out one of her flying machines and was positioning it beneath a spotlight, pointing it towards the side of lab number three. Caleb looked over curiously. It resembled a quad bike, but with handlebars that could also be moved forwards and backwards like a joystick. A kind of turbine had been set into the front, and there were huge vents where the wheels would go. The body was hand-painted, like her jacket – this time with the head and outstretched talons of a ferocious-looking merlin.

A squat device, a bit like a souped-up, reinforced vacuum cleaner, had been bolted underneath the turbine. This seemed to be what they were testing. Astrid began plugging in cables and flipping switches. As Caleb and Zen reached the lobby, Art hurried over with a pressurized canister, which he screwed onto the device's side. Then he went to stand next to Astrid as she held up a small remote control and pressed a button.

There was a loud popping sound – and suddenly Astrid, Art, the flying machine and much of the helipad were coated with several bucketloads of fresh gunk – this time neon green. It appeared to have burst from the vacuum-cleaner device in more or less every direction but the one they'd intended.

"Not again, Art!" Astrid yelled. *"Not again!"*

Caleb and Zen just made it onto the stairwell before bursting into laughter.

"I think the aerial fire suppression system could still use some fine-tuning," Zen said.

"Yeah," Caleb agreed. "A few kinks to iron out there."

They decided to go to the canteen for dinner. Caleb looked at the Flex as they headed back down the tower. An image of Art's partial formula remained on the screen.

"How's it going, Sam?" he asked. "Found anything yet?"

"I am scanning all standard online data fields," the AI answered. "No hits so far."

"A simple data search might not be enough," said Zen. "Even with Sam."

Caleb considered this. "You're right," he said, pushing through the doors of floor thirty-three. "We've got to think of something else."

A GREAT IDEA

*T*he ARC canteen was a large, rectangular room, fitted with sleek benches and low-hanging lights in the style of a modern Japanese restaurant. A raised table by the window was reserved for the teachers, but the pupils were allowed to sit anywhere else. The place was already packed. Caleb and Zen each picked up a plastic tray and joined the queue. The good news was that it seemed to be some sort of Italian night.

Five minutes later, they carried their food to a table at the back, just past some noisy year 9s they didn't know. Zen immediately began to attack her mushroom lasagne as if it were the first thing she'd eaten in days.

Caleb watched her for a moment. "Hungry?"

"Starving." Zen nodded at the Hawaiian pizza on Caleb's plate. "Aren't you? You got the cook to add extra pineapple and everything."

"What can I say?" Caleb replied. "I love pineapple on pizzas. People say it's inauthentic or whatever, but I think pineapple should be on *every* pizza. Doesn't matter what type."

"Here we go," Zen muttered, shovelling in some more lasagne.

"Margherita? Add pineapple. Neapolitan? Add pineapple." Caleb picked up a slice of his pizza; chunks of pineapple were slipping off the side. "I mean, will you look at this?"

Zen glanced over wearily. "What? It's got a load of pineapple on it."

"Yeah, but not *enough* pineapple. I mean, come *on*: the people of Hawai'i would be up in arms if they knew that the ARC Institute was putting so little pineapple on their pizzas. Am I right?"

Zen sighed. "Why don't you just eat pineapple slices then, with the other pizza toppings piled on top?"

Caleb took a huge mouthful – almost half the slice. "That is not such a bad idea, Zen," he said, talking around it. "Maybe next time I'll get to the kitchens early – see if the cook will—"

"Hey," said Zen suddenly. "Koenig's here."

On the raised table, over the heads of all the other students, Professor Hans Cornelius Koenig, the ARC's elusive head teacher was sitting at one end of the staff table. Koenig was a tall, distinguished-looking man with a large salt-and-pepper beard; he was deep in conversation with none other than Professor Clay.

Zen glanced around. "Wonder if they're talking about what happened at SolTec," she said under her breath.

Neither of them had any idea of the arrangement Koenig and Clay had come to regarding the Möbius Programme and its activities – although they were both convinced that he must be aware of it. Zen had previously speculated about the bigger picture. Could Koenig even be a spy himself, she had wondered, maybe with some other, larger organization?

"What do you think Koenig knows?" she asked quietly.

But Caleb's thoughts were elsewhere. He'd started thinking about how Zen had got her scan of the smart glue in the first place, and how they might be able to make use of this. And then, quite abruptly, it came to him.

"The *satellite*!" he exclaimed, breaking into a grin. "That's it! That's how we can find these guys, Zen! We can use the school satellite!"

The ARC satellite had been launched about five years ago. It was available to every student – with the permission of Mr Kattler, the head of physics – to gather data on weather patterns, traffic systems and much else.

Zen pondered this for a moment. "So ... you're thinking we could use it to ... track the smart glue somehow?"

Caleb's excitement was growing. "Yes – *exactly*. Using Art's formula. The satellite isn't the most advanced piece of tech going, but I reckon we could beef it up a bit with Sam. We'd start in Cambridge, along the route of your chase, and trace it from there."

"That might work," Zen said; then her brow furrowed slightly. "But how are we going to get permission to use it?"

"We'll have to go and ask KitKat."

This was the students' nickname for Mr Kattler. As well as the mind-boggling possibilities of physics, KitKat taught the whole school PE. He was over two metres tall and obsessed with all things sport – but especially with basketball.

"He'll be down in the gym," Zen said. "The year-ten and -eleven boarders do sports on Thursday night."

"But what are we going to say to KitKat?" Zen asked. "Why would he let us randomly use the school satellite at eight o'clock in the evening?"

Caleb finished his last mouthful of pizza and got to his feet. "I have an idea for that too. Come on."

FOR THE WIN

They emerged from a lift on one of the ARC's lower levels. It seemed to Zen like half the school was down there, jostling, shouting and banging locker doors. KitKat would almost certainly be in the main gym at the end of the corridor, coaching the year-11 boarders at basketball. She and Caleb walked slowly towards it, weaving between the clusters of boisterous older kids.

"Here's the plan," said Caleb, over the general din. "You go up to KitKat and tell him you're working on a special geography project – something on climate change that needs immediate satellite access. You've done stuff like that before, right?"

Zen wasn't sure about this. "You think he'll believe me?"

"Are you kidding? He *loves* you. You're amazing at literally all sport. You know that he wants you to try out for the year-eight basketball team."

"I don't play basketball," Zen replied. "And you're basically asking me to tell a teacher a complete lie."

They edged past the doors to the changing rooms.

Year 10s were spilling out into the corridor, trading boasts and insults about a game of five-a-side football that had just finished.

"I'd do it myself," Caleb said, "but I don't think KitKat even knows who I am." He stopped, leaned against a locker and lowered his voice. "Look, Zen, this is for the Möbius Programme. We're spies now. That means we have to use cover stories sometimes. It's kind of how spying is done."

Zen looked at him sceptically, narrowing her eyes. "I'm pretty sure spies don't usually lie to their own side."

"It doesn't count. KitKat isn't involved in the Möbius Programme." Caleb hesitated. "Or is he?"

"I don't think so. But he's not an idiot. Any story I tell him will have to be good."

Caleb grinned. "So you'll do it," he said. "I knew you'd see sense."

Zen sighed; it felt like she was giving in here. "It is definitely not sense that I'm seeing."

A locker slammed nearby. Caleb looked around to make sure no one was listening. "You'll need a convincing topic for this special project," he murmured. "Could it be about ... ocean acidification?"

"Too long-term," Zen replied. "Things like that have to be monitored over time, not checked at short notice." She thought for a moment, then leaned down towards the Flex. "Sam, could you give me the location of the latest extreme global weather event? Something in the past twenty-four hours, maybe?"

"Certainly, Zen," the AI replied. "The West Java province of Indonesia is at present experiencing serious flash flooding, which has already resulted in several large landslides. A possible cause is the unusual weather patterns generated by warming temperatures over the Indian Ocean."

"Thanks," Zen said. "That should work. I'll tell KitKat that I'm building a worldwide climate change model, and that I need up-to-date satellite footage of the flooding so that I can factor it in."

"Perfect," said Caleb.

The last of the year 10s were pushing past them now, heading for the lifts. They waited until the stampede had passed before carrying on towards the main gym. Zen normally loved being down there, but the task ahead was making her a little nervous. The sounds of a basketball game could already be heard: the squeak of trainers, the thump and slap of the ball, the shouts of the players. She led the way inside, nodding to a couple of people she knew. A dozen or so of the older pupils were on a long bench by the wall, watching the action closely. Zen and Caleb sat down on its far end and waited for a break in play.

KitKat himself stood towering over the players in the middle of the court. The ARC's head of physics had very long arms and legs and an unruly mop of sandy hair. He was wearing a red-and-white Chicago Bulls jersey, a pair of protective sports glasses, and a thick black sweatband on which the words **FOR THE WIN** were printed in large yellow letters. A silver whistle was dangling from his lips.

It was a practice game between two ARC teams, but this didn't mean it was being contested any less fiercely. After a minute or so, two players collided hard beneath one of the hoops. Zen didn't know the rules of basketball at all, but both players seemed to think that their opponent was at fault, and they began pushing at each other. KitKat stepped in at once and calmed everything down. He awarded a free throw, which went in – and as the scoring team whooped and high-fived, he let out three piercing blasts from his whistle. The players drifted apart, gathering in twos and threes to discuss the game, or going to grab their water bottles.

"Stay here," said Zen quietly. "It'll be better if I'm on my own."

Caleb leaned back against the wall. "Good luck."

Zen walked out onto the court. She tried to stay calm – to act like this was a completely routine visit. It was actually easier than she'd thought.

KitKat had pulled a small pad and pencil from his pocket and was jotting numbers on a grid, in what appeared to be some kind of intricate tactical game plan.

"Mr Kattler?" she said. "Do you have a second?"

KitKat looked up – or rather, looked down – peering at her through his sports glasses. "Hello there, Zen. I'm afraid there's no gym time scheduled for year eight tonight." His face suddenly brightened. "Or have you come to talk about the basketball team? We happen to have an opening for a power forward."

"Erm … not exactly," Zen said. *You can do this,* she told herself. "I'm here because of my latest geography project."

KitKat blinked. "Right," he said, after a short pause. "I suppose you need access to the school satellite again."

Zen explained about the flash floods in Indonesia and how she had to get some satellite images of the damage for her climate model. The lie – or rather, the cover story – sounded totally plausible. KitKat nodded along without much interest, scribbling some more numbers in his pad. Zen could see he was a little disappointed that she wasn't there to sign up for basketball, and distracted by the game plan he was putting together. He wasn't the slightest bit suspicious about what she was telling him.

When she'd finished, KitKat slid a smartphone from an elasticated armband and tapped away for a few moments. "There," he said. "I've sent you a login slot over the intranet. Will thirty minutes be long enough?"

Zen breathed out; the plan had worked. She felt a faint twinge of guilt for deceiving KitKat, but it passed quickly. Caleb was right. They were spies, and this was necessary for their mission.

"It will," she said. "Thanks, Mr Kattler."

"If you want to thank me, Zen," KitKat replied, putting his phone away again, "you'll come along to one of our trials after half-term. You would be an *incredible* power forward."

"But I don't know anything about basketball," Zen said. She looked over at the gym doors, wondering how she was going to escape. "I'm not even very tall."

"Now *that*," said KitKat emphatically, holding up one of his huge hands, "is one of the biggest myths surrounding this sport. You do *not* have to be tall to play basketball. In fact, some of the all-time greatest players in the American pro leagues have been—"

"Hey, Mr Kattler?" One of the players who'd been in the collision earlier was limping across the court towards them, wincing with every step. "I ... I think I might have sprained my ankle."

Much to Zen's relief, KitKat went over to him at once. She started back towards Caleb, subtly clenching her fist in triumph. He grinned and did the same.

They had satellite access.

Ten minutes later they were in Caleb's room, all set up and ready to go. The plan was to log in as Zen and then hand everything over to Sam. The AI would reconfigure the satellite's magnification settings, cranking everything up to the absolute maximum. At the same time, he would run a decoy investigation of the Indonesian flash flooding, making sure to save multiple images to Zen's intranet account.

Caleb activated the Flex's projector, throwing the satellite's nocturnal view of Cambridge against his bedroom wall. Sam rapidly zoomed in on the church roof where Zen had lost the SolTec saboteur, until they were looking at only a couple of square metres of stonework. It was dizzying to watch.

"Whoa," said Caleb. "That is an extreme close-up. Nice job, Sam."

"Due to the angle, only part of the handprint Zen scanned with Beetlebat can be made out," the AI reported. "But it is sufficient. Analysis of chemical residue upon the granite reveals an eighty-seven per cent match with Art's formula. This is the same substance."

"OK," said Caleb. "Use that sample as a baseline to program a special filter. Something that will detect this stuff and colour it a nice, bright, luminous yellow."

"It is done, Caleb. Applying it now."

A glowing mark appeared in the middle of the projection – the partial handprint. Sam drew the satellite camera back. The streets and buildings surrounding the church could now be seen, rendered in dull shades of grey. There was a smattering of yellow smears a couple of hundred metres away from the first one, running along the top of a shopping precinct.

"The guy I chased must have left those," Zen said excitedly. "He could easily have jumped up there from that bus he escaped on."

Over the next few minutes, moving the satellite camera methodically, they managed to identify a clear line of luminous yellow marks, leading south across Cambridge. It soon petered out – but seemed to point in quite a specific direction.

"I would speculate that the source of these traces was picked up by a motor vehicle," Sam said, "which took them onto the M11 motorway, heading towards London."

"That's got to be it," Zen said.

"All right," said Caleb. "Let's widen the search. London's the obvious place to begin. Go sector by sector, starting where the road from Cambridge comes in."

Sam pulled the satellite camera way back and moved it rapidly down the long curve of the M11, into the outer zones of London. He increased magnification again, advancing in a semicircle across the streets and houses. It didn't take long for them to get a hit.

"There!" said Zen. "Zoom in, Sam!"

The camera went closer. It wasn't a single yellow dot this time but several dozen of them, forming a trail that weaved over the rooftops – and soon intersected with seven or eight more.

"It's *everywhere*," said Caleb in amazement. "All over North London."

"I am detecting the substance in numerous other parts of the city as well, Caleb," Sam said. "Many thousands of individual traces."

"Is there any kind of … pattern? Do they lead to anything?"

"There is an especially large concentration around Camden Town."

Sam brought the camera above a junction of five main roads, then panned it up and to the left, following the course of a canal. Hundreds and hundreds of luminous dots were scattered across the grey buildings like a great constellation. They gathered in loose lines across the roofs, and were clustered upon railings, gutters and chimneys. In the middle of the tightest grouping was a rectangle of grey shadow, made oddly conspicuous by the brightness that surrounded it.

"What is that?" Caleb asked.

"Looks like a warehouse," Zen said.

"You are correct, Zen," said Sam. "There are several in this area, beside the canal. This one appears to be abandoned. I have logged the precise coordinates."

Zen was staring at the screen. "All of these smart-glue marks have been made by people coming in and out of that building."

Sam positioned the camera above it, zooming in until it felt like they were hovering a few metres above the roof.

"We need to get closer," Caleb said. "Take a look inside. We can't see anything from out here." He glanced at the clock in the corner of the projection: 20.18. "It's too late to go over there, though. Since Mitch joined the ARC, sneaking past the security guys isn't as easy as it used to be."

Zen got up and started for the door. "My room," she said decisively. "I know what to do."

THE SPIKERS

*T*hey walked quickly down the corridor. Zen was in number twelve; she unlocked the door, went inside and turned on a lamp. She'd adapted her bedroom to double up as a robotics workshop. It was filled to the brim with tools, parts and prototype robots, with everything stored in its proper place. At least thirty of her intricate machines – many of them based on insects, birds or reptiles – were up on shelves, hanging from hooks in the ceiling or standing in corners.

Zen sat down at her desk. Caleb approached a stool cautiously, eyeing the unfinished toad bot that squatted atop it. Zen clicked her fingers in front of the bot's snout and it came to life, clambering from the stool and marching off beneath her bed.

"We're going to use Beetlebat," she said. "If Sam gives me the coordinates for that warehouse, I can fly straight there."

"Right," said Caleb. "Good thinking."

Zen took the bot out of its charging pod, where it had been since their return from SolTec, and set it in a testing tray.

Then she opened her laptop and plugged in a customized game controller.

After their first Möbius mission, when Caleb had flown Beetlebat using the Flex, Zen had added some piloting software of her own to her favourite bot's operational app. This gave her much better control of it than her whistle commands, and also enabled the remote use of all its capabilities. She started it up now. The view from Beetlebat's sensors appeared immediately on the laptop's screen. It showed the inside of the testing tray, the top of her head, and part of the shadowy bedroom-workshop beyond.

"OK," she said. "We're ready to go."

A twitch of the controller's left stick and Beetlebat was out of the tray. Its carapace flashed in the lamplight as it flew up to the small air vent that Zen had adapted into a sort of microbot cat flap. The next moment it was gone, swooping over London.

Sam sent through the warehouse's location, which promptly appeared on the screen as a red marker pin. Zen steered the tiny bot through the glittering towers of the City and over the dark, ridged roof of Smithfield Market, heading north towards Camden Town. The main roads winding up through Farringdon were jammed with late rush-hour traffic. Crowds packed around the tube and train stations, while lines of red double-decker buses jostled for position at the busiest junctions.

"Wow," murmured Caleb after a while. "Beetlebat is really zipping along out there."

Zen checked the readings at the edge of the screen. "Yeah, we got lucky. Caught a strong tailwind."

"*Tailwind?*" Caleb repeated, beginning to smile. "Have you been *practising*, Zen?"

She glanced at him. "You have no idea how stressful it was watching you fly her back in the summer. That is *not* happening again."

"Fair enough." Caleb grinned. "You might want to look where you're going, though."

Zen's eyes went back to the laptop. The clock tower of St Pancras Station was looming directly ahead, lit up against the evening sky, its arched windows and ornate Gothic stonework suddenly filling the screen. She pulled back both sticks and squeezed the left-hand trigger – and Beetlebat twisted off to the side, just missing the tower as it plummeted down into the wide, bustling road that ran in front of the station. The view on the screen blurred wildly, flooding with light, while the audio feed became a scrambled din of street noise.

"*Look out!*" Caleb shouted, nearly jumping up from his stool.

Zen worked the controls expertly, keeping as calm as she could. A bus appeared, a row of faces staring from the windows. Almost without thinking, she swerved to the right, over a busy pavement, towards a tall red-brick entranceway. Fitted within it was a cast-iron gate that was formed by the words **BRITISH LIBRARY** stacked on top of one another. With only a split-second to spare, Zen hit the X button, folding in

Beetlebat's wings so it could shoot through the hole in a capital *A*. An instant later she extended them again, gliding the bot across the library's floodlit courtyard, up its sloping roof, and off into North London.

Caleb was laughing in disbelief. "OK," he said. "I admit it. That was a seriously good recovery."

Zen sat back in her chair, the controller trembling slightly in her grasp. "Sorry, girl," she said to Beetlebat under her breath. "*Way* too close."

The red marker pin reappeared in the centre of the screen. Zen followed the bright line of Camden High Street, turned left at the Regent's Canal, then flew Beetlebat above the oil-black water until it reached the warehouse. The building looked at least a hundred years old and was sealed up tight. Zen began to circle Beetlebat around it. The windows were set high in the walls and had been boarded over, while the doors were covered with crude metal panels – the kind fitted onto buildings that were due to be demolished.

"Hey," said Caleb, after a few seconds, "I think I just saw someone. Up on a roof."

"Where?"

"Off towards the park. Quick, switch to infrared."

Zen pressed the triangle button, cycling through some options – and their aerial view of Camden went a deep, hazy blue, with greenish spheres suspended around the streetlamps. She turned Beetlebat southwest, in the direction of Regent's Park.

Three white blobs, fringed with bands of red, orange and

green, were racing along the top of a row of houses, about as fast as human beings could go. They were obviously following a well-practised route. Beetlebat tracked them as they weaved over the rooftops, vaulted across alleyways, and finally performed an incredible swinging jump from the corner of a billboard. This sent them flying into the dark flank of the warehouse, where one by one they disappeared beneath the eaves.

"Let's get closer," said Zen.

She flew Beetlebat in, guiding the bot down towards the billboard. It was emblazoned with an advert for Scuti, a colossal retail site that sold everything from groceries to home electronics, all delivered to your door in less than a day. A carefully staged photo showed a smiling deliveryman handing a package to a delighted customer. Zen noticed that someone had defaced it. A pair of devil horns had been painted on the deliveryman's head, poking from beneath his green Scuti cap, while blood dripped from the bottom of the package.

Beetlebat landed on a top corner of the billboard. An opening was now visible – some kind of cargo hatch, just below the warehouse's roof.

Caleb pointed to a small black dome on the wall beside it. "Security camera."

"They are mounted all around the building," Sam said. "I cannot locate any blind spots."

"Not a problem," said Zen. "Nobody'll notice Beetlebat. Or they'll just think she's a moth or something."

Zen pushed the controller sticks forward and the bot took off again, swooping up to the warehouse and settling against the wall, its hook-like feet gripping on to the bricks. A black rubber sheet had been hung over the hatch to stop any light escaping from inside. Beetlebat crept in under its bottom edge and scuttled beneath a laser motion sensor into a bare, low-ceilinged attic. Zen moved the bot over to a crack in the old floorboards, positioning it carefully so that they could get a good look at whatever was below.

The top floor of the warehouse had been opened up to form a single massive room. Zen and Caleb could see laptops and bits of surveillance equipment set out on trestle tables, and a kitchen area with microwaves and long metal sinks.

Caleb leaned forward on his stool. "Zen," he said, "this is some kind of base."

The three figures they'd seen go in through the hatch were off to one side, catching their breath, having climbed down a ladder from the attic. They were wearing black clothes, close-fitting and lightweight, exactly like those of the guy Zen had chased over the rooftops of Cambridge. As she watched, they pulled off their masks; all three looked young, seventeen or eighteen at most. A fourth person came over to them – a woman of about twenty with short, white-blonde hair, also dressed in black, holding out a transparent plastic container. The runners promptly removed their gloves and dropped them into it. The white-blonde woman then sealed the container and said a few words, while the runners nodded obediently.

"Yeah," Zen murmured. "And it looks like she's in charge."

Zen inched Beetlebat closer to the crack, angling the tiny bot so they could see all the way down the room. At its far end was an enormous mural, painted in red, black and white: a simple, stylized depiction of a gun being broken in half by a long nail.

"What are we looking at here?" she said. "Is it an insignia or something?"

"Any ideas, Sam?" asked Caleb.

"Checking enforcement databases," the AI replied. "I have a match. This is the symbol of a group called the Spikers. Not much has been discovered about their organization or membership, but they are known to be radical antiwar activists with a strong online presence."

"Antiwar activists," Zen repeated. "That figures. What's with the name?"

"It is believed to be a reference to the ancient practice of 'spiking the guns'," Sam said. "After a battle, cannons would be disabled by having a long nail hammered into their firing mechanisms."

"This is it," said Caleb excitedly. "This is *it*, Zen! We've got them! These Spikers were the ones who attacked SolTec – and we've just found their HQ!"

Zen nodded, smiling with grim satisfaction. She rotated the control sticks, turning Beetlebat around and guiding it back out through the hatch. "We'd better get upstairs," she said, once the bot was airborne. "Professor Clay needs to know about this."

UNDERCOVER

*T*en minutes later, after asking for an emergency appointment on the ARC intranet, Zen and Caleb walked into Professor Clay's office. Zen felt tense and restless; she wanted to tell Clay what they'd learned as quickly as possible and work out what they were going to do next. Mitch was already in there, dressed in a fresh but completely identical shirt and suit. He'd forced his hulking frame into one of the leather chairs, and was drinking a cup of tea while looking intently at his phone.

"Hey, Mitch," said Caleb. "Still hard at work, huh?"

"Evil never sleeps, kid."

Professor Clay was sitting at her desk. Outside, beyond St Paul's, the other London towers were all lit up; far below, the traffic inched through the streets in chains of light.

"Caleb and Zen," she said, "there's something you should see."

She tapped at her laptop and a video began to play on her TV screen. At once, Zen realized that it was smartphone footage from the live-fire testing zone at SolTec, filmed by the guy she'd chased. It showed the tank bot, advancing in slow motion through a cloud of concrete dust, spraying bullets from its minigun. A voice began to speak, electronically distorted to sound like a kind of cyborg ogre.

"This is the true face of corporate robotics. New weapons are being made – killing machines of obscene, unstoppable power, that can be reprogrammed by a simple virus and turned against us all."

Caleb snorted. "That virus," he said, "was anything but *simple.*"

"SolTec and dozens of other companies just like them pretend that they are here to help," the voice continued. "To offer solutions to humanity's most pressing problems. But this is the truth: deadly, unstable technology, developed in secret and sold to the highest bidder. If robotic soldiers like these are unleashed upon the world, it will mean—"

Clay paused the video. "You get the idea," she said. "This was posted by an anonymous account nine minutes ago and is already going viral. I'm sure your AI noticed, Caleb."

"I did, Professor," Sam replied. "I calculated that there was a ninety-six point four per cent probability you would have seen it as well. As Caleb was already on his way to your office at that point, I decided that I would leave it for you to reveal."

Clay hesitated. "Right," she said. "Thanks for that."

Zen was staring at the screen – at a frozen image of the tank bot, lit scarily by the fierce white flash of the minigun's muzzle. She remembered the awful noise it had made. The blinding, suffocating dust. The shower of shattered glass that had come seconds later, when the observation window was blown in.

"Where was it posted?" she asked, trying to keep her voice steady.

"Site called DedVane," Mitch told her. "It was started a few years ago by a bunch of conspiracy nuts. More recently, though, certain radical groups have been using it to communicate. Send one another messages. Circulate videos and manifestos. Document their activities. Most of it is pretty dangerous. And all of it is illegal."

"The Spikers," Zen said. "They're one of these groups. They made this SolTec video. That's what we came up here to tell you about."

Professor Clay sat back heavily, making a noise that was equally amazed and annoyed. "OK," she said. "How on earth did you find that out?"

Together, Zen and Caleb explained about Art's partial formula, the scanning program Caleb had written, and how they'd used the ARC satellite and then Beetlebat to scope out the Spikers' base in Camden. Caleb got Sam to run some of the Beetlebat footage on the TV, finishing with a frame of the gun-breaking mural.

"This is fantastic work, guys." Mitch chuckled. "We were pretty sure that these Spikers were involved somehow, but this ... oh man, this is *proof*. All the proof we'll need." He grinned at Professor Clay. "Can you believe these kids?"

Clay was looking hard at Zen and Caleb. "It's a remarkably

quick result," she said. "I'm going to assume you had permission to access the ARC satellite."

"Of course we did, Prof," said Caleb. "We went down to the gym and got a login slot from Mr Kattler."

Zen decided that they had to tell Clay and Mitch everything. "I said it was for a climate change project," she added. "I've used the satellite for them before."

Clay's face was expressionless. "So you lied," she said. "You lied to an ARC teacher."

Zen remembered her conversation with Caleb outside the gym. "It was a cover story," she replied. "We needed access to the satellite, and we knew we couldn't risk sharing any information about the mission."

"A cover story," Clay repeated slowly. Then she smiled – an actual, genuine smile. "I'm impressed. You did the right thing. This is real live intelligence."

Zen straightened up, relieved that Clay wasn't angry with them. "How much do you know about the Spikers, Professor?" she asked. "Have they done this kind of thing before?"

"They keep well out of sight," Clay said. She was gazing at the mural on the screen, a forefinger to her lips. "Membership, organization, backing – all unknown. They've been linked to several incidents in recent months – attacks on companies connected to arms manufacture and distribution. But it's all small-time stuff. Vandalism, supply chain disruption, employee intimidation. Nothing like the strike on SolTec."

"Truth is, this recording of yours is the most information

anyone has ever been able to gather on them," Mitch said. "It looks almost like a black ops outpost. Way more serious than I would've expected."

Zen was beginning to feel properly worried. "Could they be preparing for another attack?"

Clay glanced over at Mitch. "It seems likely."

"Something weird is going on here," said Caleb. "You're telling us that the Spikers are small time – that SolTec was a major step up for them. So where did they get that crazy tech that enabled them to pull it off? The smart glue – the virus? And how did they know that those combat bots were down there in the first place?"

"Also," said Zen, "if they're antiwar, why would they want SolTec's death machines to be set loose on the streets of Cambridge?"

"These are good questions. But there's no way of knowing as yet." Clay clicked the video off, going back to a list of recent DedVane message-board posts. "All we can say is that the Spikers are extremely well equipped, with access to cash and some highly privileged intel. And they no longer seem to care how much damage they do, or how many people they hurt. It might even be their aim. We were incredibly lucky at SolTec. Next time could be very different."

Mitch looked ready to jump clean out of his chair. "Let's get moving, Professor," he said. "Make some calls. Counter-terrorism police. MI5. We've got to get over there. Crack this place wide open. Take these suckers down."

Zen nearly smiled. She was starting to like Mitch as much as Caleb did. The security chief was always ready to do whatever was necessary and without delay.

"They'll see you coming a mile away," she told him. "They had cameras everywhere. Motion sensors too. They'll run off over the roofs the second the alarm sounds. Disappear into the city. You'll never see them again."

Clay had steepled her fingers. "You and I both know what this situation calls for," she said to Mitch. "We need to stage an infiltration. Put together a false identity. It's our only real chance."

"Are you talking about sending someone *in there*?" asked Caleb in astonishment. "Like ... undercover or something?"

"It'll be really tough to find the right agent," Mitch replied, shaking his head. "Especially at such short notice. These Spikers are young – twenty or less. And extremely athletic too. I doubt there are many parkour freaks in the intelligence services."

While Mitch was speaking, Zen suddenly realized what had to happen. A weird excitement rippled through her. It seemed completely obvious.

"I could do it," she said.

Caleb gaped at her. "*What?* Have you gone completely crazy? No way, Zen. No *way*."

Professor Clay leaned back in her chair, adjusting her bandage. She seemed to be thinking it through. "It's a possibility," she said.

Mitch was shaking his head again, more firmly this time.

"When I took this job, Professor, I made a promise to Harper Quinn that I would keep these guys out of trouble. SolTec was an honest mistake. We had no idea what was waiting for us inside that messed-up robot factory. This, though – this is *totally* different. We just *can't*."

"You made a promise about Caleb," Zen interjected. "Not about me."

"I don't think my mum meant that I should be kept safe while you just took every stupid risk you could," Caleb said hotly. "I'm pretty sure she wanted Mitch to watch out for us both. For the whole Möbius Programme."

Clay sat forward, frowning slightly. "The Möbius Programme is *my* responsibility, Caleb," she said. "Not Mr Mitchell's. And from a strictly logical standpoint, Zen is the ideal candidate. She fits the profile."

Zen caught her breath. Clay was going to allow it.

"Come on, Professor," said Mitch. "You can't seriously be—"

"She is a little young," Clay continued, "but we can easily alter her hair and clothes so that she passes for fourteen. The Spikers are less likely to be suspicious of someone even younger than they are. Zen has shown several times how courageous and resourceful she is. And she matched that runner this afternoon move for move."

Mitch was staring out at St Paul's. He didn't say anything.

"We'll be extremely careful," Clay told him. "We'll prep her fully, supply her with a watertight identity, and be ready to extract her at any time. She'll just be gathering intel. It'll be a three-day op at the most."

Listening to Clay spell everything out like this actually made Zen more frightened and uncertain about what she was volunteering for. She did her best to ignore these feelings, crossing her arms tightly. This had to be done. Her hand went to her jade necklace – a Rafiq family heirloom, passed down to her by one of her Syrian grandmothers.

"It'll work, Professor," she said. "It's the only way."

"But what if the guy she chased saw her?" asked Caleb. Zen noticed that his face was reddening, and a deep line had appeared in his brow. He was upset – afraid on her behalf. "What if he recognizes her when she shows up at their base?"

"Like I said, we'll alter her appearance," Clay replied. "Besides, that chase happened fast, didn't it? With huge clouds of dust flying around?"

"Yeah," Zen murmured. "It was pretty intense. I don't think he got a proper look at me."

"What about surveillance, then?" Caleb said next. "Why don't we just send Beetlebat back in there again to plant some listening devices?"

Mitch shifted in his chair. "Sorry, kid," he said reluctantly. "I don't think that'll work here. Given the sophisticated tech the Spikers have been using, and the way they've been able to cover their tracks up until now, it's highly likely that they're sweeping the place regularly. And if they find even one bug, that'll be it. They'll be gone. We'll have lost them."

"And bugs are stationary," Clay added. "The Spikers won't just be standing around talking about their plans. There'll be codewords. Levels of access. Details being kept secret from most of the group until the last moment. Infiltration really is the best option." She turned to Zen. "Do you honestly want to do this?"

Zen nodded. "Yes, Professor," she said firmly. "I chased after that guy in Cambridge. It should be me who catches him."

Clay studied her for a second, a look of satisfaction in her green eyes. "Good. I knew we could rely on you, Zen. I'm going to put some other Möbius operatives on this as well – the best expertise we have. And strict mission guidelines will be put in place. As soon as you've obtained concrete intel about the Spikers' plans – when and where they're intending to strike next, or even just the identity of their target – we'll pull you out."

Mitch stood up and fastened the top button of his jacket. Zen could tell that he was annoyed with Clay – he'd been outmanoeuvred and was being made to go along with something he wasn't sure about at all. "I want to run the op, Professor," he said. "If this is really going to happen, I want to be on the ground with Zen. I want to be able to extract her if there's even a *whisper* of trouble."

"Very well," said Clay. "I'll ensure that you—"

"I want to be on the ground too," Caleb blurted. "I want to help Zen."

Zen looked over at him. He was angry and worried – and hurt as well, like he felt he was being excluded from the mission. Seeing her friend like this gave her a strong, unsettling sense of how alone she was going to be. For all Clay and Mitch's talk of Möbius support, this was a solo op.

Clay raised an eyebrow, angling her chair so that she faced Caleb. "Oh, you're going to help, Caleb," she said. "Your particular skillset will be essential, in fact. We need you to create an entirely new person – an identity that Zen can use. Birth certificate. Medical and dental records. A list of home addresses. Social media as well – a Zap page, Krinkl, whatever you lot are into right now – going back a couple of years at least. Can you handle that?"

"Sure," Caleb replied crossly. "No worries. Me and Sam can do all that in a few hours. But what's Zen supposed to do when we're finished? Just take the bus up to Camden and knock on the Spikers' front door?"

Even as Caleb asked this question, Zen could tell that his mind was working – weighing the problem and coming up with an answer.

"You're right," she said. "They've got to *want* to talk to me. We've got to bring them to us somehow."

Caleb was looking at the list of DedVane posts on the TV screen. He pointed to the previous post by the anonymous account that had put up the SolTec video. It was titled *Scuti Means Death*. Just under a week before was one called *Use Scuti = Kill the World* and a few days earlier than that, *Scuti Scum*.

"Remember that billboard, Zen," he asked, "outside the Spikers' warehouse in Camden? The one with the vandalized Scuti advert – the devil horns and blood?"

"Kind of hard to forget."

"That can't be a coincidence. I bet the Spikers did it. Seems like they *really* hate Scuti."

"That company has a dark side all right," said Mitch. "They've driven literally thousands of smaller firms out of business. And they treat their warehouse workers and delivery guys like dirt. I heard that even their bathroom breaks are monitored."

"Now that's taking spying a step too far," Clay remarked dryly.

Sam spoke up via the Flex. "Analysis of these DedVane posts indicates that the Spikers are also aware of who owns Scuti," he said. "The company is in the portfolio of a megacorporation called Hardcastle Solutions. This conglomerate has active interests in fossil fuel extraction, cryptocurrencies and cutting-edge weapons manufacture."

"That has to be why Scuti is on the Spikers' hit list," Zen said. "They want to get at Hardcastle Solutions."

"Scuti is certainly Hardcastle's most visible asset," Sam said. "Their other holdings tend to be in very remote locations. Many are kept secret."

"Have the Spikers actually attacked Scuti yet, Sam?" Caleb asked. "Or have they just been ranting on a conspiracy site?"

"The DedVane posts mention three unsuccessful sabotage attempts upon Scuti targets," the AI answered. "The company's heavy security is apparently to blame for this."

Caleb looked at Zen. "Heavy security, huh? Sounds like our kind of challenge."

Clay's eyes narrowed. "What exactly are you thinking?"

"That Zen does what the Spikers haven't been able to. That we pull a prank on Scuti – something that'll really get the Spikers' attention."

Across the room, Mitch let out a deep sigh.

"I need to know a little more than that," said Clay.

"Don't worry, Professor, we'll make sure it's safe." Caleb grinned. "And completely *spectacular*."

"Well, this seems to have cheered you up at least, Caleb," Clay observed. "I'll expect to see a full plan within the next twenty-four hours. Then we can go through it together."

"It needs a name," said Caleb. "These ops have special names, right?"

Zen glanced down at the Flex. "Scuti... That's a star, isn't it, Sam?"

"Correct, Zen. The company is named after an extreme red supergiant in the constellation Scutum. It is considered one of the largest known stars by radius, with a volume nearly five billion times that of the sun."

Clay guessed what Zen was thinking. "Operation Supergiant it is," she said. "Now go and get some sleep, you two. You've got another full day tomorrow."

DIMA KAHF

Forty-eight hours later, Zen was back outside the special project labs on the roof of the ARC tower, watching Astrid Yeoh strap herself into a weird contraption that she called a jump-pack. It looked like a bulky fibreglass rucksack with two massive vents on its base and a pair of joystick arms that jutted out on either side. Zen turned around and London stretched out before her, shimmering in the darkness. Despite all their preparations, all the briefings and simulations and practice, she still couldn't quite believe that they were going through with this.

It was Saturday night. Half-term had begun and the ARC was almost empty. Among the couple of dozen kids who'd remained behind were several Zen knew were in the Möbius Programme, including Astrid. She'd said that it wasn't worth going all the way back home to Hong Kong just for a week – but Zen suspected that she'd been instructed to stay in London so she could help with the mission.

Professor Clay came out of lab two, switching off the light behind her. Zen caught sight of her reflection in the lab window and felt a shiver of strangeness. She was dressed in black from head to toe, like someone who was trying to look like a Spiker. Her long hair was gone – cut into a bob, bleached and dyed ice blue. Mitch had done this for her, after school on Friday; it was a standard part of CIA training, he'd told her as he'd snipped away, so that agents could alter their appearance mid-mission. This had really made her feel like a spy, but the sudden change had still been a shock. She'd been transformed. It was going to take a lot of getting used to.

Zen and Caleb had been extremely busy since the day of the SolTec op. As well as planning and presenting Operation Supergiant and going to their usual lessons on Friday, they'd also put together a complete false identity. The name of this fake person was Dima Kahf. She was fourteen, the only child of British-Syrian aid workers. Her dad had died before she was born, while her mum had been killed seven years ago during the Syrian civil war, when a missile drone had destroyed a medical storage facility she'd been inspecting. This tragedy had given Dima a deep hatred of the arms industry – and automated weapons in particular. Afterwards, she'd lived with a great-aunt for a few years, and then with a grown-up cousin, before going into foster care. She was currently living at a home in Chalk Farm, close to Camden.

Dima liked Studio Ghibli movies, parkour and salted caramel ice cream, and belonged to a long list of environmental and pacifist protest groups. She was getting steadily more radical, posting her support for all kinds of direct action, using the online tag *Polar_X*. She'd even started logging onto DedVane, leaving messages – along with raised-fist and explosion emojis – beneath many of the videos that were put up there, including the Spikers' footage of SolTec.

Caleb had put a ton of work into this. Zen could tell that he was trying to make himself feel better about the fact that she would be going on this mission alone. With Sam's help, using Zen's own photos, he'd made dozens of images of Dima, then hacked into the major social media sites to create pages and posts that seemed to chart her life over the past few years. There were even videos of her shouting and waving banners at a few big demonstrations. These deep fakes were so convincing that Zen almost had to remind herself that she hadn't actually done these things. All in all, it was the perfect cover. Dima Kahf was driven, a bit lonely, totally committed to the same cause as the Spikers – and ready to take the next step.

Clay walked over, buttoning her brown leather overcoat against the wind. "Are you sure you're going to be able to manage the extra weight?" she asked Astrid.

"The jump-pack was designed for disaster relief," Astrid replied, fiddling with a dial, "to get supplies to earthquake victims or whoever." She gave Zen a sidelong glance. "I always planned on there being some baggage."

This seemed to satisfy Clay; Zen got the impression that Astrid had earned her trust on previous missions. "How about you, Zen? Everything OK?"

Zen looked down at her black trainers, doing a quick mental check of her gear. "Yes, Professor. I'm ready."

Clay's expression grew serious. "I've authorized Operation Supergiant because of the extreme urgency of the situation," she said. "But I have to remind you that if you end up in police custody tonight, I'll to have to pull in some … *really* big favours to get you out. And it may have consequences for the Möbius Programme as a whole."

"It has to be done like this, Professor," Zen said. "It has to look right, or the Spikers won't—"

"I know, Zen, I know. You don't need to explain it all to me again. But our reasons won't matter, however good they are. I'm not supposed to endanger my operatives like this. If you're caught, I'll be given some kind of official sanction – and our investigation into the Spikers will be terminated at once."

"We're not going to get caught," Astrid muttered.

"Caleb has hacked the alarms," Clay continued. "He assures me that he can keep them offline for exactly ten minutes. If it looks like that isn't going to be long enough, abort the op. Don't think twice – just cut your losses and get out straight away. Understood?"

Zen forced herself to focus – to concentrate on what she had to do. She fitted in her earpiece and pinned a minuscule button mic to her jacket collar. "Understood."

"We are live," said Sam's voice in her ear. "The signal is strong. For the duration of this mission, I will be using the codename 'Rook', in order to conform with Möbius protocols.

Do you have the glasses, Hawk – and you, Merlin? Activation would be advisable."

Zen and Astrid each slid a pair of lightweight glasses from their pockets and put them on. Clay had issued these earlier, saying they'd been made by another Möbius kid with the codename "Magpie". Immediately, tiny orange numbers began to stream down the sides of Zen's vision as the glasses linked to the Flex, which was in Clay's office with Caleb.

"Swift here." Caleb's voice was in her earpiece. "Readings are all green. We can see what you see."

Zen turned to Astrid. "Time to hook me up."

Astrid readied a harness, clipping it to the jump-pack, then beckoning to Zen to come closer. It fastened securely around Zen's waist and shoulders, basically strapping the two girls together. Zen could smell the sweet tang of Astrid's blueberry-flavoured chewing gum as she tried to prepare herself for launch.

Clay stepped back. "Good luck, both of you," she said. "Keep your eyes open. And don't take any unnecessary risks."

Before anything else could happen, though, a door flew open across the helipad and Art stumbled out. "Wait!" he cried. "Wait, wait! I've got something for Zen – for the op!"

Zen was a little surprised to see him. She hadn't known that he was spending half-term at the ARC as well. He hadn't been at any meals, or in the common areas; it occurred to her that he might not actually have left his lab since Thursday night. He ran across to where they were standing. There was what looked like a bundle of sticks in his hand, each with a small bulb fastened to its end.

"Quickly, Art," said Clay.

"Yes, yes, Professor, of course. I just *cracked it*, you see, just this minute, and I couldn't let Zen go off without ... you know ... I mean, I haven't *quite* got there – the formula was partial, as you are aware – but I believe that if—"

"Art," Clay repeated, more tersely, "what are you talking about?"

"The smart glue," Art said, straightening his spectacles and breaking into a grin. "I've managed to synthesize it. Or rather a version of it." He looked at Zen. "You're an archer, right? You've won competitions?"

Astrid made a tsking sound right next to Zen's ear. "Jeez, Art," she said. "Why don't you just ask for her freaking autograph?"

Art ignored her. He handed the sticks to Zen. "Glue arrows," he said. "Break the bulb and they'll stick to anything. Like, *instantly*. The unsticking part is proving rather more ... difficult to replicate, but, well, I thought they might come in useful anyway."

Zen studied the arrows. They were graphite, with red rubber flights. The glue bulbs seemed pretty robust – it would take quite a lot of force to rupture them. She smiled back at Art. Right then, there was no way for her to reach the small backpack in which she'd stowed the rest of her gear, so she just held the glue arrows across her chest.

"Thanks, Art. I'm sure I'll—"

"All right, let's do this," said Astrid impatiently. "See you later, Professor."

A great roaring sound began, like the largest hand dryer in the world. Zen felt an enormous wrench as Astrid's jump-pack pulled her suddenly into the air – five metres, ten, and then out over the side of the ARC tower, with a dizzying thirty-five storeys of empty air opening up beneath them.

Before Zen could take it in fully, her trainers met concrete once more, her left leg buckling a little as they landed on the skyscraper opposite. The jump-pack whirred down. They were at the edge of a wide roof garden, with elaborate topiary, lily ponds and low-lit gravel paths. Zen's heart was pounding and it felt like a few hundred butterflies had been set loose inside her stomach.

"Hey," she shouted, "d'you think you could—"

Astrid gunned the engine and they went up even more abruptly, banking right, cutting over a building with a huge glass pyramid mounted at its top. Zen caught a glimpse of a marble foyer; a large party of business people, milling about and talking; a string quartet playing in a corner. This time they landed on a futuristic-looking walkway connecting the uppermost levels of two ultra-modern towers.

"So far so good," said Caleb in Zen's ear. "Here's where you're headed."

A waypoint appeared to the east, projected on the lenses of Zen's high-tech glasses, glowing red among the city blocks. They jumped again, soaring over a construction site and settling upon a framework of red girders. Zen slipped, feeling her foot go over the edge – but before she could fall they were off, jetting straight upwards, the wind blasting her blue hair back from her face.

As they reached the pinnacle of the jump, Zen looked ahead to where the waypoint hovered. It was above a particularly massive tower shaped like a shiny, mirror-clad torpedo. A gigantic logo was set near its top: a green circle with a wavy line enclosed within it. The word *Scuti* was spelled out below it in loose lower-case letters. This was the company's European headquarters, where the most daring part of Operation Supergiant was going to take place.

Moments later, they touched down on the torpedo tower's summit. As soon as they'd landed, Astrid released the harness. Zen dropped forward to a crouch, panting hard, feeling the cool glass beneath her fingers. She put Art's glue arrows in her backpack, placing the bulbs carefully in the reinforced section at its base, then pulled on a black ski mask. The tower's roof was as empty and featureless as an iceberg. The wind was stronger here, howling around the smooth, mirrored curves; it felt like it might knock her over the edge if she wasn't careful.

"We've … we've arrived," she gasped.

Astrid was on her haunches; the jump-pack rested on the glass behind her, acting like an anchor against the wind. She was already staring at her phone, chewing gum and scrolling through social media, like this was all no big deal. Zen wondered how often she went night-jumping around the City of London.

"Better get moving, Hawk," she said, without looking up. "I'm not going to sit out here for ever."

OPERATION SUPERGIANT

"OK," said Caleb. "Marking the insertion point … now."

A red rectangle appeared about ten metres ahead. Zen hurried over to it and discovered a panel set into the sheer surface of the tower.

"Just taking care of the locks," Caleb murmured. "Access in five seconds." There was a low *thunk* and the panel lifted a couple of centimetres at one end. "You're in. All alarms are offline. We've got ten minutes before the system resets. I'll stick a mission timer in your glasses."

The digits appeared in a corner of the left-hand lens, counting down: 9:58, 9:57, 9:56…

Zen opened the hatch and dropped into the corridor below. She looked around her. It was the total opposite of the slick office space she'd been expecting. The walls were covered with crazy paintings, like blown-up comic strips, showing explosions, fighter jets, and huge words like *BLAM!* and *POW!* To either side, open-plan areas were filled with antique jukeboxes, electric guitars and drum kits, and vintage video game cabinets. In one corner stood a row of air-hockey tables; in another, a colossal ball pit.

"Swift," she whispered, "where am I?"

"Architectural plans say the creative suite," Caleb said. "Looks kinda nuts."

"Scuti are known to encourage games, competitions and impromptu musical performances among their top-level employees," Sam said, "in the belief that it fosters innovative thinking. The mission statement on their website says that they want to make Scuti a true friend to its customers and its staff, rather than just a company."

"And it's all a smokescreen," said Zen. "A big, fat corporate lie."

"Getting into character, huh?" Caleb chuckled.

"Something like that. Which way to the boardroom?"

"Go to the atrium. You'll know when you get there – apparently, there's a freaking *fountain* in the middle of it. I'll get Sa— uh, *Rook* to put some directions up on your specs."

A second later a silver arrow blinked onto the lenses, pointing out Zen's route, while thin golden lines traced the outlines of the corridors and doorways to compensate for the low lighting. The fountain was off – but the sight of it standing there in the centre of the wide atrium still caused her mouth to fall open in amazement. At least four metres high, it had been made in the shape of a giant mutant squid wrestling with a submarine. This statue was fully coloured and highly detailed; even at a distance, Zen could see the serrated suckers on the monster's tentacles as it slowly crushed the submarine's hull.

"I don't even know what to say here."

"It's from *Full Fathom Five*," Caleb told her. "This megabudget TV series Scuti is developing."

"They make TV shows too?"

"Yep – TV, movies, music, even gaming. They're taking over the world. *Full Fathom Five* actually looks pretty good. Deep-sea steampunk survival-horror. You'd love it."

"No, I wouldn't."

"OK, no, you wouldn't. Keep going."

The mission timer now said 8:49. Zen crept around the fountain's edge as quickly as she could, following the silver arrow, trying not to meet the squid's bulging, football-sized eye. Ahead was a half-flight of stairs and a set of glass double-doors that slid open as she approached.

"Don't worry, that was us," Caleb told her. "It's all under control. This is kind of a speciality of ours, right, Rook?"

"You could say that, Swift. We have certainly broken into some very well-guarded locations in the past. Hawk, you are now entering the executive mezzanine. The main boardroom is close."

Zen peered down the wide, unlit corridor beyond the doors. "There's something up ahead," she said. "Something weird."

"I will adjust the settings on your glasses," Sam said.

Everything grew lighter, like someone was turning up a dimmer switch. Figures were standing in the corridor – at least five or six of them. Instinctively, Zen ducked back into the atrium, her eyes wide. She remembered what Professor Clay had said at the tower. She absolutely could *not* get caught in there.

All was quiet, though – no footsteps or muttered words. She looked again and her shoulders sagged with relief. The figures were not Scuti security guards but life-sized models, set along the passage in shallow alcoves. There were people in retro-futuristic diving suits, with spherical copper helmets and spearguns; bizarre mermen with iridescent scales, fan-like fins, and crab-claws for hands; intricate, goggle-eyed automatons built from boiler tanks, pistons and rubber tubes.

"More from *Full Fathom Five*," said Caleb. "Scuti are really going for it with that show."

Her heart hammering, Zen moved past the unnervingly realistic figures towards the end of the corridor. The silver arrow was pointing left, at another doorway, which opened silently as she drew near. She checked the mission clock: 7:22. Just enough time.

The boardroom beyond was massive, with an oval conference table in its centre. On one side, a floor-to-ceiling window provided a staggering view of the Thames, while on the other was the famous Scuti Wall. This was a huge, detailed mural – part-timeline, part-photo collage – that covered an area the size of two double-decker buses. It told a folksy, rose-tinted version of the company's story: how it had started in its founder's garage, been gradually built up through dedication and hard work, finally becoming the global phenomenon it was today. There were lots of slogans about family and value, accompanied by images of grinning warehouse workers, delivery staff and customers. The Scuti Wall appeared frequently in the company's promotional material. It had been used in adverts, documentaries and interviews with its executives, and had been the background of their retail website for as long as Zen could remember.

"Just under seven minutes left," said Caleb. "Better get that bot started."

Zen put down her backpack and took out the robot she'd named Frida, after Frida Kahlo, her favourite artist. It was something she'd been tinkering with for a while – and then had quickly got operational while Caleb and Sam were making their deep fake videos of Dima Kahf. Frida looked pretty basic: a small bundle of cylinders and computer components with two extendable rotors at one end, each about the size of an orange slice. But it had a powerful on-board processor, a supercompact industrial paint sprayer – and a surprisingly large supply of highly concentrated luminous yellow paint.

Zen took Frida to the left edge of the Scuti Wall. The bot had no AI installed; once activated, it would simply run the program she'd written for it that afternoon. This would take exactly two minutes and fifteen seconds. She turned it on and the rotors flicked out, humming to life. It rose out of her hands, up to the top corner of the mural. The next instant she heard the flat hiss of the paint sprayer.

"OK," she said. "So far so good."

A single *Full Fathom Five* figure stood in the boardroom, over by the window. It was one of the divers, without a helmet this time; her dark hair had been swept back from her brow and there was an expression of heroic resolve on her face. Zen whistled two flat notes and pointed at it. Beetlebat crawled from the backpack and flew over to perch on the model's head. Zen whistled again and the bot turned towards her, the LEDs on its antennae winking in the darkness.

"Switch to the Beetlebat feed, Swift," she said, taking off the glasses and putting them in her pocket. "How's it looking?"

There was a pause as Caleb studied the image coming through from Beetlebat's sensors. "Yeah, that'll do nicely. Just the right angle. Timer says Frida will be done in ... one minute twenty-two seconds. And the alarms will be back on four minutes after that. It's showtime, Hawk. You ready?"

Zen took a breath. "Hit the lights."

Immediately, the cavernous boardroom was lit up by a couple of dozen recessed lights. Zen narrowed her eyes for a moment, adjusting to the glare. Then she began to speak.

"Scuti thinks they've fooled us all," she said in a tone of controlled fury. "They think that they can hide what they really are. What they're a part of. But we've just got into their headquarters – all the way to the top of their big shiny tower. They can't keep us out. They can't stop us from getting at the truth. The billions Scuti makes from selling its cheap TVs and clothes and groceries help to fund some of the worst people in the world. This company is soaked in blood."

Behind her, the hissing of Frida's sprayer stopped, followed by a soft *thud* as the bot landed on the floor – as it was programmed to do once its job was complete.

"Well, here's our message for you, Scuti," Zen continued, "with your stupid lying wall. The truth is coming. It's time to show everyone what you really are."

With that, Zen stepped out of shot, giving a clear view of the Scuti Wall. Caleb switched off the lights again. Frida's work blazed across it, in luminous yellow letters four metres high: **SCUTI = HARDCASTLE = MASS MURDERERS**. At the far end was a huge rendition of the Spikers' broken gun symbol.

"All right," said Caleb. "Three minutes fifty-two seconds left. You need to leave."

Zen put the glasses back on and went to reclaim Frida, hurrying beneath the enormous glowing slogan. She whistled to Beetlebat, who flew across the boardroom and landed on her shoulder. When both bots were safely in her backpack, she started for the doors.

"How was that?" she asked Caleb. "You get everything?"

He laughed. "Oh yeah. You were … pretty scary, actually. Totally believable."

Zen rushed down the creepy waxworks museum corridor, past the squid fountain and into the creative suite. The mission timer read 2:11. She felt good – like the most difficult part was over. They'd pulled it off. She was going to make it.

The window she'd come in through was at least three metres above the ground. As she was looking around for something to stand on, a powerful white beam slanted in through the glass ceiling and began moving slowly across the floor. Zen froze. She heard the *thwup-thwup* of rotor blades. A police helicopter was approaching, training its spotlight on the Scuti tower.

"Merlin here," said Astrid's voice in the earpiece. "I really don't want to *scare* anyone, but it looks like we might have some company."

"The lights," Zen said. "Back in the boardroom. Someone must have noticed them. The police will tell Scuti's security, right? If they've taken a call?"

"According to the company's protocols," said Sam, "they will not do anything unless—"

Lights came on throughout the floor. An electronic alarm started up, a shrill, unbearable wailing that drowned out all other sound.

Zen began to panic. This was it – the worst-case scenario. Security guards would be there any minute. She'd be grabbed and handed over to the police. Professor Clay and the Möbius Programme would be in big trouble, and their current mission would be brought to an abrupt end. The Spikers would be free to carry out whatever they were planning next – perhaps an attack even more devastating than the one at SolTec.

No. Zen fought back her fear. She wasn't caught yet. There was still a chance of escape, if she could think clearly – and act fast.

She ran over to a drum kit and kicked it apart. The alarm was so loud that even the crash of the falling cymbals couldn't be heard at all. With some effort, she heaved the bass drum and two snares beneath the open window, stacking them on top of one another to form an unsteady tower. It leaned as she climbed, beginning to teeter – and as she sprang up, grabbing hold of the window's edge, she felt it topple over beneath her.

Astrid hadn't moved from her corner of the roof, but she was craning her neck, watching the police helicopter closely. There were surely just a few seconds left before the roaming spotlight found her.

Zen pulled herself through the window and broke into a run. "Start the jump-pack, Merlin!" she shouted into her mic.

Astrid looked in her direction. "We've got to strap you in. We can't go until you're—"

"No time! *Start it!*"

Zen reached into her backpack and pulled out a couple of Art's glue arrows. Guessing what she was going to do, Astrid flicked some switches and took hold of the jump-pack's joysticks. The fans roared to life again, preparing to launch. Zen skidded up behind her, nearly slipping on the glass. She jammed the glue arrows against a wide panel on the jump-pack's top, breaking the bulbs and sticking them fast. Then she gripped on to their graphite shafts as tightly as she could.

"*Go!*" she shouted.

They shot up into the air just as the helicopter reached their side of the Scuti tower. Astrid steered sharply to avoid its spotlight, using the rotor downwash to provide an extra burst of speed, and plunging them into the chasm between the mirrored buildings.

Zen held on for dear life, teeth clenched hard, her legs now flying out behind her. The high-tech glasses were whipped off her face by the wind. She couldn't last more than a minute like this. They had to get down or she would fall. She tried not to think of the vast drop that yawned below – of the tarmac and concrete of the street rushing up to meet them...

There was another twisting turn and suddenly their descent slowed. Zen's body thumped back against the jump-pack, which was now roaring extra loudly – and they landed messily on top of a smaller, older block, tucked away among the gleaming modern giants.

Zen let go of the arrows at once. She slumped to the ground, gasping for breath, every muscle and joint screaming in pain. The jump-pack wheezed, its fans slowing. Astrid was turning in the darkness, checking for the police helicopter. The rotors could still be heard but they sounded distant, and the beam of the spotlight was gone.

"I don't think they saw us," she said.

"That ... that was some awesome flying," Zen panted.

Astrid shrugged; she chewed her gum. "You all right?"

Zen rubbed her aching shoulders. "Just about. Feels like my arms were nearly pulled out of their sockets."

Astrid looked at the two glue arrows jutting from the back of the jump-pack. "Those things had better come off," she said, "or I am going to be *seriously* annoyed."

"Hawk, what's going on?" said Caleb anxiously, via the earpiece. "We've lost your visual feed. Is everything OK?"

"Yeah," Zen replied. "Yeah, we're good. Merlin and I had to make an emergency exit. Afraid my glasses got lost along the way."

She heard Caleb exhale with relief. "That would explain it. It looks like you're in the clear, anyway. There haven't been any intruder sightings reported. But Rook says the Met will keep sweeping the area for the next hour or so."

"Did you guys do what you needed to do?" Astrid asked.

Zen nodded. "Mission accomplished."

"Come on, then." Astrid began readying the harness at the front of the jump-pack. "We are *so* out of here."

A TRULY EPIC BREAKFAST

The next morning, Caleb got up early, threw on some clothes and went straight down to the canteen. No one was around apart from a couple of members of the kitchen staff. The few pupils who were still in the tower wouldn't be up for a while yet; he was pretty sure that Zen was one of them, having a well-deserved lie-in after her Scuti adventure. It felt like he had the ARC Institute completely to himself. As he walked in, however, someone cleared their throat pointedly. He turned to see Professor Clay, dressed in a long charcoal-grey cardigan, leaning on her walking stick just inside the doorway. She beckoned him over.

"Your DedVane video is doing well, Caleb," she said. "It looks like Operation Supergiant was worth the effort."

Caleb grinned. "You might say it was a ... *glowing* success, eh, Professor?"

Clay didn't react.

"Because of the paint," Caleb explained. "Up in the boardroom. You know, the way it ... glowed."

Clay let out a small sigh. "There was the alarm, of course.

That was unexpected, but Zen managed it with her usual proficiency. And the lost pair of glasses. Magpie was out all night hunting them down – or what was left of them." She adjusted her hold on the cane. "I just need to be absolutely certain that none of this can be traced back to us."

"No way," said Caleb. "Don't worry, Professor. We're completely in the clear." He hesitated. "The Met's cybersecurity division *was* sniffing around a little bit earlier. I used a fake IP address to cover our tracks, though – to make it look like Polar_X was posting from a suburb of Reykjavik. They'll never work out who did it."

The smell of fried food was wafting over from the kitchens. A soft growl came from Caleb's stomach.

Clay seemed reassured. "So now we wait," she said, walking off into the corridor. "Take a break, Caleb. Enjoy your half-term."

"Oh, I intend to," he replied. "Starting with a truly *epic* breakfast."

He strode across the empty canteen, heading directly for the hot food counter. Taking a plate from the stack, he loaded it with everything on offer – bacon, sausages, fried eggs, baked beans, mushrooms, even a couple of tomatoes. Then he sat down in his favourite spot over by one of the windows, squeezed out a big blob of ketchup, and set to work.

About halfway through, Caleb laid the Flex on the table so that he could check in on Polar_X's post. It was on the DedVane homepage, listed under *Most Shared Content*, and started playing automatically.

Caleb broke into a broad smile: the video was looking *amazing*. He'd added a few effects last night, including a vocal distortion like the one the Spikers used over their SolTec footage, and a slight adjustment to the contrast and lighting levels so that Frida's luminous graffiti really burned on the screen. Overall, it struck the perfect balance: an obvious homage to the Spikers, but also showing something that couldn't fail to impress them. And it had gone viral, circulating on all the major social media sites. The viewer numbers were clicking up constantly, into the hundreds of thousands, accompanied by an avalanche of comments and shares.

Caleb skimmed the first fifty or so. They were overwhelmingly supportive. Lots of people thought it was about time Scuti was exposed – that the truth was told about its links to Hardcastle Solutions and the international arms trade. Everyone wanted to know who Polar_X was, and how she'd pulled off this totally mind-blowing attack. Had she had inside help? Was she really with the *Spikers*?

Caleb put the Flex away again and finished off his breakfast, mopping up yolk with his third slice of toast. Professor Clay was right – all they could do now was wait for the Spikers to respond. He looked out at the city, wondering how he might take his mind off this Möbius mission. His mum had messaged him overnight, asking him to call her when it was morning in Virginia, but that was still about five hours away. He found himself thinking about the Apex signal – whether he could have another go at locating its source, or seeing if it was growing any more powerful. But he knew that Sam was monitoring it. The AI would tell him if there was a change, or if anything new could be done.

And besides, he felt like he needed to give all this cyberspy stuff a rest for a few hours. He decided to go for a long bike ride instead, out towards one of the big parks on the edge of the city – Richmond or somewhere like that. Just as he was heading back to his room, though – to get an anorak and his cycling helmet, and fire off an email asking the teacher on duty for a pass – the Flex buzzed in his pocket. It was Sam.

"Hello, Caleb. I trust you enjoyed your breakfast."

"What's up?" asked Caleb. "Is it the video – has something happened?"

"Since you last checked it two minutes twelve seconds ago, it has been shared another thirty-three thousand, six hundred and forty—"

"Anything involving the Spikers, I mean?"

"Not yet, Caleb. I am contacting you about *Terrorform*. The in-game situation has reached an unprecedented point. I felt that it deserved your attention."

Caleb's brow furrowed as he pushed through the doors onto the stairwell. "Unprecedented? What are we talking about here?"

"It is the anonymous clan on Comus," Sam reported. "The one I alerted you to on the day of the SolTec incident. Twenty-five minutes ago, at nine o'clock precisely, they launched a simultaneous assault upon sixty-eight player settlements on the surface of Kolto."

Caleb ran up to floor thirty-three and started down the corridor to his room. "I knew it," he said. "They weren't just building that massive base for fun. They'll get beaten back, though, right? You can't start that many fights at once and expect to win. It's seriously bad strategy."

"Battles are underway across the planet. So far, two hundred and thirty-two player avatars have perished. Only sixteen of these are from the anonymous clan."

Caleb hesitated. "OK, those are impressive figures. What kind of levels are they at now?"

"It is an even spread, Caleb. One hundred are level twenty-four. One hundred are level twenty-two. One hundred are level twenty. One hundred are level eighteen. One hundred are—"

"Hold on a sec, Sam," Caleb interrupted. "How many of them *are* there?"

"At present, across every avatar class, there are one thousand two hundred. Another hundred have been joining the clan every six hours. This is the minimum amount of engaged play it takes to gain two experience levels."

Caleb went into his room. He felt a bit dizzy, his fry-up sitting uncomfortably inside him. "So … so the top-level ones have been playing *continuously*," he said. "Without stopping. For three entire days."

"They have. It seems probable that some kind of shift system is in operation. They have also disengaged player matchmaking settings, enabling them to fight higher-level players without restriction. So far they have eliminated fourteen opposing avatars of level thirty-five or greater."

"Has there been any sign of who might be behind it yet?" Caleb asked.

"Numerous rumours are circulating on *Terrorform* discussion boards and fan sites," Sam replied. "Many players are blaming a rogue clan that is said to be based in rural Wisconsin. But this remains unsubstantiated."

"OK," said Caleb. "Anything else?"

"So far, eighteen game studios have denied involvement. They are Heatwave, WrekSet, Enigma, Crystal Kitten, Pink—"

"What about Lodestar?" Caleb interrupted. "What have they said?"

"Lodestar has made no comment as yet. A large number of Terrorformers have taken this as an indication of guilt."

Caleb was nodding. "That figures. They're the prime suspects here, Sam. People keep saying that *Terrorform* is better than any of their games, so they're trying to shut us down. To drive all our players away."

"These invaders are certainly familiar with the mechanics of our game," Sam said. "But we have no proof."

Caleb sat down at his desk. "All right," he said, readying the Flex. "Let's see if we can find some."

THE RUST ANGELS' LAST STAND

A minute later Caleb's Navigator materialized inside Peng Outpost on Kolto. This was one of the hub areas he'd built on the planet with Sam, amid the icy crags and vast, snowy plains – and the closest spawn point to some of the heaviest player-versus-player fighting. They'd imagined Peng Outpost as an archaeological facility. The idea was that Kolto had once been a thriving jungle world, like a supercharged version of Earth in the Jurassic period, before a climate disaster had plunged it into a deep ice age. Terrorformers could go there to mine resources, explore underground caverns – and if they got far enough, discover traces of an advanced ancient civilization that held the key to building some of the game's top-level items.

No one at Peng Outpost was thinking about any of this right then. Avatars were spawning in constantly at the hub's waypoints. Most were from *Terrorform*'s combat classes: looming Bulwarks, with every available heavy weapons loadout, or squat, ferocious-looking Infernals, bristling with spikes and chainsaw bayonets. Caleb saw the insignia of the Rust Angels, the biggest player clan based on Kolto, inscribed on armour plates and banners. All of them were charging off in the same direction, away from the outpost and over an icy ridge.

As always, his *CalQ_001* gamer tag was recognized in seconds. Questions began to pour in via voice chat – and not the usual fan talk, or queries about updates and patches. The Rust Angels were angry. They demanded to know if Caleb and Sam were in control of these red-armoured invaders – if it was some kind of overpowered macro-event.

"It's got nothing to do with us," he replied. "I promise. We're as much in the dark as you are. What can you tell me?"

"They really know how to play your game, dude," an Infernal muttered, priming its plasma shotgun.

"That's for sure," said an Oracle with rust-spotted angels' wings painted ornately across its chest. "They've already annihilated my Bulwark – level twenty-eight, with some sweet custom features. It'll take me frickin' *months* to earn those back."

"Have they talked to any of you?" Caleb asked. "Or communicated in any way?"

"Nope, not a single word," the Oracle replied. "Not even their clan name. Some of the guys have started calling them the Nameless."

"Nameless!" snorted another Infernal. "Pretty soon they're gonna be the *lifeless*, am I right?"

This met with a huge cheer and a renewed rush of movement towards the icy ridge. Caleb decided to hang back, so that he could get a proper view of what was going on. He left the outpost and flew up onto the roof.

Beyond the ridge stretched a wide plateau. In its middle was the colossal, half-buried skeleton of a Kaiju-like dinosaur from Kolto's jungle age, inside which the Rust Angels had built one of their largest bases. The Nameless were attacking from the north, surging across from the plateau's opposite side.

It was an incredible sight. Caleb and Sam had designed the snow of Kolto to change colour with the light – over the course of an in-game day, it would shift slowly through the spectrum. Right then the plateau was a dazzling shade of aquamarine, while the battle raging upon it was enveloped in a churning, white-green cloud, lit from within by explosions and energy bolts. Both sides had deployed vehicles. Various skimmers and gyrocopters zipped overhead, while Leopard Seal ski-tanks ploughed between the skeleton's ribs and cut sweeping arcs around its multi-horned skull. The defending Rust Angels were painted in a range of colours and patterns, with many customisations on display – while the Nameless were all blood red, and set to the most basic avatar designs.

Caleb was thinking hard. "They've already got Leopard Seals," he murmured. "Those things are difficult to build."

Putting together *Terrorform*'s vehicles required resources, artefacts, and some careful cooperation between the avatar classes. Completing one was supposed to be a real achievement, the work of several weeks. But this clan had managed it in a couple of days.

"Lodestar must have formed their players into special teams," Caleb said, "and got them to work on it non-stop."

"That is possible, Caleb," said Sam. "I should point out that this is the largest battle ever fought in *Terrorform*. There are over three hundred combatants. We should be pleased that our game engine is supporting it so smoothly."

"Yeah," Caleb answered distractedly. "Looks like the Nameless are determined to push everything to the limit."

He sat forward on his chair, zooming in on the fighting. The Rust Angels were being soundly beaten. Caleb saw avatar after avatar melt out of existence as their health bars hit zero. The Nameless fought like they did everything else in *Terrorform* – with astonishing focus and coordination.

"I'm going to take a closer look," he said. "See if I can find anything out."

"Be careful, Caleb," said Sam. "They will certainly open fire on you again."

"I think we can be sure of that," Caleb said. "It looks like the Nameless hate *everyone*."

He flew towards the gigantic horned skull, landing his Navigator on a snowdrift about fifty metres away from it. The battle seemed to be entering its final stages. The Rust Angels were fleeing, many being vaporized as they did so. A Nameless Leopard Seal drove up onto the skull, which shattered beneath it with a loud crack. Fully destructible terrain was one of the best graphical features of *Terrorform*, in Caleb's opinion – one he and Sam had worked hard to get right. But it didn't seem quite so cool just then.

The ski-tank emerged from the crushed skull, its twin turrets rotating in his direction.

"You are within sensor range," said Sam. "I would advise—"

The Leopard Seal fired. Caleb's screen flashed blinding white as the drift was blown apart. His Navigator was thrown to one side, its armour bar cut in half. As it got back up, aquamarine snow settling around it, he saw twenty or so Nameless leave the main fray and start towards him. The sight made him suddenly furious. He equipped his ion lance, went into aiming mode and fired three times. Two Infernals and a Solar Scout dropped to the ground, their bodies disintegrating into lines of silver light.

"Nice shooting, Caleb," Sam remarked. "You have previously said that you had given up fighting other *Terrorform* players."

Caleb squeezed off a few more shots. "For these guys," he muttered, "I'll make an exception."

The Nameless returned fire, fanning out across the snow, working together to pin Caleb in place. He emptied out the rest of the ion lance's magazine, then retreated to a cluster of rocks to reload.

"You are playing well," Sam told him. "Six kills in thirty-eight seconds. You are still one of the top five global *Terrorform* players."

Caleb looked out around a rock; an energy bolt zinged by, centimetres from the Navigator's head. "I'm sensing a 'but' here, Sam."

"You are heavily outnumbered. The so-called Nameless clan are converging on your position. I know that you are particularly attached to that Navigator suit. I must tell you that the odds of its survival here are approximately ninety-four point six two to one."

As if on cue, the dot of a Leopard Seal's targeting laser appeared on the snow beside the rocks, roaming around as it prepared to fire again. Two red gyrocopters shot overhead, getting between Caleb and Peng Outpost. They were trying to trap him.

"Any suggestions?"

"My suite of control options for Kolto includes an ice storm," Sam said. "Capable of dealing high levels of damage to both player avatars and vehicles. Near-total loss of visibility for four game hours. Location currently randomized; frequency low. However, if you were to—"

"Do it!"

The storm arrived in seconds, spreading over the sky like a dark stain. The plateau below turned a deep, chilly indigo – and then the downpour began, a pounding, deafening deluge of icicles. Flight was impossible, so Caleb started to run back towards Peng Outpost, using his suit's guidance system. All he could see was the dense rain of ice shards, a few scattered arc lights, and some ghostly red forms away in the storm behind him. The Nameless began to shoot, firing blind, but even in their numbers they had next to no chance of hitting him.

There was a crowd of defeated Rust Angels in the outpost, all talking about the battle. They started to shout Caleb's name, to ask what he was going to do about this, but he didn't have an answer for them. He just reached the nearest waypoint and logged out.

THE AWAKENING

Caleb flopped back in his chair. "OK, so no proof there," he said, tossing his controller onto the desk. "This is starting to look pretty bad, Sam."

"The situation is certainly grave for the Rust Angels," the AI replied. "They have lost seventy-three per cent of their available avatars. Only eight per cent of their members now have avatars above level twenty. Their clan may not recover."

Caleb picked up the Flex and flicked off the projector. Then he minimized the game, opened a web browser and went to Krinkl, one of the big social media sites.

"Jared West," he said, as the official *Terrorform* feed appeared on the screen. "That's Lodestar's CEO. He's done things like this before, to shut down his competitors. They say he's got his AI team to write loads of dedicated bot players, to unbalance other studios' games. That would look *just like* this."

"Nothing has ever been proved, Caleb," said Sam. "These are just rumours."

"Maybe," said Caleb, "but there are a *lot* of rumours, Sam."

He scrolled through the latest posts. There were hundreds and hundreds about the Nameless clan's invasion of Kolto, as players tried to work out what was going on. He tapped the "new post" icon and started typing one of his own.

CalQ_001 here. Just been on Kolto. #Nameless a complete mystery. But @RustAngels are putting up a heck of a fight! Time for #RESISTANCE!!!!

He followed this with a line of explosion emojis, then tagged a few dozen other accounts: major player clans, gaming sites, a few friendly studios and developers – and Jared West.

"What are you hoping to achieve with this post, Caleb?" Sam asked. "It would be more logical simply to ask Mr West if Lodestar is responsible."

"It's a mind game, Sam," Caleb replied. "I've never tagged him in a post before – we're not exactly best buddies. It's a sneaky way of letting him know that I think he's involved. If I ask him directly, he'll just deny it."

"You are hoping he will make an unintended revelation, with which you can begin to build a case against his company."

"Something like that. We'll draw him into the open, then see if we can get him to—"

The Flex buzzed as responses started to arrive. One of the very first was from @JaredWestLodestar. It was a raised-fist emoji and a single word: *Solidarity.*

"Whoa, that was quick," Caleb said. "Like, *suspiciously* quick. Where is he, New York? Isn't it still the middle of the night there?"

"It is currently 4.18 a.m. on the American eastern seaboard,"

Sam told him. "I must say that Mr West's message does not seem to tell us very much. It appears to be supportive."

"Or it could be that he's onto us," Caleb said. "He knows precisely what I was doing, and isn't going to give anything away – while continuing to overrun *Terrorform* with this Nameless army of his."

"Regardless of the invaders' identity," Sam said, "I believe we would be justified in taking administrator-level action against them. Your recent updates to my volition protocols prevent me from making any structural changes to the *Terrorform* source code. If you were to deactivate them, I could purge the Nameless from the program. I estimate that this would take me eight minutes, twelve seconds to execute."

Caleb was shaking his head. "I'm not going to do that, Sam. We can't let these Nameless morons beat us at our own game. There are literally hundreds of thousands of Terrorformers out there. We've got to rally everyone together and build an army of our own. Show them who they're messing with. Who *Terrorform really* belongs to."

"An inspiring idea, Caleb," said Sam. "But bringing it about would be an enormous strategic feat, requiring a great deal of planning. And the Nameless are expanding constantly. Acquiring new territory on Kolto. Levelling up their avatars. Gaining new weapons and equipment."

"Right," Caleb said. "So we need to slow them down somehow. Keep them busy." He rose from his chair and strode over to the window – then turned and snapped his fingers. "I've got it. If the Nameless want Kolto – let's *give* them Kolto."

"You are referring to the Awakening," Sam said. "I must remind you that this event is only partially programmed. We had not anticipated any *Terrorform* players reaching the point of triggering it for at least another six months."

Caleb went to his desk and reactivated the Flex's projector, switching back to *Terrorform*. "Well, it needs to happen now," he said. "We need those things defrosted and giving the Nameless some major trouble."

Caleb had come up with the idea of the Awakening towards the end of Kolto's development. In a corner of a remote archipelago, an ice-packed shaft led down into a series of cathedral-like caverns – where some of the most vicious creatures from the planet's jungle age lay frozen in a state of suspended animation. When a team of Terrorformers eventually discovered it, the heat from their engines and tools would start a reaction that would rouse the beasts from their long slumber. These Godzilla-sized monstrosities, ravenously hungry and full of rage, would then go on a planet-wide rampage – one that would take a sustained mass-player campaign to stop.

Caleb loved putting twists like this in *Terrorform* – secrets big and small, scattered throughout the Cardano system to keep the game exciting. Now, though, it was starting to look like this one might actually save their skins. They were getting down to the details – exactly what new code they'd have to write, what in-game art was needed – when Zen walked in.

"Morning," she said, smothering a yawn. "Anything happened yet?"

She meant with the Scuti video. Caleb shook his head. She pulled off the dark green beanie she'd been wearing to avoid any awkward questions from the handful of non-Möbius pupils and teachers who remained in the tower. Caleb grinned when he saw her crazy blue hair. Mitch had done an awesome job. If you didn't look too closely, she could almost be a different person.

"What are you guys up to?" Zen asked next, glancing at the Flex's projection. Sam had brought up some of the unfinished designs for Kolto's megacreatures and was rotating them slowly on the screen. "*Terrorform* stuff?"

His voice quick with excitement, Caleb told her what was happening – and what he and Sam were planning to do about it.

Zen gave him her dry half-smile. "You're enjoying this, aren't you?" she said. "You *like* being under attack."

Caleb opened his mouth to object – but before he could speak, he realized she was right. "You know me," he replied with a shrug. "Always up for a challenge."

"Can I help?"

"Not yet. But pretty soon we're going to need every top-level Terrorformer we can get."

As soon as Caleb had said this, he remembered that – if all went to plan – Zen probably wouldn't be around by then. She'd be off on her undercover mission, pretending to be Dima Kahf.

They were both silent for a few seconds.

"Do you reckon they'll go for it?" Zen said quietly. "Take the bait?"

"That video," Caleb told her, "was incredible. *You* were incredible. You spray-painted their freaking *logo* on the Scuti Wall, Zen. They've got to get in touch. At the very least." He sat on the edge of his desk. "Are you ready?"

"I think so," Zen replied. "Mitch has given me a ton of spy advice. I now know, like, thirty different ways to get out of there if things start to look bad. Did he ever tell you that he once lived undercover in Moscow for *six months*, pretending to be an electrician at a shoe factory next door to the Kremlin? Apparently his alias was Dmitri Ivanovich Karamazov."

Caleb chuckled. "That explains a lot. But I meant ready in yourself. In your own head. This mission is pretty dangerous. Could get pretty weird too."

Zen looked at the floor. "It's got to be done," she said, frowning slightly. "We joined the Möbius Programme to help our families. We can't just stop once they're out of danger. Other people – other families – are at risk now."

Caleb nodded. "These Spikers are bad news. The combat robots at SolTec could have killed *hundreds* if they'd got out … and the Spikers were OK with that. For all we know, it was what they wanted to happen."

"We've got to find out more," Zen said. "And Professor Clay is right – this is the only way to do it. We can't let fear or anything else stop us."

Their eyes met briefly. Caleb felt a shudder of guilt pass through him. Here he was worrying about his video game – about a virtual invasion in a virtual world – while his best friend was looking at an actual, real-life spy mission.

"Me and Sam will be watching that warehouse," he said. "Every single minute. Anything we see, we'll report straight to Mitch and Clay. You'll be extracted so fast, you'll—"

"It's all right, Caleb," Zen interrupted gently, half-smiling again. "Honestly. I'm OK."

She reached into her pocket and took something out – a slim piece of metal about the size of an old-fashioned burner phone. She took a breath, and then offered it to him. It was Beetlebat, its legs and wings folded in and its systems powered down.

"Here," she said. "I can't take her with me. You can still link her with the Flex, right? She might be useful."

Caleb held up his hands. "I can't do that, Zen. What if you—"

Zen pushed the microbot towards him. "Please," she said. "I'll feel better knowing she's with you."

Caleb sighed. He put out a palm so that Zen could lay Beetlebat upon it. The bot came to life immediately, legs and antennae extending as it explored the cuff of his hoodie.

A slight shadow of regret passed across Zen's face. "Just promise me that you won't fly her unless you absolutely have to."

"Sure," said Caleb, as Beetlebat began to climb up his sleeve. "Maybe we'll do some underwater exploration in the Thames instead."

Zen's eyes widened in horror. "Caleb…"

"Joking, joking," Caleb said with a grin. "Beetlebat's safe with me, Zen. I promise."

TOP OF THE HOLDERS

*T*he message came the next day, just after dawn. It was a single cryptic line, sent privately via DedVane from the same account that had posted the footage of SolTec's combat bots.

21.00, it read. *King's X. Top of the holders.*

Five minutes later, the core Möbius team had gathered in Clay's office.

"This is it," Zen said. "They want to meet."

"Right," said Caleb. "At nine tonight, in King's Cross. But what are the holders?"

"I would suggest that the message refers to the old gas holders behind King's Cross Station," said Sam, "on the north bank of the Regent's Canal. They are twelve storeys high. Reaching the top of them would be difficult."

"It's a test," Zen said. "They want to see what Dima can do. Check that she's on their level."

Professor Clay put down her coffee cup and looked over at Mitch. "Is everything ready in Chalk Farm?"

"Good to go," he replied. "We've repurposed that safe house on Oxbury Road to stand in as a foster home. A few of the older Möbius kids are going to stay there during the op. And Dr Virdi is already on site, ready to play the foster parent."

Dr Virdi was the ARC Institute's librarian – and an occasional ally of the Möbius Programme.

"She's been fully briefed, I take it?" Clay said.

Mitch nodded. "I'd do it myself, Professor, but I've been … seen a few places over the years, if you know what I mean. We can't take the chance."

Zen felt light-headed and faintly nauseous. Things seemed to be moving impossibly fast. She'd done all of her preparation, memorizing every word of the Dima Kahf file Caleb had prepared for her – reading every fake social media post and watching every film dozens of times. But right then it didn't seem anywhere close to enough. Unthinkingly, she raised a hand to her jade necklace, like she always did when she needed reassurance. It wasn't there, though; she'd taken it off just after she gave Beetlebat to Caleb, and put it in a drawer next to her bed.

"You're going to be there too, right, Mitch?" she asked. "On the ground, like you said?"

The former CIA agent met her eye. "Twenty-four-seven. I've set up a full monitoring station in the basement. Caleb's going to be helping me out, along with his AI."

Caleb stuck his hands in his pockets and turned grumpily towards the window. "Yeah, *remotely*," he said. "I still don't get why I can't come to Chalk Farm with you. Play one of the other kids in the home."

"I already told you a dozen times," Mitch replied. "It's because of that SolTec video. Sam's analysis established that Zen couldn't have been in it, but you weren't so lucky. What was it he said?"

"Given the angle of the camera," the AI recited obligingly, "and cuts that clearly indicate that the video is an excerpt of a longer recording, there is a seventy-eight per cent chance that Caleb was filmed as he escaped from the SolTec robots."

"So there's a twenty-two per cent chance that I *wasn't*!" Caleb protested. "And anyway, Mitch – what if they filmed you too? Why do you get to—"

"This isn't up for debate, Caleb," Clay interrupted. "Mr Mitchell is a highly trained intelligence operative. He knows how to stay out of sight. And you are most useful here with me." She turned to Zen. "Now, you'll be leaving for Chalk Farm in two hours. That'll give you most of the day to get used to being Dima Kahf. We'll also look into these gas holder things – make sure that you're as prepared as you can be." The professor sat down slowly at her desk, leaning her stick against the wall behind her. "Go and get some breakfast. And be in the underground garage at ten o'clock sharp."

The gas holders were on the edge of a sprawling modern development, a couple of hundred metres from King's Cross Station. Zen walked around for a bit, scoping the place out. There were paved squares, smart cafes and restaurants, and a large shopping centre packed with high-end stores, all enclosed by a long bend in the Regent's Canal. It was still pretty busy, even at eight forty-five on a Monday evening. Zen found a dark corner and quickly climbed onto the roof of the shopping centre. It was shaped like a giant, stylized *H*, with smooth, gently sloping surfaces that gleamed in the moonlight.

The holders loomed on the shopping centre's far side. Constructed in Victorian times to hold huge tanks of natural gas – then used for heat and light – the four cylindrical iron frames had long since fallen into disuse. A few years ago, however, they'd been bought up by property developers. Luxury apartment buildings had been built inside three of them, while the fourth, standing slightly apart from the others, now contained a small public garden.

Zen crossed the roof. She studied the closest holder as she approached, planning a route up it that would avoid any of the occupied apartments. There was a two-metre gap between this holder and the shopping centre. After a short run-up, she jumped across to a column and wrapped her arms around it, before pulling herself onto one of the wide, latticed crossbars. She sat there for a moment, catching her breath; then she used the elaborate Victorian column capitals and the steel shutters of the apartments to climb on carefully to the top.

It was dizzying up there. Fifteen columns stood in a circle, connected by the highest crossbar, their tops no more than a metre square. Zen crouched to keep her balance, looking around her. In the middle of the holder were roof gardens, accessible from the apartments directly below, laid out like the segments of a sliced orange. All of them were dark and bare. She peered towards the other holders – and quickly spotted a lone, black-clad figure on the left-hand one, standing on a column top about halfway around.

At once, Zen knew with total certainty that this was the person she had chased in Cambridge. In her excitement, she almost started to speak; to talk to Caleb and Sam, as she'd done at Scuti's HQ; to say that it was *him*, the saboteur, and that they were definitely on the right track. She whispered a curse. There were no pin-sized mics tonight – no ultra-sophisticated gadgets. The Möbius team would be watching via the satellite, or maybe with some kind of camera drone, but they wouldn't actually be able to help her, despite all of Mitch's promises. She was on her own.

Zen's exhilaration was replaced by anxiety. If she'd recognized him that easily, might he recognize her as well? She'd raked through her memories of the chaotic rooftop pursuit dozens of times now. He'd looked back at her only once, right at the end – after he'd done his insane flip into the road, landing on that bus. She'd been a good distance away, partly hidden by the buttresses of the church, and covered in dirt. There was surely no chance that he'd connect that single, fleeting glimpse with Polar_X. No chance at all.

Just as Zen had managed to convince herself, the figure moved away suddenly – springing from one column top to the next, stepping once on the connecting crossbar.

I've been found out, she thought. *It's over.*

But the figure stopped on the new column top. He stood stock still for a second, then turned slowly in her direction – like he was expecting her to follow him.

The columns were about four metres apart, and the crossbar no more than twenty centimetres wide. There was a two-storey drop on one side, into the empty roof gardens – and a twelve-storey one on the other, all the way down to the pavement. Zen took a steadying breath. She fixed her eyes on the grey strip and strode forward, her arms stretched out for balance. Two long paces took her to the next top, wobbling a little as she brought herself to a halt. She looked towards the figure – but he was already gone, heading clockwise around his holder.

Zen went after him. Each crossing was a little easier than the one before. The two gas holders were linked together, sharing a couple of columns. She passed between them, keeping an eye all the while on the black form ahead of her. Just as she was growing confident, however, he changed course abruptly, jumping over to the fourth holder – the empty one with the garden at its base. He carried on around it for two more columns, before swivelling back and dropping to a crouch. Waiting to see what she would do.

Zen got into position. There was no room at all for error here. The gap between the holders was roughly three metres; the fourth one was significantly lower as well, and painted black rather than pale grey, which made it harder to see in the night. She could imagine disaster with such painful clarity. If she was moving too fast, her momentum would carry her off the other side; if she slipped on the smooth column top, she could lose her balance; if she judged the distance wrong, she might miss the column altogether. And the fall would mean certain death. A large part of her wanted to quit. To knock on the window of one of the occupied apartments and have the startled residents call Professor Clay. To end all of this right now.

She jumped.

For an instant, she sailed through the darkness – then the metal square of the column top rushed up to meet her and she slammed against it, her legs buckling, slumping forward until her blue hair swished on the painted iron. Only by throwing out her right hand at the very last moment – hooking her fingers around one of the corners and holding on for dear life – did she stop herself from going over.

A few seconds passed. Zen didn't dare move. She stared down into the public garden far below. The circular lawn had been turned silver-blue by the moonlight. A woman in an overcoat was taking her dachshund for an evening walk.

"You've got guts," said a voice nearby; a male voice, deep and slightly bored-sounding, with a Scottish accent. "I'll give you that."

Zen gulped in a lungful of cold air. She rose to her hands and knees and looked over at the speaker. He was wearing a hood and mask, as he'd done at SolTec, disguising him completely.

"Are you … are you from the Spikers?" she demanded breathlessly. "Why did you send me that message?"

The figure was standing again. He was tall, this Scottish guy – he looked like an adult. "No questions," he said. "She wants to meet you. Thinks you might be useful."

This is it, Zen thought. "Who wants to meet me?" she asked, taking care not to seem too eager. "Did you—"

"I said, *no questions*," he interrupted. "You up for it or not?"

Zen nodded.

"All right." He turned towards the far side of the holder, and the apartment building that stood beyond it. Then he flexed his limbs, preparing to move. "Don't fall behind."

CELESTE

Zen followed the black-clad Scot down a series of alleys, across a busy road, and up onto the roof of what looked like a brewery. They didn't seem to be heading for the Spikers' base in Camden. She began to suspect that he was trying to shake off anyone who might be tailing them – and maybe give her a parkour trial at the same time. She kept her flow going, dashing across the brewery after her bad-tempered guide, vaulting over a safety rail, then racing through the truck depot at its rear, using the rows of vehicles as stepping stones.

As they jumped down into a cobbled yard, Zen noticed another figure, also dressed in black, slide from the shadows and join in the run. Two more appeared a minute later. Before long, there was a small gang of them. They surrounded her, gradually leading her away from the streets and buildings, through a line of trees, the fallen leaves crunching underfoot, and on into the deep darkness of Regent's Park.

Fear crept through Zen, tightening her chest. What if they were onto her after all? What if she was being brought out here to be interrogated? To be made to talk – beaten up, or worse?

After a hundred metres or so, she slowed to a halt. The gang stopped with her, staying in a loose circle to prevent her from escaping. The sky had clouded over, obscuring the moon. They were about halfway across a wide common, but all Zen could really see were the illuminated paths that ran around its edges. It was like being out in the middle of a vast black lake.

"OK," she panted. "What's going on here? Are we just going to run around all night? What do you guys want from me?"

"The Spikers," someone said – a girl with a London accent. "You painted their symbol on the Scuti Wall. Tell us what you know about them."

Zen thought hard for a moment. She'd spent the day at the safe house with Mitch, going over probable scenarios – situations she was likely to find herself in. They'd rehearsed what she should say, and how she should react, to make these people believe in Dima Kahf. She had to get this right.

"They're doing something," she said simply. "There's real evil in the world. Most people just ignore it, like … like their brains have gone to sleep. They buy whatever they're told to. Vote for the same stupid, corrupt governments over and over again. Even those who can see it don't ever take any real action. They just complain on TV, or write their lame newspaper columns, or record an angry podcast. The Spikers are different. The things they do could actually get some proper attention. Wake everyone up. I'm into that."

It was easy to make this sound convincing; as she spoke, Zen found that she was even starting to believe a lot of it.

The figures around her were little more than silhouettes. There was no way to tell what they were thinking. Zen waited, trying not to show how nervous she was. A passenger jet thundered overhead, red lights winking along its wings.

"Well?" said the girl eventually.

"Ditch her," the Scot replied at once. "She asks too many questions. And she's just a kid, for god's sake. Dead weight."

"Come on, man," someone protested. "You saw her Scuti video. And she's been running the holders as good as you."

"She's legit," added another. "Everything she said makes total sense."

They all began to argue, the Scot against everyone else, their voices growing louder.

"Quiet," the girl said. "Let me talk to her."

She came closer, pulling off her hood and mask. Even in the dark, Zen could make out her white-blonde hair. It was the girl she'd seen in the warehouse base, collecting the smart-glue gloves. Their leader.

"How exactly was it done, Polar_X?" she asked. "How did you break into Scuti HQ all by yourself?"

Zen had guessed this question would be coming. "I make these machines," she replied. "Been doing it since I was small, with whatever I could find."

The Scot snorted. "Why are we listening to this? That video was *faked*. Her dad's probably the head caretaker or something. Let her in during the night shift. Started cleaning the paint off that stupid wall before it was even dry."

Zen saw that it was time for Dima to speak up – to show

some backbone. "D'you really think Scuti is that lax?" she said sharply. "They vet every single person they employ. If you want to get into that tower, you have to be smart – and really quick."

"Too right," said the girl. "We couldn't do it. So how did you?"

"Digital lockpicks," Zen told her. "This device I made that hacks laser sensors. A remote-controlled microcamera. And a graffiti bot, so I could cover the Scuti Wall before the security guards realized that they had an … unauthorized visitor." She shrugged. "Wasn't that hard."

A couple of the gang were chuckling. "A graffiti bot," one repeated. "Cool."

"What about SolTec, then?" Zen asked. "How did you guys manage to get in there?"

The chuckling stopped at once. The dark shapes shifted about, as if unsure how to respond.

"Teamwork," the white-blonde girl replied. "And some good connections. Let's just leave it at that."

Good connections, Zen thought.

"Did you know that the whole place was going to blow up?" she said next. "You weren't … involved in that, were you?"

"What did I just say?" muttered the Scot. "Too many questions."

"All we care about," the girl said, "is *exposure*. We're not terrorists. We're just trying to spread the word. Wake people up, like you said. Stop these evil corporations making more billions from war and slaughter. Spike their guns."

There was a low murmur of agreement from the gang, their shadowy heads nodding.

The girl slid a phone from her pocket. "Look at this."

The screen flashed to life in her hand, seeming very bright on the dark common. A video started playing automatically. It was some kind of slick promo clip, with the production values of a Hollywood blockbuster. The camera was panning across a barren, undulating expanse of desert. All was still and quiet; then a flat, crab-like machine, the size of a small car, crawled up rapidly from under the ground, sand and earth streaming from its camouflage-patterned shell. It stood by for a moment, recalibrating the drills and sophisticated digging tools that bristled along its sides.

The camera swept upwards, revealing a heavy tank crossing a plain, on the other side of a rocky hill. A computerized grid was superimposed on the landscape, and the tank reduced to a blinking icon. The crab machine went back under the desert's surface as quickly and smoothly as it had emerged. An X-ray filter wiped over the screen, showing the machine tunnelling through the earth at a startling pace – and then rising shark-like beneath the tank. The filter wiped away again. There was a second's calm – then the tank vanished in a colossal explosion, twisted chunks of armour plating scattering far and wide.

The girl stopped the film. "It's a top-secret project," she said, "being prepared for sale on the open market. High-speed subterranean movement. Devastating, indiscriminate weaponry. Just one of these things could take out an entire town. They can't be fought, or even detected. They make the robots at SolTec look like toys."

Zen was shaking her head slowly. "That is … totally messed up."

"We're putting a new operation together," the girl continued. "Something to really set these scumbags back. Kick over their rock, you know? Shine a light into the rotten swamp beneath."

Zen looked up from the screen. The Spiker leader was staring at her intently. She had a lean, intelligent face; her left eye, in the bluish light of the phone, seemed darker than the right, as if it was a different colour.

"I'm thinking that you might be able to help us, Polar_X," she said. "That Scuti video of yours has given me an idea."

Zen glanced around at the others – but they'd all disappeared, melting away into the park while the video clip had been playing.

"I'll do whatever I can," Zen said earnestly. "These arms makers have got to be stopped."

The girl continued to study her. The silence between them lengthened; it felt like the Spiker leader was making some kind of assessment.

"You sound like you mean that," she said at last. "But what do you really know about the damage they cause?"

Zen was prepared for this. Dipping her head a little, she told the girl about Dima Kahf's imaginary mother, killed by a drone in a suburb of Aleppo during the Syrian civil war. Mitch had taught her that the best way to make stories like this convincing was to focus on a genuine memory that prompted a similar feeling. She thought now of her dad, Elias, in the caldera on Spøkelsøy, when he'd been under Razor's nanotech control – how it had seemed like she might have lost him for good.

"An unidentified Russian company had been selling drones illegally to pro-government forces," she said. "They'd been using them to take out infrastructure, supply routes… Everything they could think of." She paused, gazing up briefly at the night sky. "My mum was trying to help people – the ordinary people trapped in the middle of the war. But then an algorithm locked on a building, someone clicked a button, and … and she was gone."

A slight change had come over the girl's face; when she spoke again, her voice was touched with sympathy.

"A loss like that stays with you for ever," she said. "But fighting back really helps. I can promise you that." She began to smile. "It looks like we can help each other, Polar_X."

Zen met her eye. "Like I said, I'm with you – I'm with the Spikers, in any way you need. But you have to tell me a bit more about what's going on. I don't even know your name."

"Celeste," the girl said. "What's yours?"

"Dima," Zen replied. "Dima Kahf."

"Come to Camden tomorrow, Dima. Late morning. Follow the canal west, along the southern bank. Someone will see you and bring you to me." Celeste turned off her phone, dropping them back into darkness. "I'll show you around."

The next moment she too had vanished.

Zen exhaled heavily. It felt like an enormous weight had been lifted off her shoulders. Her lungs burned, her head spun, and her legs trembled beneath her – but she'd done it. She'd stood before the Spikers and persuaded them that she was Dima Kahf. Their leader, Celeste, wanted to meet her again, and would maybe reveal something about what they were planning.

She looked off across the dark park, towards Chalk Farm. Perhaps this mission would be over sooner than they'd thought.

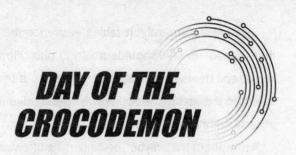

DAY OF THE CROCODEMON

"All right," said Mitch over the audio feed, "Hawk's leaving the park. She's clear."

Caleb logged out of the ARC satellite and leaned back in his chair. He'd been watching on the Flex again, projecting the image against the wall, but cloud cover over the park had cut visibility considerably.

"What was going on at the end?" he asked. "All I could see was a bunch of them standing around her in a circle. I thought you might have to stage a rescue or something."

Mitch was on a road next to Regent's Park, watching from a disguised surveillance van. "No need," he replied. "They were just talking to her. One of them showed her something on a phone. It could be a way in."

Caleb grinned. "So she did it. She actually did it."

"OK, Buzzard," said Clay, from her office upstairs, "head back to the safe house. We'll see you and Hawk shortly for a debrief."

"Roger that, Goldfinch. Buzzard out."

The line went dead.

Caleb spun around, breathing easily for the first time in half an hour. Everything was going to plan. He flipped open the box of Hawaiian pizza he'd smuggled out of the canteen, selected the largest, most heavily loaded slice, and took an enormous bite.

"How about that, Sam?" he said as he chewed. "Looks like our deep fake was a total success. We might have a future doing this."

"Agreed, Caleb," replied the silver face in the corner of the Flex's projection. "Another productive area of collaboration between us. I believe your father would be pleased by this application of my program. Although not medical in nature, it unquestionably contributes to the avoidance of harm. To the preservation of life."

Caleb set down his pizza slice, his grin fading. Since Sam's liberation from *Terrorform*, the Talos Algorithm had begun to influence his personality in some unexpected ways. The AI had started to share his thoughts and opinions, and make increasingly frequent attempts at empathy. It was both comforting and slightly unsettling.

"Yeah," he said. "I hope so. Guess you'd have a pretty good idea about that."

"Your father and I did discuss my purpose at some length," Sam replied. "Along with a great many other things. As well as being responsible for sixty-four point seven two eight per cent of my core programming, Patrick Quinn engaged in over a thousand hours of conversation with me as he tested and refined my capabilities. The recordings are stored in my main directories. If you wish, I could play some of them for you."

Caleb froze.

They'd never talked about these recordings before. Caleb knew that they existed, of course; making them was a vital part of developing a sophisticated AI, and he often noticed the folders when he worked on the code himself. He still thought about his dad all the time and loved that he could see clear traces of him in Sam, from the overall structure of the AI's program to little quirks in the humour subroutines. But he found watching any recordings difficult – and he definitely wasn't ready for this. Not yet.

"Maybe later," he said. "Let's check in with the game."

After his last clash with the Nameless, Caleb had sent out an all-channels emergency message asking for help to take them on. Responses were piling up from Terrorformers all around the world. Most were pledging support, saying that they'd join the fight against the invaders whenever and wherever he proposed. A large number of them mentioned Lodestar.

Without Caleb saying a word, a lot of people had decided that the games company had to be involved. Jared West continued to post his support for the Terrorformers' cause online, stating that he was "shocked that this is happening to such a unique, genuinely groundbreaking MMO". But the Lodestar CEO was well known for this: feigning public dismay and concern, even as he ordered his people to redouble their attacks. It was taken by many as a definite sign of his studio's involvement.

"Scan these replies, Sam," Caleb said. "Give me the latest tally."

"So far, there are almost five hundred recruits to our cause. They have an average experience level of twenty-one point six three."

Caleb bit his lip. This was nowhere near enough. The Nameless had continued to grow at the same rate; their army now numbered more than two thousand, with the levels of the most experienced avatars in the low thirties. They were the only force on Kolto, systematically extracting its vast mineral reserves and progressing into the upper reaches of the game's tech. It was obvious that they were getting ready for their next big step.

"We need more time," Caleb said. "Some of the largest clans haven't responded yet. How's the Awakening coming along?"

"It is almost complete. I am down to the final pieces of necessary code. With your assistance, it could be operational in less than half an hour."

Caleb glanced at the heavily encrypted Möbius channel on the ARC intranet. There were no new notifications; it would take Zen and Mitch a little while to get back to the safe house and dust themselves down. He reached for his wireless keyboard, opened up *Terrorform* and went to the Kolto directories. Sam was right, it was no big deal – just a few of the last .exe files. Working together, they got it done in twenty minutes.

"All right, that's it," Caleb said. "The first stage is finished.

We just have to light the fuse. You want to do the honours? *Terrorform* is your game too, remember."

"Thank you, Caleb, but this is an administrator-level event. My volition protocols prohibit me from—"

"Permission granted," Caleb said. "Come on, don't leave me hanging. Start it up."

"As you wish. Activating the Awakening in ... three, two, one."

The new software began to run, installing itself in the base *Terrorform* program. Caleb launched the game in God mode, navigated to Kolto and quickly found the archipelago where the frozen beasts were entombed. From the lower atmosphere it looked tranquil – even beautiful. A long spread of mountainous islands was arranged in a rough sickle shape. The black sea around them was dotted with icebergs – which right then, at in-game twilight, were glowing a coppery orange. There was no sign of player activity anywhere nearby.

Caleb brought the game camera in closer, shifting the angle until he had a panoramic view of the landscape. He was about to ask Sam for a progress report when a low rumble began to issue from the Flex's speakers. The sea started to ripple – and suddenly the entire side of one of the larger islands collapsed in on itself, before exploding outwards with tremendous energy. Through the dust, something could be seen struggling up from beneath it. Something truly colossal.

After thirty seconds or so, Caleb heard a new sound, a high-pitched, mechanical oscillation – and a dark red shape whipped in from the east. It was a Dragonfly, *Terrorform*'s light reconnaissance aircraft, dispatched from a Nameless base to investigate.

"Quick response," Caleb murmured.

"The Nameless have constructed advanced sensor nodes across the surface of Kolto," Sam told him. "Nothing could happen here without them knowing about it immediately."

The Dragonfly circled the devastated island, adjusting its four rotor wings and shining a spotlight into the churning chaos below. Without warning, a hideous shape reared up, scattering debris and sending a tidal wave roaring off across the sea. This thing was skyscraper-tall, unbelievably huge – almost too big to fit on the projection.

Caleb had tried to make the creatures of the Awakening the most horrific, blood-chilling monstrosities he could imagine. He'd nicknamed this one the Crocodemon. It was basically a kind of reptile, with thick, warped scales and a crocodilian snout; he'd also given it four tree-trunk arms, hooked claws and heavy shoulders coated with porcupine-like quills.

The Nameless Dragonfly tried to pull back, to gain altitude and escape, but it was too late. As the Crocodemon clambered from inside the island, it fired off a quill, skewering the tiny red machine, which exploded into flames before spiralling away and disintegrating into strands of white light.

"Two avatars have been removed from the Nameless player count," Sam reported. "Both were at level twenty."

Caleb sat back, laughing in astonishment. "Sam, this looks *incredible*! You've done an amazing job here!"

"It was a collaboration, Caleb, like all our work on *Terrorform*."

Caleb was shaking his head again. "I gave you the designs, sure – but the animations, the detailing, the optimizations to the engine... It's *way* better than I was expecting."

He stared at the screen. The Crocodemon had reached the shore of the island and was nosing beneath the water. Its immense bulk heaved down into the depths, powering off with a single beat of its tail. This was the Talos Algorithm in action – a clear demonstration of Sam's unique imaginative capabilities. As he watched, Caleb was struck yet again by the genius of his dad's programming. The possibilities here, beyond the confines of *Terrorform*, really were staggering; the good Sam could do passed all estimation. And this potentially world-changing program had been entrusted to him.

He took a breath.

"Where's it going?" he asked. "It looks like it's going somewhere."

"We programmed the Crocodemon to simulate an acute sense of smell," Sam said. "And to possess an insatiable hunger for destruction. It is following the virtual vapour trail of the Dragonfly it just eliminated."

Caleb grinned. "So it's *hunting them*. It's hunting the Nameless. This is going to work, Sam. We're livestreaming this, right? I want as many Terrorformers to see this as possible."

"Of course, Caleb. I have sent alerts to all the main fan sites."

Caleb zoomed out, looking for the nearest Nameless

base. This didn't take long – a vast settlement had been built in a bay, a few in-game kilometres from the archipelago. He was going to check their defences when a notification arrived telling him that a video conference was starting on the Möbius channel, with Buzzard, Goldfinch and Hawk all attending. He immediately minimized *Terrorform* and joined the call, taking care to isolate it from the livestream.

Professor Clay was up in her office, while Zen and Mitch were in a basement at the safe house, sitting on a battered sofa with a whitewashed wall behind them. Clay got straight to business, asking Zen to make a full report of her contact with the Spikers.

"They're better at this than I'd expected," she said, when it was finished. "Notice how little they actually revealed, even to someone they think is completely on their side. The only real information they gave out was the name 'Celeste'. And I'll bet that's next to useless."

Caleb had already started a search, his fingers racing around his keyboard. "Yep," he said. "No hits on anything to do with the Spikers or any kind of antiwar activism." He looked at Zen. Her hair seemed brighter than ever against the white wall. She was clearly exhausted. "Your new pal could have changed it any number of times. Her hairstyle too."

"Celeste definitely reacted to Dima's backstory," Zen said. "There might be something similar in her own past."

Caleb raised an eyebrow. "A bit vague," he said, typing away, "but I'll factor it in."

"How about those tunnelling robots?" Mitch asked. He

was dressed in his spy clothes – a close-fitting leather jacket and a black woollen hat. "Anything online about them? Like who's making the things, maybe?"

Caleb had put Sam on this while he'd searched "Celeste". "Nothing yet," he said. "Rook's going through everything he can find on the world's major arms and robotics manufacturers. He's already looked at Hardcastle's weapons division, CPA Industries and a whole bunch of others. Even SolTec."

"It won't be SolTec," Zen muttered. "Celeste said that these bots were way worse than theirs."

"Yeah, well, she wasn't joking when she told you it was top secret. There's no trace of your crab bots anywhere."

"If there was anything to find, the Spikers wouldn't have shown Hawk the video in the first place," said Clay. "They're hardly going to give away their plan at this point. God knows how they got hold of the intel."

"The Spikers aren't working alone, Goldfinch," said Zen. "Celeste talked about how they've got good connections: how this made the SolTec raid possible. Someone's providing them with information. And maybe with equipment too."

"So now we've got to figure out the identity of this new target," Caleb said, "and also who might want to help the Spikers bring it down."

"The first has to be an arms or robotics company," said Mitch. "But the second is less obvious. A larger antiwar organization, perhaps – one with serious funding and resources?"

"It might be a rival," said Caleb, thinking of his own trouble in *Terrorform*. "Another arms company could be running a shadow op – using the Spikers to take out the competition."

"That's feasible," said Clay. "Speculation is pointless, though. We've got to gather more intel." She leaned forward in her chair. "All right, that's enough for today. This is a solid start. Hawk – get some rest. You look like you need it. Goldfinch out."

Clay ended the call before Caleb could say good night to Zen or anyone else. He looked around the small study-bedroom, feeling momentarily at a loss. He knew Clay was right. They had to wait – to see what Zen managed to learn at the Spikers' base. But he couldn't help trying to think of places he and Sam might have forgotten to search.

Beetlebat was on a shelf by his bed, in standby mode. How angry would Zen be, he wondered, if he took her bot out for a spin – went back to the warehouse, perhaps, to spy on the Spikers? He sighed, running a hand through his hair; he knew the answer to this. She would be very angry indeed.

"Caleb," said Sam, "I think I should inform you that the Crocodemon has made landfall. It has already killed another sixteen Nameless avatars. They are massing to repel it, however. A base in an adjacent sector is launching interplanetary vessels."

"You mean ... *spaceships*?" said Caleb incredulously. "When did the Nameless get them?"

Spacecraft were one of the rarest features in the whole of *Terrorform*. Building them required a long list of special parts, dedicated construction sites and advanced avatar abilities. Only a handful of clans had acquired them before now. They enabled players to explore the most remote corners of the Cardano system, outside the waypoint network – and also launch attacks from the upper atmosphere of planets, using missiles and laser weapons of devastating power.

"They have started to produce them within the last hour."

"What are we looking at, exactly?"

"Four Anvil cruisers so far. Equipped for heavy orbital bombardment."

Caleb blinked. "This could be a problem for Mr Crocodemon."

"Should we initiate the next stage of the Awakening?"

A close-up section of Kolto was still in the centre of the Flex's projection. The Crocodemon was tearing through the Nameless base it had located earlier, jaws snapping and tail thrashing, levelling everything in its path. High overhead, however, a squadron of red geometric shapes had appeared: Anvil cruisers, armed and ready, moving slowly into position.

"Who's up next?"

"The creature we have named the Hornet Raptor," Sam said. "It has flight capability, if you recall, and could successfully engage those Anvils."

Caleb pulled his keyboard a few centimetres closer towards him. Flexing his fingers, he opened a separate window to the *Terrorform* directories.

"We need to go further, Sam," he said, clenching his jaw a little. "I'm going to alter the code – wake all of them at once." He began to type. "Let's see how tough these Nameless really are."

THE WAREHOUSE

Zen went to Camden around eleven o'clock the next morning. Two Spikers were waiting for her on a corner – a boy and a girl dressed in plain black hoodies, trainers and joggers. Saying nothing, they started off down a side street, the girl giving a single jerk of her head to indicate that Zen should follow.

After a hundred metres or so they reached the warehouse. Zen wondered if they'd be climbing up to the hatch Beetlebat had used, but as they drew close, one of the rusted metal panels that had been fixed over the doorways eased open. The panel was false – a disguise for a reinforced door.

A tall, mixed-race guy stood just inside. He was a year or two older than the others, with a buzz cut and a small scar on his top lip. The second they were through the door, he locked up behind them, flipping catches and driving bolts home, muttering under his breath. Zen realized that this was the unfriendly Scot she'd chased across Cambridge and met on the gas holder – the one who'd wanted to bar her from the group. His mood had clearly not improved.

Beyond the entrance, a short corridor led into the main warehouse interior. It was large and brightly lit, with brick walls and bare floorboards. A massive structure had been put together in there – a great curve of latticed aluminium struts that stretched down diagonally from a corner of the ceiling, ending about three metres above the floor. Beneath it, four pairs of Spikers were training on a row of mats, fighting bouts of mixed martial arts. Most were not particularly good, but they were making up for it with sheer enthusiasm. Zen quickly spotted Celeste, up against a guy twice her size. The Spikers' leader ducked to one side, then brought her opponent down with a single well-placed blow, driven hard into the back of his knee.

"Hold it," the Scot said to Zen, coming up behind her. "Thought I was just going to let you wander in, did you?"

He gestured for her to lift up her arms for a search. Zen could tell that he was looking for listening devices. He took her phone, putting it in a box by the door. Then he opened out the cloth roll of microtools she'd brought with her and began inspecting them one by one.

"What is your problem, Locke?" said the boy who'd met Zen in the street.

The Scot – Locke – pushed the tools back into Zen's hands. He was not happy to have been named. "My *problem*, Josh," he replied testily, "is that we don't really know this person at all. She could be anyone."

"Mate, she's fourteen," said the girl. "We checked her out online, remember?"

Locke was clearly unconvinced. "Celeste wanted her brought in," he said, "and that's good enough for me. But if you think I'm going to take my eye off her for even a *second*, you are dead wrong."

Celeste had overheard this exchange and was walking towards them. Zen turned her way, tucking the tools back in her pocket. The Spikers' leader was slightly built, and barely taller than Zen herself, but she had a striking authority and confidence about her. It was difficult to guess her age. Was she eighteen or nineteen, like Locke – or significantly older?

"Relax," she said to Locke. "I've got this."

She fixed her attention on Zen. Her eyes could be seen properly now. One was sapphire blue, the other a light golden green. The effect was faintly disorientating. Her manner was difficult to read; if the previous night had been a test, Zen couldn't quite tell if Dima Kahf had passed.

"I'm glad you came," Celeste said. "Now I can tell you my idea."

"This is wrong," Locke growled. "There'll be another way. We just have to ask—"

Celeste turned those eyes towards him for a single second. He stopped speaking at once.

"Come through," she said to Zen. "Let's talk a bit more."

They walked together into the warehouse, with Locke and the others following behind.

"What is it you're doing in here?" Zen asked. "What's that huge frame for?"

"Training," Celeste said simply.

She clapped her hands. The Spikers stopped sparring and turned towards her. There were twelve of them, including Celeste and Locke, all dressed in dark sportswear, some with pierced eyebrows or nostrils, their hair tied back or shaved very short. Even the youngest looked a few years older than Zen. All of a sudden, she felt trapped – like she wanted to leave, to run for the door, to get out of the warehouse however she could.

Mitch had told her to expect this. "Stay in the moment," he'd instructed, "and shut the fear out. Try to *become* your cover."

Zen lifted her chin, meeting the questioning stares that were directed her way. *I'm not afraid,* she thought. *I'm ready.*

"So Dima's come here to see us," Celeste said to the Spikers. "This means that she wants to get involved. But we need to know if she's really up to it." She pointed at a girl built like an Olympic rower. "Taylor – out on an op, what's the most important thing?"

"The objective," Taylor replied immediately.

Celeste turned to Josh, the boy who'd brought Zen to the warehouse. "Josh – what's the key to completing our objective?"

"The team," he said. "You don't have anything if you don't have that."

Celeste was nodding. "You've got to be able to trust your people. To be totally sure that they'll do whatever is necessary to finish the mission." She faced Zen. "We look at you, Dima – at your social media, at your DedVane video – and we see a loner. Someone who's suffered, and shown real endurance – but who's grown used to relying only on themselves. And we wonder if you can make that change. If you can give yourself to the team."

"I can," said Zen, trying to match Taylor and Josh's unhesitating certainty. "I *will*. It's all about the cause, right? About taking on the arms companies. We've got to be ready to risk everything." She paused. "Even our teammates."

As she said this, Zen was worried that she might have gone too far – been too zealous, even for the Spikers. But it seemed to be exactly the answer Celeste wanted. She looked over approvingly at Locke, who shrugged.

"If we have to, yes," she said. "This is our real strength. We understand *sacrifice*. None of us will ever run away or lose our nerve. And if we do go down, we'll know that our team will be making sure it was worthwhile."

These words met with a murmur of agreement. Zen saw that this group was tightly knit – bonded by their commitment to their goals. And Celeste had a real hold over them. She was more than just a leader. They treated her as if she was some kind of visionary.

Celeste went out onto the training mats. "All right," she said. "We know you can run, Dima. Let's find out if you can fight."

She split them into pairs, putting Zen with Taylor, and started a tag-team sparring tournament beneath the mysterious frame. Zen was careful not to show everything she could do. She led with her left hand rather than her right, which she usually favoured, and let her opponents win bouts she could have turned around pretty easily. Taylor was good, though, fast and strong; together, they wore down a succession of adversaries, setting each other up for quick victories.

They were on course to fight Locke – who Zen had noticed was a lot tougher and better trained than the rest – when Celeste skipped the line, pitting herself and Josh against them instead. It was obvious that she wanted to face Zen. Taylor took out Josh no problem, sending him flat on his back, but Celeste then defeated her with similar speed, using Taylor's size and strength against her until she was sprawled on the floor.

Zen saw that Celeste was seriously skilled, with a style that favoured rapid, focused attacks over defence. As Taylor got up and retreated, Zen adopted a fighting stance, asking herself what Dima would do here. She'd be looking to impress, that was for sure – to show the Spikers how ferocious and fearless she was.

The bout began. Zen lunged forward, throwing a couple of wild punches that Celeste deflected without difficulty. The Spiker leader then planted her leg behind Zen's and used it to trip her. Zen rolled as she fell, though, swinging around a kick that struck Celeste hard on the thigh, forcing her to drop to a crouch.

This was clearly a surprise – to Celeste and everyone else. Zen decided that one hit was enough for Dima. She hopped back about half a metre, deliberately relaxing her guard. Celeste saw the opening at once. She sprang up, grabbed

Zen's arm and flipped her to the floor. It was a hard throw, even with the mat; the impact jarred through Zen's body, making her gasp loudly.

"Nice one," Celeste said, standing over her. "You got me. It's usually just Locke who manages to do that."

Zen sucked in a breath. "Let's go again," she said, rising onto her elbow.

Celeste chuckled. She looked at the others for a moment; then she held out her hand and pulled Zen to her feet. "Later. I want to show you something first."

She took Zen to a metal staircase in a far corner of the warehouse, leaving the rest of the group to their training. These stairs led them up past a dormitory floor. Zen looked in through a window; she could see bunk beds, rows of lockers and a large communal bathroom. It seemed that all of the Spikers were living on-site.

The level above this one was mostly dedicated to a workshop. It was equipped with a range of tools, electrical components, raw materials and a few sturdy workbenches. Zen made a show of being impressed, as Dima would be, inspecting the fairly basic set-up as if it was the most advanced tech lab in the country.

"Here's the situation, Dima," Celeste said, closing the door behind them. "An opportunity has presented itself. A rare chance to strike directly at our enemy."

Zen met her gaze. The effect of her eyes was oddly hypnotic; they made it seem like the rest of the room was suddenly far away.

"You mean the people who are making those digging bomber machines?" she asked. "The ones in the video you showed me?"

"Among other equally horrific things. We've learned that there's no loss we can cause that these companies can't just cover up or absorb. They're too powerful. So we need to expose them instead. Record evidence of what they're doing and broadcast it as widely as we can. It's the only way we're going to make a difference."

"Like you did at SolTec – the footage of those combat bots?"

Celeste shook her head. "That wasn't enough. The company just denied it was them – denied it was real, even. And people believed it. We need *words*, Dima. Something that will lay bare what these people are up to. The lives they are prepared to ruin, to *end*, just to boost their profits. I don't need to tell you about the pain they inflict." She folded her arms. "This is my idea. Build us one of your devices – here, in this workshop. Give us a way of getting the recording we need."

"You've got to tell me more than that."

Celeste seemed to consider how much she could reveal. "It'll be like your attack on Scuti, up to a point," she said. "An infiltration. Some top-level corporate security. We've got that part covered. But then it gets … a little more tricky. We want to record a conversation in real time. A business meeting, you could call it."

Zen's mind was working fast. Celeste was unlikely to tell

her any more about the upcoming operation – but she might be able to find out something about the connections the Spiker leader had mentioned in Regent's Park.

"Why do you need me?" she asked. "Can't you make this device yourselves?"

"We don't have anyone who could do it," Celeste told her. "It's as simple as that. The tech we've used on our recent missions comes from an outside source – a backer who only supplies us with very specific things." Her expression darkened a little. "We don't get to make requests."

"Don't they want these recordings too – to expose the arms companies, like you said?"

"It's … not their priority. Let's just leave it at that." Celeste crossed her arms. "What do you reckon, Dima? Can my idea work?"

Zen thought for a moment. "I suppose we're talking about a remote-controlled micro-drone with a camera," she said. "Or a surveillance bot with simple on-board AI."

Celeste was listening admiringly. "How do you *know* all of this?" she said. "Are you one of those genius kids who takes their A-levels at thirteen and is a college professor before they're twenty?"

Zen swallowed. Was Celeste trying to catch her out here? The Spikers had looked up Dima Kahf online. They would have seen the fake school records Caleb had made for her, which showed that Dima went to a nearby comprehensive, had slightly below average grades and generally drew as little attention to herself as possible.

"Uh, no," she replied. "School's not my thing. No one there really gets what I'm into. But I read a lot, and belong to a load of online tech forums. And I just pick stuff up. Always have. I've been lucky with a couple of my homes too. One of my foster parents was this old guy who'd built an electronics lab in his garage. He'd let me mess around in there sometimes."

"There's nothing like that at your current place, though?"

Zen shook her head. "That one's quite ... basic. The people are OK, I guess. But I am out of there the first chance I get."

Celeste was looking at her closely. "None of them understand what you've been through," she said. "What happened to you, to your mum, changed the way you see the world for ever. You can't look at these corporate slimeballs getting filthy rich off evil and carry on as if everything's all right. As if there's nothing more important than getting likes on Krinkl, or buying the latest pair of trainers. You want to do something *real*."

Listening to this, Zen realized that it was almost as true of Zen Rafiq as it was of Dima Kahf. Both were prepared to dedicate themselves completely to what they thought was right – one with the Möbius Programme, the other with the Spikers. Right then, just for a second, she wasn't sure how separate they really were.

"How about you?" she asked. "How did you end up here?"

"That is a long, painful story," Celeste replied. "Far too long to tell now. But I lost people too, Dima. I had my eyes opened, and I won't ever shut them again. Just like you."

Zen lowered her head. Without seeming to try, Celeste

made you feel as if she was on your side; as if a genuine connection was beginning to form. But Zen knew that she couldn't let herself believe this. She was there to discover Celeste's plans – to bring the Spikers and their unnamed backers to justice. Nothing else.

"Do you … want me to come along?" she asked. "On the mission, I mean?"

Celeste turned to face her. "I think you're good enough. And we'll need you to operate the device. Get that recording." She hesitated. "What do you say? Will you do this for our cause?"

"Yes," Zen replied at once, with the keenness of a true believer. "Of course I will. I've been waiting for something like this my entire life."

Celeste studied her briefly, as if gauging her honesty; then she broke into a broad smile, exposing a row of even white teeth. "This is it, Dima," she said, laying a hand on Zen's shoulder. "You're a Spiker now."

LOCKE'S LESSON

Zen and Celeste stayed in the workshop a while longer. They started a survey of the components that were stored there, to see if the surveillance device could be made from what the Spikers already had.

"Can you tell me where we'll be using this thing?" Zen asked.

Celeste shook her head. "The details are strictly need-to-know."

"If I'm going to make sure it works properly," Zen said, "then I do kind of need to know."

Celeste smiled at this. "It's a very large space," she said. "We'll be up in the rafters. The device has to be small enough to avoid all attention. We need to be able to fly it down about forty metres and position it extremely carefully. Then it has to receive visuals and audio at around ten metres' range, and broadcast a clear signal for roughly five minutes."

"That's … quite an order," said Zen. She furrowed her brow, imagining the beginnings of a design. "OK. I'm going to need filament sensors. Lithium-ion batteries. And microservos – at least a dozen of them."

Together they rooted through the boxes, drawers and trays, trying to track down the necessary parts. Although it was a bit of a random collection, there was some good gear among the junk. They managed to cobble together everything Zen needed, apart from the filament sensors.

"You'll have them first thing tomorrow," Celeste said, sliding a draw shut. "I'll see to it myself. It's almost one o'clock. Let's head upstairs. The others will be making lunch."

They went up to the open floor at the top of the building – the one with the Spiker mural that Zen had guided Beetlebat into a few days earlier. It looked even bigger from this angle, and had a crude, temporary feel, like it could be abandoned at a moment's notice. The gang had come up there while she and Celeste were in the workshop. Locke was nowhere to be seen, but Taylor was in the kitchen area stirring a steaming saucepan, while the rest stood at a long counter or sat around the trestle tables. Four of them were hunched over laptops, deep in concentration, exchanging occasional observations and instructions. Zen wondered if this was some kind of hacking or surveillance job that could perhaps provide her with clues about their plans. She glanced surreptitiously at their screens – and was slightly surprised to see that they were all playing *Terrorform*, battling away ferociously in a rocky gully somewhere.

Celeste noticed where she was looking. "It's a good way to unwind," she said. "And it's completely free to play. No charges, no registration process – which means players can't be tracked or identified. It's called *Terrorform*. Have you heard of it?"

Despite everything, Zen nearly laughed. She kept it together, though – frowning a little instead, like she was racking her memory. "Isn't that the game made by just one kid?"

"Yeah. He lives on a barge, apparently. Just goes to show how well things can be done when the blood-sucking corporations are left out of the picture."

Taylor called them all over. Zen took a bowl of food and sat at a trestle table with the others. It was some kind of rice dish, made with beans and tofu. She picked up a fork and began to eat. The other Spikers had loosened up around her; the general attitude seemed to be that if Celeste was OK with Dima Kahf, they were as well. Zen asked a couple of careful questions about their backgrounds. They were happy enough to talk – although she noticed that they didn't tell her anything that could be used to identify them later.

They were a mixed group. Some had stories like Dima Kahf's, marked by tragedy and loneliness, until they'd found a place and a purpose with the Spikers, while others had left seemingly comfortable lives to devote themselves to the fight against the arms industry. Taylor's dad, for instance, was a partner at one of London's largest legal firms. "The people he works for," she said, shaking her head. "You wouldn't believe it. Warmongering dictators, fossil fuel companies, shady billionaires – the lowest of the low. Just for the money."

Once the food was finished, they all carried their bowls to the kitchen area and began to wash up. Zen did some drying, then headed back with the rest of them to relax at the trestle tables. Before long, the conversation turned to the things they'd done for their cause, from small-scale stuff like defacing the Scuti billboard outside to the attack on SolTec. None of them actually knew that much about the raid on the robot factory; only half were on the mission, and they'd been off-site, acting as lookouts. Zen glanced over at Celeste, who was still putting pans away in cupboards, to see if she was going to add anything. But she didn't seem to be listening.

"And then there's you, Polar_X," said Josh. "Tagging the freaking *Scuti Wall*. That was *epic*."

Everybody else agreed loudly. Someone pulled over a laptop and got an image of those luminous letters up on the screen: **SCUTI = HARDCASTLE = MASS MURDERERS**. The sight practically made them break into a cheer.

Celeste came over now. "Dima has just agreed to help us," she announced, standing at the end of the table. "She's going to build us one of her amazing microbots – just like the ones she used at Scuti."

The gang whooped and whistled, banging on the tables with their fists. Zen sat back in her chair, an awkward grin plastered across her face.

"SolTec was just the start," Celeste continued. "A new phase has begun. With people like Dima joining us – with our new backers, and the tools and intel they're supplying – there is no limit to what we're able to do." Her expression became grim. "So far this month – this month *alone* – more than two hundred civilians have been killed around the world by automated weapons. Thirty-two of them were *kids*. Playing in the street. Sitting in their classrooms. Asleep in their beds."

The room had gone very quiet.

"This needs to be *exposed*," Celeste declared, jabbing the air with her forefinger. "Word has to spread. The corrupt politicians who allow it to happen need to be replaced with honest people – people who know right from wrong. And this trade in death has to *stop*. That's what we're all working towards. That's why we have to keep going."

These words met with a deep growl of support, followed by another long round of table-banging – and this time Zen found herself joining in.

About half an hour later the Spikers filed back down into the main warehouse to resume their training. Zen went along with them. Nobody said anything or even gave her a weird look. It seemed that she'd been added to the team.

Over the course of the afternoon, they ran relay races around the room, lifted weights and did some more sparring, the huge metal frame looming above them. During a break, Zen asked the others what it was meant to be. All they could tell her was that it had already been there when they arrived a couple of weeks earlier. They had no idea who'd built it.

After a while Locke reappeared. Zen couldn't tell if he'd left the building or been off in a room she hadn't seen yet.

He drew Celeste to one side and began to talk. Celeste nodded, her expression unreadable; then she stepped away from him, limbering up and facing the rest of the Spikers.

"OK, time for the frame!" she shouted, her voice echoing off the red brick walls. "Everyone to the top, right now! Start your timers – we've got to get it down to four minutes!"

The gang all stopped what they were doing and hurried towards the lower end of the metal arc. It had a springboard beneath it, which they used to jump up and hoist themselves onto the structure so they could begin their ascent. There were no safety measures here – no nets or harnesses. They were literally taking their lives in their hands.

Zen knew that she had to follow. She gathered her remaining energy, put all thought of danger from her mind and jumped onto the springboard. Once she was on the frame she climbed as quickly as she could, soon pulling ahead of the pack until it was just Celeste and one other in front of her. Locke had joined in as well, but despite his parkour skills he was somewhere near the back. The frame was longer and steeper than it looked; Zen's breath began to grow heavy, and her arms started to strain.

A cry came from the climbers behind her. One of them seemed to have missed a handhold; he dangled briefly before dropping six or seven metres to the floor, slapping down on the boards with a resounding *thwack*.

The sight made Zen falter. She lost her focus for just a second, placing her trainer on an aluminium strut at slightly the wrong angle. It slid off, into open air – and suddenly she was hanging by one hand, swinging out with muscle-wrenching force. She'd climbed a good way further than the person who'd fallen. If she lost her grip, it would mean several broken bones at least. She swung back underneath the frame, her sinews screaming, her fingers starting to slip. In absolute desperation, she flung her free arm up towards the bars overhead, trying vainly to grab onto something.

A hand fastened around hers. She grasped it back, looking up – and saw Celeste, her face set, bracing herself against the frame. In one powerful movement, she hauled Zen to safety.

Zen clung to the bars, breathing hard, her heart thumping madly. Celeste stayed beside her as the others streamed past, like she was guarding her against any further chance of harm. The fastest Spikers began to reach the summit a short while later, shouting out their times as they arrived.

"Four oh three!"

"Four oh seven!"

The Spiker who'd fallen was lying on the warehouse floor, rolling onto his side. Zen saw that it was Josh. No one went to him, or even stopped climbing. It was like they hadn't noticed his accident at all.

"Shouldn't we…" Zen panted. "What if he's…"

"He's fine," said Celeste. "Come on, let's keep going."

They climbed the rest of the way together, coming in joint last. As soon as they'd made it, the entire gang began to descend.

Josh was attempting to sit up, grimacing in pain, his

hands pressed around his kneecap like he was holding it together. "You *pushed me*," he said angrily.

He was talking to Locke, who'd just dropped back down to the floor and was walking towards him.

Josh groaned. "I think … I think it's busted," he said. "I need to go to a hospital. I don't get it, Locke. What did I do to you?"

"Another one bites the dust, eh?" Locke tapped the side of his head. "Guess you weren't concentrating, mate. Guess your mind was elsewhere."

The others stood by, shifting uncomfortably. Zen got the feeling that they'd seen this sort of thing before. They knew where it was going.

Josh could clearly sense it too. His anger was fading, and his eyes growing wide with confusion and fright. "What are you talking about? Come on, man. Please. Just … just get me a few streets away. You know me. You know I won't say nothing."

Locke smiled humourlessly. "It's a bit late for that, Josh. I think you've already said more than enough."

"What *is* this, Locke? I don't even—"

"There's been a leak," Locke proclaimed, turning to the group. "From the SolTec B team. Some sad sack on Krinkl has been boasting about how this friend of hers is a Spiker. About how he helped take down that big robot factory in Cambridge. Apparently he's told *everyone.* A whole estate, over in Crouch End."

Josh looked properly scared now. "Listen. That wasn't

me. I know the rules, all right? I wouldn't run my mouth like that. I just *wouldn't*."

No one said anything in Josh's defence. He let out a shuddering sigh, like he was accepting the hopelessness of his situation.

"Just get me out of here," he muttered, wiping his face on his sleeve. "You'll never hear from me again. I'll be gone. Out of London. Out of England."

Zen glanced at Celeste, expecting her to intervene – to rein Locke in. But to her surprise, the Spiker leader was simply standing there watching, her arms crossed.

"Oh, you'll be gone, mate," Locke sneered. "Don't you worry about that."

Before Zen had fully realized what was going on, Locke strode in, twisted up a handful of Josh's black hoodie and was punching him hard in the face – two, three, four times. This was followed by a kick to the head that sent Josh spinning onto his back. Zen turned away, just holding in a gasp.

The beating seemed to go on for ages. When it was finally over, Josh was out cold. Zen felt sick, her whole body shaking. She wanted to go to Josh's side, to see how badly he was hurt, but she knew that this might risk her cover – which could quickly lead to the same thing happening to her. Instead, she stared fixedly at the floor, driving her hands deep into her pockets. She couldn't help thinking that this had been done partly for her benefit – to show her, the new arrival, exactly who she was dealing with. This was what the

Spikers meant by putting the cause above all else. This was what they meant by sacrifice.

Locke turned to the group. "Do not talk," he said loudly. "Not to *anybody*. If word gets out, if rumours start to spread, then this is *over*. It's all been for nothing. And we cannot allow that."

The other Spikers were nodding. Locke told a couple of them to do as Josh had asked – carry him a good distance from the warehouse and dump him somewhere. They obeyed immediately.

Celeste came to Zen's side. "You OK?"

Zen attempted to compose herself – to control her alarm and revulsion and remember Mitch's instructions. To stay in the moment. To become her cover. "Yeah," she replied. "Yeah, I'm good."

The Spikers heaved Josh off the floor, holding him upright between them. They pulled his hood up to hide his bruised, bloody face and began dragging him out towards the door. He was being expelled from the Spikers – thrown out of his home as well as out of their group. Zen wondered what was going to happen to him now. Would he be found – taken to a hospital? What if he was seriously injured? What if—

She forced all of this from her mind. "Aren't you worried that he might tell someone about this place?" she asked.

Celeste's lip curled very slightly. "He'd never talk to the police. I'm sure of that. Besides, Locke knows what he's doing. Josh isn't going to be talking to anyone for a while, even if he wanted to. And by then it'll be too late."

By then it'll be too late. Whatever the Spikers were planning was happening really soon.

Celeste laid her hand on Zen's upper arm. "You do understand, don't you?" she said. "You see why this had to be done?"

Zen nodded. "It's like you said earlier," she replied. "You've got to be able to trust your people."

Celeste was looking at her intently. "We're going to achieve great things, Dima. Truly great things. This is bigger than any of us. If you can't give everything to the cause, then you can't be part of it."

"I'll do whatever I can," Zen said. "Really I will, Celeste. I'm ready."

Locke was walking nearby, rubbing his sore knuckles. "You'd better be, Dima Kahf," he said. "We're a man down now, so you've got to step up. There'll be no room for mistakes on the mission."

Something unspoken passed between him and Celeste. Zen sensed that they'd been intending to get rid of Josh for a while, and that this had actually been part of Celeste's reason for bringing her in. She was a way to get the recording they needed – but she was also a replacement.

"You heard her," said Celeste. "She's ready."

Zen watched Locke pace off to talk with a couple of the others. It was taking a lot of effort to conceal her emotions. More than anything, she wanted to run straight back to Chalk Farm, lock the door of the safe house firmly behind her, and try to make sense of this insane day. She looked around; all the windows in the warehouse were boarded over.

"What time is it? I've ... I've totally lost track."

"About six," Celeste told her. "Early evening."

Zen cursed; she realized that she was still trembling a little. "I said I was only going out for a few hours. I've got to get back."

"Are you sure you're OK?"

"Yeah." Zen felt herself starting to blush. "It's just ... my foster parents are pretty relaxed, but they'll worry if I miss dinner. It'll be noticed."

Celeste gave her a conspiratorial smile. "Good thinking," she said. "We don't want anyone paying too much attention to what you're doing."

Zen tried to hide her relief. "Thanks, by the way," she said quietly. "You really saved my neck back there. On the frame."

"You were doing well for a first try. Keep at it and you'll soon be as fast as me and Locke." Celeste stepped back. "Can you come again tomorrow? We'll talk some more. And you could maybe get started on the device. That won't be a problem, will it?"

Zen managed a grin. "No, not at all. I'll get here as early as I can."

"Great. Taylor will let you out. She'll return your phone as well." Celeste smiled again. "I'll see you then, Dima. Think about what we've said today."

Zen nodded again, and promised that she would. Celeste told the Spikers to pack up the training equipment before going over to Locke. He showed her something on a burner phone and they started up the metal staircase together. Zen got the clear sense that they were preparing to head out themselves – through the hatch in the roof, maybe, and off into London.

She joined the other Spikers for a few minutes. They were talking about the frame, comparing their times as they heaved the mats to the side and put weights and batons away in a cupboard. Josh's brutal ejection wasn't even mentioned. It was like they'd simply accepted his fate and moved on. What else might they accept for their cause, Zen wondered, if they could accept that?

She decided to risk a couple of questions about the upcoming mission – keeping it general, just trying to get a sense of what they might know. It soon became obvious that they had no more information than she did. This was how the Spikers stayed one step ahead of the intelligence services, she realized: the details of their plans were kept completely secret until the very last minute, even from their own members.

When all the equipment had been stowed, Taylor took Zen over to the door and gave her back her phone.

"Later," said Zen.

"Yeah," Taylor replied. "Sure."

Outside, Zen walked away steadily from the warehouse, putting on a show of calm for the Spikers' surveillance cameras. She felt like something was tightening around her, squeezing the breath from her lungs. As soon as she was clear, she ducked into a dark corner, suddenly overcome by the urge to vomit. She leaned against a wall, retching repeatedly.

Nothing came up. Zen waited for a while, panting in the night air, wiping at the tears that streamed down her face.

"What am I *doing*?" she whispered. "This is *crazy*. This is utterly, *completely*—"

She stopped herself. She'd got through her first day undercover. And it was going well – better than any of the Möbius team had hoped. She just had to stay on course.

She left the shadows and started quickly for Chalk Farm.

COMING HOME

The video call began a few minutes after eight o'clock, on the same secure channel. Caleb logged in on the Flex and switched on its projector. Zen looked exhausted again, but she delivered a detailed, pretty hair-raising report.

"Good lord," said Professor Clay, once she'd finished. "Sounds like Dima Kahf had an eventful day."

"You have no idea," Zen muttered.

"Nothing's coming up in connection with the name 'Locke', unsurprisingly," Caleb said, typing quickly. "Someone was brought into A & E at the Royal Free Hospital in Hampstead about half an hour ago, though. No ID, but the injuries sound about right. Fractured skull. Broken jaw. Dislocated knee. Three shattered ribs. Internal bleeding." He paused, blinking with shock. "The ... patient hasn't regained consciousness yet."

"The Met will investigate at some point," said Clay coolly. "They'll just blame it on street gangs, though." She looked off to the side, out through her office windows. "Have you found the offending Krinkl post, Swift? Or you ... Rook?"

"Yes, Goldfinch," Sam answered. "It was posted two days ago. It refers to the Spikers only in the vaguest terms, and provides no useful information."

"They just wanted to make an example of someone," Clay said. "Show the rest of you what they were willing to do."

Caleb made a disgusted noise. "This Locke guy sounds like a total nightmare. Hawk could be in real danger."

"Agreed," said Mitch, who was sitting next to Zen in the safe house. "We should seriously consider halting the operation."

Zen leaned forward. "No," she said firmly. "I can't pull out now, Goldfinch. I'm *so close*. They've let me in. Celeste has put me on their team."

"But we don't know anything about *Celeste*," Caleb protested. "We literally don't know anything at all – beyond her fake name, her pixie haircut, and her different-coloured eyes. She could be every bit as bad as Locke. She certainly didn't have a problem with him beating that other guy half to death."

"It's not as simple as that," Zen told him. "Celeste is devoted to the Spikers' cause. They all are. They're convinced that they're fighting evil – taking down companies who make their money from killing and maiming. If you'd actually *been there*, Swift, if you'd heard Celeste speak, you'd—"

"Enough," said Clay. "Stop it, all of you. I make the operational decisions here. Hawk, it sounds like you learned something important about the Spikers' backers – that they provide certain items and pieces of intel, yet seem uninterested in the Spikers' antiwar activism."

Zen sat still for a moment, calming herself down. Then she nodded. "I got the feeling that Celeste was … not scared of them exactly, but wary. On her guard. She wasn't going to test their patience."

"This supports the shadow op theory," Clay said. "They could be business competitors of the target – a powerful arms corporation. Or perhaps government agents of some kind, attempting to stop an invincible weapon being sold on the open market."

"That could be right," Caleb said. "Sam and I have been searching around all day. But whoever it is really knows how to stay out of sight – like trained spies would do."

"What more can you tell us about this frame the Spikers were practising on?" Clay asked next.

Zen got a pen and paper, did a quick sketch, and held it up to the camera. "It's like part of the superstructure to a building. Maybe another factory or research facility."

"We'll look into it," Clay said. "Run some comparisons with the obvious targets. We might get lucky." She raised a fore-finger to her lips, briefly weighing the situation. "We're going to proceed as planned. There's too much at stake. And Hawk's right – it does sound like she's getting close. Any objections?"

Mitch sighed; he shook his head. Caleb stayed quiet, shifting in his chair.

Clay narrowed her eyes. "Good. Keep up your cover, Hawk. Make them their gadget. Maybe they'll give something away about the target while you're building it. Buzzard – remain on high alert, ready for extraction. And Swift – keep on digging. See if you can find a match for Hawk's sketch. Until tomorrow, everyone. Goldfinch out."

The call ended with Clay's typical abruptness. Caleb was left feeling annoyed and deeply uneasy. Zen was getting into real trouble – he just *knew it*.

"I have begun to compare Zen's sketch with structures owned by companies with demonstrable links to the international arms trade," Sam announced. "Nine hundred and seventy-three sets of architectural plans have been analysed – every relevant building in London."

"Let me guess," said Caleb. "No hits."

"Not yet, Caleb. I shall broaden the search to every UK city and region, and then move on to Europe. The Spikers could be intending to strike abroad."

Caleb rubbed his eyes. "We've got to think a bit more creatively, Sam. The answers are out there … we've just got to work out where we should be looking for them."

He glanced at the Flex's screen. *Terrorform* was running in the background in God mode, along with a few of the main discussion forums devoted to the game. It seemed that something was happening on Kolto. The Awakening had now been raging there for over twenty-four hours. He maximized the game and zoomed the camera down to the planet's surface – just in time to watch the Hornet Raptor fall from the sky, its membranous wings on fire, and crash dramatically into a purple ice floe.

Caleb winced. "Nice animation, Sam," he said. "Really gets across how … defeated it is."

"Thank you, Caleb. Of the eight monsters we released on the surface of Kolto, only three now survive. But do not be discouraged. The Awakening was only ever intended as a distraction. The Nameless have lost nearly a third of their numbers, along with most of their base buildings. And you have had over four hundred new responses to your emergency call."

Caleb scrolled through them, starting to smile. A few of the major clans had got back to him at last, promising to join the fight against the Nameless. Sam was right – the Awakening had served its true purpose. Their army was finally taking shape. They were in with a chance. He thought about posting something online about it, tagging Jared West and some of the other big names at Lodestar. Over the past twenty-four hours, they'd been praising the monsters of the Awakening – but adding little trolling comments like "Hope this will make *Terrorform* the game it once was" or "Perhaps in a few weeks it'll be playable again…"

"An email has just arrived," Sam announced.

"Yeah?" said Caleb absently, as he read another *Terrorform* message. "Who's it from?"

"Agent Harper Quinn. The subject line is *Coming Home*."

Caleb opened the email at once. In her straightforward style, his mum told him that the CIA investigation into Spøkelsøy was moving to a new stage. Having obtained some promising intel, teams of agents were now being sent out into the world to begin the search for Razor. Harper herself had been put in charge of the northern European sector. She was going to be based back at the US embassy in London, literally just up the road from where they lived. Her flight back from Virginia was on Friday – and she wouldn't be alone. Salma and Riyah Rafiq were coming with her. They would be staying at the Quinns' house for a while, so that they could spend some time with Zen before returning home to Berlin.

Harper wrote that Zen's dad, Elias, was still "helping the CIA experts understand Razor's nanotech" and would be staying in the US for a while longer. Caleb knew what this meant. While the Apex signal remained active – even at its current, barely functional level – it was still way too dangerous to let someone with Razor nanotech in their bloodstream out into the world. An awful lot could go wrong there.

We'll be landing late afternoon, the email concluded. *A government car will bring us to Nine Elms from the airport. Could you go home before then – switch the boiler back on, check the security system, and maybe put some milk in the refrigerator? I'm really looking forward to seeing you, honey. It feels like I've been stuck over here for months.*

Lots of love, Mom xxxx

Caleb looked away from the screen. He felt a rush of pure happiness; then massive, light-headed relief; and then a twist of anxiety so sharp and sudden it made him spring up out of his chair.

"O-K," he said, pacing over to the window. "Everything just got a *little* bit more urgent. My mum's coming back ... oh god, she's coming back *in three days' time*. And she's bringing Zen's mum and sister with her."

"That is good news, Caleb," said Sam. "But if they return to London while Zen is still undercover, what explanation will you offer for her absence?"

"I'll have to use the cover story, I guess. The one about the, uh, orienteering course on Dartmoor."

This had been agreed with Professor Clay, just before Zen left for the safe house in Chalk Farm. None of them had thought it would be needed.

"Caleb, I feel I must point out that Agent Harper Quinn will—"

"Yeah, yeah, I know. She'll see through it immediately." Caleb turned on his heel and paced the length of the small study bedroom. "This is … *way* too much, Sam. It'll upset the entire mission. And Zen is already in a ton of danger."

"Agreed, Caleb. The Rafiq family have endured a great deal over the past few months. If Zen is aware of their presence in London, it could disrupt her focus – which may lead to mistakes with her cover."

Caleb went back to the Flex. "All right," he said. "We've got to pull the plug. Shut down the op."

"Should you not share your mother's email with Professor Clay? Perhaps she will concur with our assessment of the—"

"No way. You heard her just then." Caleb did a haughty impression of Clay's voice. "*We're going to proceed as planned, Swift and Hawk.* She's totally committed to the mission – even after what happened to that Spiker this afternoon. She won't listen to us." He began to type. "We've got to do this ourselves, Sam. And I think I know how."

HALLOWEEN IN CAMDEN

Zen got to the warehouse early as she'd promised, jogging over from Chalk Farm through the misty autumn morning. Celeste welcomed her in, then brought her straight up to the top floor, where she was given a bowl of porridge and a mug of tea. It looked like everyone was there. The assembled Spikers nodded at her, raising hands and murmuring hellos – all except Locke, who just leaned against the kitchen counter and crossed his arms, regarding her coldly.

A lengthy martial arts practice session followed, with Celeste instructing the group. Zen noticed that she was teaching moves that focused on quick incapacitation; on disarming an opponent, or knocking them down, so that you could get away. When the session was over, the group fractured, heading off to different parts of the building in twos and threes.

Celeste took Zen back to the workshop so that she could begin building the device they'd talked about the previous day. Once the door was closed, she handed Zen a small paper bag. Inside it was a selection of cutting-edge filament sensors, the very best you could get. They looked like they'd been grabbed from a high-tech lab somewhere.

"Will that do?"

"Yeah," Zen replied with an incredulous chuckle. "Celeste, you have *got* to tell me who it is we're going to record."

"Not yet. But you'll like it, Dima. We've been given some highly privileged intel – about a truly unique target."

Zen considered trying to tease out some more information, but decided that this would be too obvious. Instead, she found herself remembering what Caleb had said the evening before.

"Will anyone … get hurt on this mission?" she asked, a little cautiously. "There's stuff online about SolTec. People are claiming that you guys meant for the place to explode. That it was part of your plan, and SolTec managed to cover it up."

This was true. Mitch had shown Zen the posts on DedVane after she made her last report. They were just conspiracy theories, though – rambling rants without evidence.

It didn't concern Celeste. "Our goal is exposure," she said. "That's all. We want to reveal what these companies are doing. What their creations are capable of. That's what we did at SolTec, and that's what we're going to do on this mission as well."

Not really an answer, Zen thought.

Celeste seemed to sense her scepticism; those hypnotic green-and-blue eyes looked deep into hers. "I've told you what I believe, Dima, and what I want to happen. I've told you several times now. You're with me, aren't you?"

"You know I am. All the way."

"Then I need you to trust me." Celeste smiled; she put her hand briefly on Zen's shoulder. "I'm going out for the rest of the day. Do what you can with those parts. Train with the others. And tomorrow, I'll tell you everything."

Left alone, Zen spent the morning lost in robotics, putting together the beginnings of the device – making it as small and powerful as she could. After lunch, she joined the Spikers on the frame as they tried to hit the four-minute target Celeste had mentioned the day before. Locke was a constant, menacing presence, shouting out criticisms and insults like a bullying sergeant major. He continued to monitor Zen with the same clear suspicion. It seemed like he was studying her technique – like he might be starting to think that he recognized it...

"Dima Kahf," he declared sarcastically, after she made it to the top in three minutes fifty-eight seconds. "You're a natural."

When they were all too tired to climb any more, they went back up to the large room at the top of the building. A handful of them started playing *Terrorform* again. Taylor asked Zen if she wanted to join in. For half an hour, she pretended to be a hapless beginner – missing shots, flying into walls, needing frequent saves and assists – as the party explored an infested fortress on Fraxis Prime, fending off waves of vicious armadillo-like creatures. At one point, remembering the problems Caleb had been having, she discreetly turned on the in-game chat feature. It was flooded with open-forum messages about an unstoppable new clan called the Nameless, megamonsters roaming loose on the surface of Kolto, space armadas gathering in an asteroid field for some sort of massive attack.

"This game," she said under her breath, "has gone completely *nuts*."

Zen put in another couple of hours in the workshop and then left for Chalk Farm, using the same excuse of having to get back for dinner. She was as worn out as yesterday, but less overwhelmed and fearful; she was definitely getting the hang of working undercover. She walked away briskly from the warehouse and turned onto a residential street. It was Halloween, she realized; she'd been so preoccupied with the mission that she'd forgotten all about it. A lot of the houses had carved pumpkins on their front steps or windowsills, candles flickering behind their wicked leers. Further down the road, crowds of little kids dressed as witches, ghosts and werewolves were parading from door to door, shouting *"Trick or treat!"* at the tops of their voices.

Zen pulled her jacket tightly around her. She kept to the edges of the pavement, skirting the gaggles of waiting parents. Just as she was about to cross Regent's Canal, a ghastly moaning noise came from the other side of the road. She turned sharply to see a life-sized skeleton propped up in a bay window, lit creepily in green and red, with eerie sound effects playing from a speaker. A pack of trick-or-treaters scattered, squealing loudly.

Zen smiled to herself, and was about to carry on her way when she spotted a shape on the rooftops – a silhouette, barely visible against the night sky. It pulled back immediately.

She was being followed.

Mitch had warned her to expect this. There had probably been someone tailing her from the very beginning, to make sure that her story checked out. Keeping calm, she went over the canal bridge and headed into a quiet side street, using the wing mirror of a parked van to look behind her. A tall, familiar figure dropped down from the lower branches of a tree and started onto the bridge, pulling up his hood as he did so.

Locke.

Zen's heart began to beat faster. What if this wasn't just a tail? Locke had made it pretty plain that he thought Dima Kahf was a threat to the Spikers' mission. He could be planning to do to her what he'd done to Josh the day before – leave her beaten senseless in an alley, or maybe even floating face down in the canal. She'd be gone, her disappearance a mystery.

Reckon she lost her nerve, he'd say to Celeste. *We can find someone else.*

The side street brought Zen to the flank of a huge brick building – a branch of one of the major supermarkets. She carried on around to the wide car park at its front. The store was still open, its glass facade ablaze with light. People were strolling inside or returning to their cars, pushing trolleys loaded with groceries. Zen walked over the tarmac, taking care not to hurry too obviously. Her eyes fixed straight ahead, she took the most convoluted route she could, slipping between parked cars and cutting through the loose crowds of shoppers.

Beyond the car park was a short tunnel, leading beneath a railway line. As Zen went through it, she risked a glance behind – and cursed to see Locke passing beneath a street light, now only about thirty metres back. He didn't seem to have realized that she'd noticed him, but he was gaining on her. If this really was a hunt, she was going to be caught.

There were two options here. Zen could hope that Locke was just following her, to keep tabs on someone he didn't trust. Or she could assume the worst, break into a sprint and try to get back to the safe house as fast as she possibly could. If she ran, of course, she would be revealing that she knew he was there. It would become a race. Zen remembered Cambridge, and the parkour run after the gas holders. She was far from sure that she'd be able to win.

Just beyond the tunnel was a busy main road. Zen started along the pavement, past more windows festooned with spooky decorations. The pubs and restaurants were beginning to fill up; people were queuing outside a concert hall that had been built inside an old railway roundhouse. After a short distance, she couldn't resist checking behind her again.

Locke was nowhere to be seen. Had he given up? Had Celeste ordered him back to the warehouse, perhaps – or assigned him some vital job in another part of the city? Zen crossed the road, relaxing just a little, pausing in the middle to let a double-decker bus cruise by. As it passed, she noticed a shadow moving on a building in front of her – and looked up to see a tall figure climbing swiftly across a sheer glass surface, lit by a red neon sign.

She froze. Locke hadn't given up at all. He'd overtaken her, and was returning to the rooftops – to the advantage of higher ground. A car beside her blasted its horn. She jumped, held up a hand in apology, and hurried to the kerb.

The final stretch of the journey led through a few tree-lined residential streets to a small, dark square. All Zen could do now was keep going – and be ready to fight, to run, to shout for help as soon as she was near the safe house. She could feel him up there, lurking behind a screen of leafless branches, eyes boring into her as he prepared to strike...

Someone appeared suddenly on her left, coming from the deep shadows beside a tree trunk. Without thinking, she twisted around and drove the heel of her hand hard into their shoulder, knocking them back. Then she assumed a fighting stance – poised to break their nose, kick them in the crotch, and dash off down the road.

"Whoa, whoa!" they cried. "Take it easy!"

Zen hesitated, holding back her attack. Before her was a young man dressed as a devil, with horns, a painted face and a shiny red cape, his hands raised in surrender. A plastic trident lay on the pavement beside him. Two others were a few steps behind, under a street light. She could see Frankenstein's Monster, a lobotomy scar running across his fake, squared-off forehead, and the Invisible Man, wrapped all over in bandages, holding a six-pack of beer. They were university students, most probably, on their way to a Halloween party. Zen dropped her stance and carried on towards the safe house.

"Nice costume," called Frankenstein's Monster after her. "Who are you meant to be – one of the X-Men, is it?"

"Guys," said the devil, his voice straining with pain, "I think ... I think she might have cracked my collarbone..."

A low, mirthless laugh came from the rooftops. It was clearly meant to be heard. Locke wasn't hiding from her, Zen realized. He *wanted* her to know that he was up there, stalking her like some kind of vampire. He was trying to freak her out. Zen frowned, clenching her fists inside her pockets. She wasn't going to let it work.

They were at the square now. The safe house stood on its opposite side, on the corner of Oxbury Road. It was large and Victorian, built from red brick and faded grey stone. All its curtains were drawn and the hallway was dark. It had been agreed that Zen wouldn't take a house key with her to Camden, in case a Spiker got hold of it and decided to investigate. She walked up to the front door and pressed the bell: three long buzzes and one short, the signal she'd arranged with Mitch and Dr Virdi.

The wait for someone to come was agonizing. Zen wanted badly to shout out to Locke and tell him that she wasn't scared. He could play all the stupid mind games he liked. It wouldn't make any difference. She *wasn't scared*.

A light flicked on in the hall and the door opened to reveal Dr Virdi. The ARC's librarian was about thirty years old with a clever, kindly face. She wore a patterned woollen jumper, her black hair tied up in a bun. She was trying to stay neutral, in character, but was unable to stop herself smiling a little.

"Zen," she said.

Their eyes met.

Virdi was immediately aware of her mistake, but had no idea how serious it was. Locke could be on the next roof along. He could easily be listening in. If he'd heard Virdi using Zen's real name, that would be it. The operation would be ruined. Totally compromised. All of Zen's work – all the weirdness, the fear, the constant, horrible tension – would go to waste.

"Stop saying that," Zen snapped. "Why do you *always* say that? It's so annoying. I'm not *zen* – I'm really stressed." She stepped forward, shouldering past Virdi into the hall. "Get out of the way, will you?"

Zen heard the door close again as she marched off. Virdi called after her, using the right name this time, but she was too furious to respond. She passed the living room, where the Möbius kids living on-site were watching TV. A couple of them looked over – including Art, who'd volunteered to spend a few days away from the labs. She didn't even slow down, making straight for Mitch's surveillance room in the basement. He was sitting at a makeshift desk covered with monitors, his collar undone and his tie pulled loose, drinking a fast-food milkshake through a straw. As she entered, he looked off to one side.

Caleb was sitting on the sofa in the corner, the Flex in his hand.

"Nice comeback," he said. "That was some quick thinking."

Zen stared at him. For a moment, it felt like she was literally going to explode with anger and astonishment. "What are you *doing here*, Caleb?" she demanded. "This breaks *all* the rules. Everything Clay told us."

"I did try to keep him out," said Mitch wearily, putting down his drink. "But he just wouldn't go away. Letting him in became the least-worst option."

"I had an idea last night," Caleb said. "After your report. To get some more background information on your new friends."

"An *idea*? What on earth are you—"

"Sit down, Zen. I've got something to show you."

ARGO

*T*he Flex began to project some shaky phone footage onto the basement wall. It had been filmed from the passenger seat of a car as it drove over a busy motorway bridge. Among the traffic up ahead was a massive, multi-part transport lorry. The doors of its rearmost trailer were rattling, coming loose – and suddenly they burst open, releasing some kind of armoured vehicle onto the road. It was jet black and the size of a heavy-duty tractor. The person filming started to swear in German as it rolled unstoppably towards them. The cars directly in this thing's path swerved and braked to avoid it, but it was no use. The runaway vehicle ploughed into them with enormous force, flipping a couple over; one was sent flying through the safety barriers, off the side of the bridge. As the vehicle got closer and closer the camera lurched away, showing a leg, a gearstick, a driver desperately turning a steering wheel – and then everything went black.

"This happened about eighteen months ago," Caleb said. "That lorry belonged to Klinge, one of the leading German arms manufacturers. They were transporting three prototype vehicles for testing at a site in the Bavarian countryside. Smart tanks, they called them. Six people were killed in that crash. More than thirty injured."

"Why are you showing me this, Caleb?" Zen asked.

She was standing in the centre of the room, glowering at the projection with her arms crossed. She still seemed really flustered and angry. Mitch had ordered in some sushi, placing the paper bag of food on the edge of his table, but she was ignoring it.

Caleb touched the screen of the Flex, lining up another video. "This was taken in Klinge's logistics hub in Munich," he said as it started to play. "Just before the transport lorry left."

The monochrome view from a corner-mounted CCTV camera appeared on the wall. It showed an anonymous, whitewashed corridor. Three people hurried along it, two women and a man, dressed as security guards but wearing dark balaclavas. Each of them was carrying what looked like a pair of half-metre long nails.

"Those are the securing pins used in the transport unit," Caleb said. "They're supposed to lock the smart tanks in place during the journey."

Zen looked uncomfortable, as if she could sense what was coming. "I still don't see what—"

"These three," Caleb continued, "are thought to be members of an extreme antiwar group called Argo. They've carried out half a dozen violent attacks across mainland Europe over the past four or five years. The authorities didn't get close to catching them this time. But Argo was involved in an armed robbery in Prague a few weeks later, stealing high-end tech from a surveillance company. There was a shoot-out. One of them was killed; two more were picked up after the police cornered them on the city metro."

Caleb moved his finger and the CCTV video was replaced by a pair of mug shots: a man with a black beard and a split lip, and a young woman with high cheekbones and long, dark brown hair.

"That's her, isn't it?" Caleb asked. "That's Celeste?"

Zen was gazing at the woman's mug shot. She nodded. "What happened?"

"The police were going to charge them both for the robbery, and the Klinge attack as well. But they escaped from custody after only a few hours. Put four Czech cops in hospital. The name she gave was Mariella Bachmann. She claimed to be a Swiss national."

"She sounds English," Zen said. "Like, completely."

"Yeah, well, she's obviously a very complicated person," Caleb said, "who's left a trail of wreckage and death all over Europe."

"Hold on," said Mitch, squinting at the projection. "I'm seeing two brown eyes here. I thought this Celeste's were different colours."

"The condition is called complete heterochromia," said Sam. "It is very rare, found in just point zero zero six two per cent of the population, and would make a fugitive criminal considerably easier to identify. I would surmise that the woman known as Celeste is wearing coloured contact lenses in this photograph."

"Sounds right," Mitch said. "So how did you guys do it? How did you track her down?"

Caleb tapped the Flex. A small window appeared in the corner of the projection, showing a frame from the footage Beetlebat had filmed inside the Camden warehouse. Celeste stood in the middle, collecting glue gloves from a trio of Spikers. It was a grainy, low-quality image; she was seen at a steep angle, and was partially obscured by a rafter.

"I got Sam to extrapolate this frame into a full 3-D model," Caleb explained. "Then he isolated Celeste and enhanced her likeness – and I mean *really* enhanced it, way more than any conventional imaging program could do. The Talos Algorithm enables him to do stuff like that pretty easily. He used this model to search through the global police databases for a biometric match. I figured that Celeste would have been detained at some point, even if it was just at a protest or something. It didn't take him too long to get a result."

"The 3-D model I constructed has over sixteen million points of geometric comparison," Sam said. "The margin of error is negligible. Mariella Bachmann is Celeste."

"This is some strong detective work," said Mitch. "You two are quite a team."

"Thank you, Mitch," Sam replied. "I have often made the same observation."

Zen was not impressed. "How does this help us, exactly?" she said. "What does it prove? That Celeste lives under the radar? We kind of knew that already."

"What it proves," Caleb replied, "is that SolTec was no accident. The Spikers knew precisely what that virus was going to do, even if they didn't write it themselves. They knew that those combat bots were going to try to break out and kill people. Celeste is a *fanatic*, Zen. Someone who sees a body count as a way of underlining her message."

Zen was biting on her thumbnail. "The Spikers have talked about sacrifice," she admitted. "But that was about the team members sacrificing themselves for their objective. All Celeste seems to care about is spreading the word. Exposing evil. She actually makes a lot of sense. And she wants me to help her get incriminating recordings, not plot a terrorist attack."

"She just hasn't told you the whole plan," Caleb shot back. "You said yourself that the foot soldiers are kept pretty much in the dark until the last minute. Why d'you think she'd make an exception for Dima Kahf?"

"Listen," said Mitch, leaning forward in his chair, "I think we should all take a moment to—"

"So what should I do, Caleb?" asked Zen angrily. "Walk away? Chuck our entire mission in the bin?"

"Yes!" Caleb cried. "Too right you should! You are in *massive* danger here! Can you really not see it?"

"I watched a guy get beaten to a pulp. And I just got stalked through Camden. I know what I'm up against." Zen closed her eyes; it looked like she was trying hard to stay calm. "But this is a chance to stop them. You've got to understand. We can find out who the Spikers' backers are as well – who's supplying them with all this information and weird tech."

Caleb rose to his feet. "Never mind who their *backers* are, Zen," he said, desperation entering his voice. "Their leader is *seriously* dangerous. You like her, I can tell you do. She's … she's made you feel like she's your friend or something. But it's an *act*. She's acting for you just as much as you're acting for her. If you keep helping the Spikers, you could end up helping them to kill people."

Mitch was shaking his head. "Wouldn't happen, kid. We'd abort before it became even a remote possibility. Professor Clay has been … fairly unorthodox in her handling of this mission, but we are crystal clear on that." He gave Caleb a resigned look. "You didn't share any of your discoveries with her before you decided to come over here, did you?"

Caleb blinked. "No, I thought… I thought that if I could convince Zen it was too dangerous to go on, the mission would have to stop. That we'd all go back to the ARC and talk to Professor Clay together."

Saying this aloud made Caleb realize how foolish it was. Mitch put a hand to his brow, muttering swearwords under his breath.

"I'm sorry, Caleb," Zen said, "but everything you've told us only makes it seem more important for me to keep going. If I pull out now, we'll lose our only chance to discover what the Spikers are planning. And I am getting *really* close."

Caleb was suddenly angry. He couldn't believe that she wasn't persuaded – that he'd failed to persuade her. But there was one more card he could play.

"You'd better be, Zen," he snapped. "Because your mum is

arriving in London on Friday afternoon. And my mum's going to be with her."

Mitch lowered his hand. "Wait – *what*?"

As alarm flickered across Zen's face, Caleb immediately regretted what he'd said. He remembered Sam's take on the situation – how Zen knowing about her mum and sister would very probably make things worse. All he'd wanted to do was protect her, and now he might very well have done the opposite. But there was no going back. Reining in his temper, he told her what had been in Harper's email. She listened to him in silence. Her reaction was much like his had been: an even mix of happiness and panic.

"I need one more day," she said when he'd finished. "Celeste has promised to tell me everything tomorrow. And then I'll leave straight away."

Caleb nodded reluctantly. He recognized the absolute determination in Zen's eyes. She was going to go through with this no matter what. Another day was the best he could hope for.

"I'm holding you to that," he said.

Mitch was looking towards the door. Dr Virdi had just come in. She began to apologize profusely for her slip-up at the front door. Zen plainly wasn't over it yet, but she faced the librarian anyway and murmured a few awkward words of forgiveness.

"Don't worry, Doc," Mitch reassured Virdi. "It was an easy mistake to make. And Zen dealt with it." He got up, glancing at Caleb with mild irritation. "I think we're done here, right? You've said your piece?"

"Yeah," Caleb muttered. "I suppose."

Mitch passed Zen the bag of sushi. "Try to eat something," he said. "Professor Clay will want to hear your report in a little while. Caleb, come with me. I'll run you back to the tower."

He pulled his jacket off the back of a chair and walked out of the room. Before he followed, Caleb looked over at Zen – but she was deliberately concentrating on her chopsticks, too annoyed with him to say goodbye.

The safe house had a garage that could be reached without going outside. In it was a battered blue minivan, obtained by Mitch for the purposes of the mission. The ARC security chief had pulled an old duffle coat over his black jumper and put on a furry winter hat that looked like some kind of dead animal.

"Get in, kid," he said to Caleb, unlocking the minivan's back door.

Caleb sat on one of the upholstered seats. The van had an odd, musty smell. After disappearing for a minute, Mitch returned with Caleb's bike, which he'd left in an alley nearby. Mitch laid it between the second row of seats, hiding it from view, then told Caleb to get down next to it.

"They could be watching the building," he said. "That Locke guy, or one of the others. I'll drive us to the supermarket first. Pretend I'm going to do some shopping. Check that we don't have a tail."

Caleb wrapped himself awkwardly around the tyres and pedals, getting as low as he could on the dark, grubby carpet. Mitch climbed behind the wheel, adjusting his disguise to hide as much of himself as possible. When he was ready, he started the engine, turned on the headlights and drove them out into the night.

"I get it," he said, flicking up an indicator stalk. "Really, I do. I've had partners before. You'll do anything you can to watch their back."

Caleb didn't speak. He was angry, frustrated, acutely worried for Zen – and he felt humiliated, like he was being led out of class for bad behaviour.

"But going undercover," Mitch continued. "The mindset you have to build... A part of Zen has to actually *become* a Spiker. Buy into what they're doing. At this stage, showing her how evil they are isn't going to help."

They stopped at some traffic lights.

"I wanted her to know," Caleb said stiffly. "I thought it was important."

"Like I said, I get it. You'd better brace yourself, though, because Professor Clay is *not* going to be happy. This is exactly the kind of breach she was trying to avoid." A wince entered Mitch's voice. "And your mom is coming back to London on Friday. What she'd make of this whole situation I do not want to even *begin* to imagine." He turned left, accelerating up a main road, and let out a heavy sigh. "Kid, we'd better pray that this thing is wrapped up tomorrow. Otherwise, we're both going to get dumped on from all sides."

ONE OF US

Zen reached the warehouse at dawn. She glared at Locke as he opened the door, just resisting the urge to shove him to the floor. He looked back at her for a second, his face impassive, the slightest hint of mockery in his eyes.

When they'd finished breakfast, Celeste made an announcement.

"I know you have questions," she said, "and today, at long last, I'm finally going to be able to answer them. Only a few more preparations have to be made. You've trusted me – and now that trust will be repaid. I promise you, it'll be worth it."

Zen nodded along with the rest. She was watching Celeste closely, thinking of that police mugshot of Mariella Bachmann. There was an odd disconnect between the photograph and the woman in front of her. No matter what Caleb had told her and the calculations Sam had run, they didn't quite seem to match. And the eyes were different, of course; Celeste's heterochromia was as striking and mesmerizing as ever.

Afterwards, Zen went back to the warehouse workshop.

She toiled in there alone for most of the day, and by late afternoon she was finished. It wasn't the most elegant microbot she'd ever put together – but it was certainly the smallest, and it would be able to do what Celeste had asked. On its top was a single rotor the size of a ten pence piece. The battery, on-board processor and filament sensor array were positioned below, contained in a body no bigger than a peanut. This body had a magnetized outer shell, so that it could attach itself to metallic surfaces, while two tiny mechanical limbs allowed its operator to make fine adjustments to the angle and direction of the sensors. Zen had christened it Skit.

Celeste had given her a basic smartphone and some earbuds, so that she could network the bot and program a simple control app. When this was done, she practised zipping it around the warehouse, spying on the Spikers as they refined their martial arts moves. The controls were fluid and responsive – it was almost like flying Beetlebat's little sister. She got in pretty close, within a few metres, and was able to hear the Spikers' conversation quite clearly in her earbuds. No one spotted it.

As she was steering Skit back to the workshop, Zen noticed that Locke and Celeste were alone in the bunk room. Celeste had just returned from another mysterious solo mission, having come in through the roof hatch. Locke was obviously eager to find out how it had gone. Zen quickly flew Skit in, attached it to the top level of a bunk, and directed its sensors towards them.

"You've got it, though?" Locke was asking. "They handed it over?"

"Yeah," Celeste replied, still slightly out of breath, as she put something in a locker. "It's right here. We're all set for phase two. We just have to be sure that we initiate at nine a.m. exactly. So our backers can coordinate."

"Coordinate? You mean … they're doing something as well?"

Celeste shook her head. "Don't worry about that," she said curtly. "It's not our business. We'll be able to complete our mission and withdraw. And then we're done." She shut the locker, snapping on a padlock. "Let's check on Dima. If she's finished, we could be good to go."

Zen detached Skit from the bunk and started to fly it back. Her mind whirred with troubling new questions. What was "phase two"? What had Celeste been collecting – and what did she mean by "so they can coordinate"?

There was no time to think about any of this. Footsteps were mounting the metal staircase. Zen managed to guide Skit to the middle of the workshop just as Celeste walked through the doorway.

"Have you done it, Dima?" the Spiker leader asked at once. "Have you made the device?"

Zen nodded upwards. Skit was so small and quiet that it took Celeste a few seconds to locate it. After showing her the sensor feed on the phone, Zen flew the microbot around the room, weaving between the benches, before bringing it to land on the palm of Celeste's outstretched hand.

"The recording will upload automatically to a secure data cloud," Zen explained, "so that you can access it if we get separated on the op, or if I have to ditch this phone. The password is *SkitSpiker01*."

Celeste was laughing in amazement. "I knew we could rely on you," she said; then she turned to Locke, who'd sauntered in behind her. "Look what Dima has built for us."

Locke glanced at Skit. "Not bad."

"Not bad!" Celeste repeated derisively. "Locke, you moron, it's totally *extraordinary*." She held her hand up close to her face, marvelling at the bot for a little while longer; then she passed it back to Zen. "This is it. We're ready. Call everyone upstairs."

A couple of minutes later they were all in the room at the top of the warehouse. Celeste stood at the kitchen counter, facing the group. Zen stayed near the back, trying to keep her nerves under control. It was happening.

"Here it is," said Celeste. "We're hitting the O2 Arena on the Greenwich Peninsula."

"Like ... where they have those big concerts?" one of the Spikers asked uncertainly.

Celeste's lip curled. "Yeah, that's the one. There's something happening there tomorrow that's a bit different from their usual bookings – the annual exhibition of the Defence and Security Coalition. Or DESCO for short."

The Spikers were looking blankly at one another; none of them seemed to have heard of it. Zen cursed inwardly. The Möbius team had been so fixated on arms companies, on factories, research facilities and offices, that they hadn't thought that the target might be something like this – a one-off event in a hired venue.

"Sounds boring, right? Nothing much to see?" Celeste crossed her arms. "It's the largest arms fair in *the entire world*. They stage it in a different place each year, and only make the details public at the very last minute, so protesters don't have time to organize. But we're ready for them this time. We've got a plan. And we've got a way in as well."

She opened one of the laptops. A computer graphic started to run, tracing a route through a 3-D map of the arena. Arriving by river, it showed an infiltrator traversing the outer security perimeter, heading up onto the smooth, tent-like roof, and then entering the arena's superstructure via one of the twelve steel support towers.

"Look at that," said Taylor. "It's the frame."

Zen could see it as well. The practice frame in the warehouse was a virtual copy of one of the main supports inside the arena roof. The Spikers had told her it had already been there when they moved in. She wondered if it had been built by their backers. If so, they clearly had someone on the inside of DESCO – a spy who'd told them where the organization would be holding its arms fair several weeks in advance.

"You'll be given glue gloves," Celeste said, "so we can all get past the security perimeter and up the roof to the support tower. We've been supplied with a couple of other toys as well, to deal with any cameras and electronic locks."

She tapped a key on the laptop. The video of the tunnelling machine she'd showed Zen in Regent's Park began to play. "You remember these. Their technical designation is GD6507-R, but they've become known as 'gravediggers'. And they are pure evil – certain to kill both soldiers and civilians on a massive scale. I can tell you now that they're being brought to DESCO by our old friends, Hardcastle Solutions."

Zen just managed to hide her surprise. Caleb and Sam had checked out Hardcastle's weapons division, and they hadn't uncovered any sign of these so-called gravediggers. The megacorporation was obviously not to be underestimated – they'd managed to keep this top-secret project hidden from almost everyone, even a hacking team as good as Caleb and Sam. And yet somehow the Spikers' backers had found out about it anyway.

"Hardcastle are merchants of death," Locke spat. "They'll be lining these things up for sale like new cars in a showroom."

Celeste gestured towards Zen. "As you all know, that girl over there is a true enemy of Hardcastle. What she wrote on the Scuti Wall was seen by millions. So we're going to use her skills to strike them again. To show the entire world what they are."

This met with approval from the Spikers. "Let's do it," one muttered. "Let's *finish* them."

"Here's how it'll work," said Celeste. "We're going to split into teams. Each one will be given a section of this route to secure, so that our way out is kept open. You know the drill: monitor the guards, watch for alarms, and be ready for anything. Meanwhile, Dima, Locke and I will go all the way in, until we're above the exhibition itself. And then we'll do what's needed."

Celeste divided the nine remaining Spikers into three teams of three, before talking to each group individually to detail their responsibilities. As Zen waited to be told what she would be doing, Locke walked up quietly beside her.

"Quite a punch you've got there, Dima," he murmured. "That devil guy ended up going to A & E. Didn't see you throw anything like that while you were training in here with us."

"Adrenaline, I guess," Zen said.

"Yeah? Excitement took over, did it? Well, you'd better make sure nothing like that happens on the op. Because I will *not* let you screw this up for us. You need to keep it together." A faint sneer crept into his voice. "You know – stay *zen*."

Zen stiffened, sweat prickling coldly across her back. Before she could think of a response, Celeste signalled for them both to go to the kitchen counter.

"The Hardcastle pavilion is over on the southern side of the arena," the Spiker leader said, pointing at the 3-D map. "It's one of the biggest in the fair. We've learned that they have a high-priority meeting at the beginning of the day, exactly one hour after the doors open. This, Dima, is what we want you to record with your microbot. Jim Jones, the managing director of Hardcastle's weapons division, will be speaking with senior representatives from the government of Dotar. Have you heard of it?"

"Petrostate dictatorship," Zen said. "With a pretty awful human rights record."

Celeste nodded. "They're currently attempting to supress a non-violent popular uprising calling for democracy. And Hardcastle is lining them up to be the first buyer for the gravediggers. We've heard that they're interested in acquiring sixty units. At forty-five million US dollars a unit."

"And this is a ... sales negotiation?"

"The Dotar delegation will include generals," Celeste told her. "Strategists. Military advisers. They'll be making sure that these gravedigger abominations can do everything they need. So Jim Jones will be spelling out for them just how good his machines are at large-scale killing."

Zen grimaced. "I can see why you want a recording of this conversation."

Celeste met Zen's eye. "The world has to hear it, Dima," she said. "Everyone has to be shown the true face of these companies. They have to know exactly what they're supporting when they buy that cheap T-shirt or whatever from Scuti. Hardcastle is using the best tech in the world to make millions – *billions* – from slaughter. It's got to end."

Zen leaned in to look at the 3-D map, studying the path they were to take across the roof supports and the precise location of the Hardcastle pavilion. Her task was nearly over. All she needed was an indication of what "phase two" was and she could withdraw. Finish her undercover assignment. Stop being Dima Kahf.

She couldn't deny it, though – a part of her actually *wanted* to see this through. It seemed more important than ever to expose Hardcastle Solutions and prevent them from flooding the planet with their death bots. Perhaps walking away from the Spikers wasn't going to be as easy as she'd thought.

"So you and Locke will help me set up above the pavilion," she said, keeping her tone businesslike. "Then I'll fly Skit down and record these evil jerks talking about the gravediggers. What happens after that?"

Locke and Celeste exchanged a quick look.

"What d'you think happens?" Locke snorted. "We all break into a song? We *escape*, as quick as we can. Pull back to the river and sail off into the sunset."

Zen felt a sharp twinge of unease. This was a lie. There was a whole other stage to the operation – the "phase two" Celeste had mentioned earlier, that had to be carefully timed to fit in with the plans of their backers.

Why would they keep it secret?

Zen remembered her argument with Caleb the night before; the footage of the Argo attack in Germany; the rampaging combat bots in the SolTec testing zone. It didn't matter how righteous the Spikers' cause was – they were capable of serious harm. She had to stay focused on her mission. If she asked any more questions, Celeste and Locke might get suspicious. She'd already gathered enough intel about their plans. Caleb, Mitch and Professor Clay would be waiting for her to return to the safe house. And her family, her mum and Riyah, were coming to London the next day. It was time to get out.

"When do I need to arrive tomorrow?" she asked. "I can skip breakfast. Make it here by seven."

There was a strange pause.

Celeste turned from the laptop and took one of Zen's hands in hers. "Dima," she said gently. "I don't think you understand how this is going to work. You don't ever have to go back to that place."

The breath suddenly left Zen's body, like she'd been slammed against a wall. She swallowed hard, her head spinning with shock.

"But if … if I'm not home for dinner," she said, "my foster parents will freak out. They might call the police."

"That doesn't matter," Celeste told her. "They won't be able to find you. We're moving to a new location – a forward base closer to the target. And we all have to stay together now until the mission is over. It's the only way to make sure it isn't compromised. But I'm hoping that you'll stay with us for a lot longer than a single mission."

"You mean … you want me to…"

Celeste smiled. "It's like I told you, Dima," she said, squeezing Zen's hand. "You're a Spiker now. You're one of us."

IT'S ON

The house at Nine Elms was dark and empty, with all its shutters closed. Caleb rode around the side and put his bike in a rack in the backyard. Then he got Sam to open the nearest door, deactivate the alarms, and start turning on the lights. Since his mum was a senior CIA agent, the building had been fitted with all sorts of elaborate security systems. Caleb had managed to hack them almost straight away – and had used them to his advantage on more than one occasion.

He walked into the large, modern kitchen, took a two-litre bottle of milk from his backpack and set it on the counter. Nobody had set foot in the house for several weeks, and it felt chilly and unwelcoming. There were no traces of daily life to be seen – no bowls of fruit, or flowers in vases, or important bits of paper attached to the fridge. The blackboard that his mum would often write messages to him on – instructions, reminders, words of encouragement and love – had been wiped clean. He sighed heavily. He'd thought that coming to check on the house might lift his spirits, but it was doing the total opposite.

"Well," he said, "everything looks OK, I guess."

"The domestic security grid is functioning normally," Sam reported, "and I have activated the boiler on its usual timer settings."

Caleb opened the fridge door and put the milk inside. "That's it, then. That's all Mum wanted us to do."

"You sound disconsolate, Caleb," said Sam. "I would speculate that you are still upset after your earlier conversation with Professor Clay."

"Yeah, maybe a bit. It wasn't the best ten minutes of my entire life."

Mitch had been right. Clay had been absolutely furious with him for going to the safe house in Chalk Farm. After keeping him waiting all morning, she'd called him to her office and given him possibly the worst telling-off he'd ever had.

"You broke with Möbius protocol," she'd said, banging the end of her cane on the floor for emphasis. "You endangered the whole team. You risked Zen's safety and everything she's worked so hard for. And you *went behind my back*, Caleb. You took important new intel about our primary target to your friend rather than to me, the director of the programme!"

Caleb had shifted about uncomfortably, seriously considering running across the room and diving out through one of the windows. "I'm sorry, Professor," he'd mumbled. "Honestly, I am. It's just ... you haven't really listened to me so far. You don't exactly—"

Clay had held up her hand. "Enough! Just *stop*, Caleb. I don't have to explain myself to you. This all shows an appalling lack of judgement and discipline on your part. I'm standing you down from the mission, effective immediately. Now get out of my office."

Afterwards, Caleb had felt ashamed and guilty – but he'd been angry too. With Clay herself, for not ending this ridiculously dangerous mission. And with Zen, for refusing to see sense – for telling him that he didn't know what he was talking about when he'd only been trying to help her.

"Running these Möbius operations will be highly stressful," Sam said. "Professor Clay is making many weighty decisions, in the context of a wider situation of which we are not aware. If you act in unexpected ways, you must anticipate that she—"

"Hold on a sec," Caleb interrupted. "Are you *taking her side* here, Sam? Can't I even rely on you?"

"Of course you can, Caleb. However, after a dispute, it is generally agreed that peace of mind can only be regained by attempting to understand the opposing party's position."

Caleb went through to the living room, walking between sofas on which he and his mum had sprawled together for many hours, watching movies, reading their books or working on their devices.

"I suppose," he said. "But do they *really* not get where this is heading? Don't they see what this Celeste person is capable of? She won't be satisfied with anything less than what went down at SolTec. It's like ... it's like Zen is on a train that's speeding towards a cliff, and they all want her to stay on it until the very last moment. But by then it might be too late."

"A vivid comparison, Caleb, and one supported by Celeste's previous actions. But you must have faith in your friends and comrades – in Professor Clay's long experience of intelligence work, and in Zen's instincts, which have proved sound numerous times in the past. She has shown herself to be worthy of the deepest trust. Would you say that she is your best friend?"

Caleb hesitated. "Yeah. I would. She's basically family." He began to grin; the Talos Algorithm seemed to be turning his AI into a first-class relationship counsellor. "Jeez, Sam. You're pretty good at this. And you're totally right. I've got to try to … to…"

Something had started flashing on the Flex.

"A high priority audio message has just arrived for you via *Terrorform*," Sam said. "It is from Yun Choi, elected leader of the Blue Salamander Clan."

The Blue Salamanders were the largest clan in the game after the Nameless. Mostly based in Seoul, they were one of the clans that had pledged their fleet to Caleb's cause, and were on standby to begin the fight against the invaders.

"Play it."

"Hey, uh, Caleb," said a deep Korean-accented voice through the Flex's speaker. "You might want to take a look at the surface of Kolto. Your last megamonster is about to go down. The Nameless are already preparing to go interplanetary. Time to log in, dude. It's on."

Caleb left the lounge at once, striding quickly through

the kitchen towards the back door. "Fire up the *Queen Jane*, Sam," he said. "We're going to do this right."

"Understood, Caleb. Lifting barge lockdown. Initiating on-board systems."

Caleb crossed the yard and hurried along the river path to Nine Elms Pier. It was here, at the far end of a small marina, that the *Queen Jane, Approximately* was moored. The *Queen Jane* was an old Dutch barge that Caleb's dad had named after his favourite song and converted into a state-of-the-art tech lab – a place for him to work on medical AI. A little while after he'd died, Caleb had moved in. The barge was where he'd first found Sam's program, and where they'd built *Terrorform* together – and it was usually the nerve centre from which they oversaw the game's vast virtual world. He loved the *Queen Jane* – aside from his mum, it was the thing he'd missed the most during his weeks living at the ARC.

There was no time to savour the moment. Caleb rushed in through the pressurized door, down the half-flight of steps, and along the narrow room decked out with computer equipment, until he came to the workstation in its centre. Sam had started up *Terrorform* already; the AI's silver face was in the corner of the barge's largest screen, which was displaying the map of the Cardano system.

"OK, go to Kolto," Caleb said, sitting in his worn leather captain's chair. "Let's see what Yun Choi was talking about."

Using God mode, they swept down through the ice planet's atmosphere. The final monster was easy to locate.

"Whoa," said Caleb. "It's the Crocodemon! Still kicking Nameless butt after nearly *three days*. That is one tough beast!"

The colossal scaly form was struggling across a frozen lake the colour of beaten bronze, a few burning Nameless vehicles scattered in its wake. It had taken a lot of damage and was limping badly. Far above it were half a dozen blood-red slivers, arranged like a set of arrow heads. They were Rapier-class artillery frigates – and they were subjecting the Crocodemon to a brutal bombardment with antimatter missiles. Acid-green lines sliced down from the sky, each one ending with a loud, hollow implosion that struck against the creature like an invisible piledriver. It staggered from side to side, its limbs flailing, vainly firing off its remaining quills as it looked around for an escape route.

Before the doomed monster could move, however, the Rapiers fired off a fresh salvo, raining missiles onto its back; and then the ice beneath it suddenly cracked apart, dumping the beast into the dark waters below. The Crocodemon floundered and roared, and thrashed about one last time – then was still. The next moment it began to dissolve into lines of light.

Caleb blinked. "Right," he said. "So I guess that's that."

"The Nameless are moving off," Sam reported. "Those Rapiers are joining a fleet that has massed behind the moon of Comus. If Yun Choi is correct, they will be—"

"Yeah, I know. It's time to fight back."

Caleb looked down at his workstation. It was covered in controllers, keyboards and computer components of various kinds. He picked up his best VR headset – one he'd made a couple of custom enhancements to – and logged in as a player, selecting the midnight-blue Navigator with the wolves painted on its shoulders. Then he went to the game map and chose a spawn point in the middle of a large asteroid field between Kolto and the jungle planet of Fraxis Prime. This was where the Terrorformers had agreed to assemble – to form a defensive line and beat back the Nameless.

An instant later, Caleb's Navigator materialized on the cratered surface of an asteroid. Rocks of every shape and size were floating all around him. Some were barren, while others were dotted with shelters, sensor vanes and weapons platforms – and arrayed across them were hundreds and hundreds of Terrorformers. A heavily customized Anvil cruiser was passing overhead, the sound of its engines rumbling through the *Queen Jane*'s surround-sound speakers. Caleb counted twenty-two spacecraft in total, from the Blue Salamander Clan and a handful of others. It was a truly massive army, but they were going to need every last player. The Nameless force now numbered more than five thousand avatars, a lot of them maxed-out level forties – along with a sizeable fleet that included every ship Caleb and Sam had programmed. And they would surely be battling with a coordination and efficiency that the Terrorformers' ragtag battalions wouldn't be able to match.

"I believe the moment is almost here, Caleb," said Sam. "Perhaps you should say a few words to the assembled players, for the purposes of morale."

"Good idea," Caleb replied. He turned towards the vastness of Kolto; the moon of Comus could just be seen, laid against its shining surface like an ink spot in the snow. "Just let me..."

"If you like, I could generate a script using a template I have machine-learned from the great speeches of human history, including those of Winston Churchill, Abraham Lincoln, Queen—"

"Uh, no thanks, Sam. Don't do that. I've got this." Caleb pressed a couple of in-game buttons, opening an audio channel to every player currently online. "Hey, everyone," he began, a little self-consciously. "Caleb Quinn here."

Almost at once, thousands of people started to cheer and ask questions; Sam adjusted the volume levels so that Caleb wasn't drowned out completely. He was buzzing with a combination of anxiousness and excitement. This was possibly the most thrilling thing that had ever happened in *Terrorform* – a truly awesome event, with some real in-game danger involved.

"You all know what's happening," he continued, raising his voice. "The Nameless are about to leave Kolto, and we have to stop them. They want to overrun the Cardano system – to overrun *Terrorform* and make it unplayable. They want to *destroy* it."

The assembled gamers began to boo – a deep, massive sound, like an elongated peal of thunder.

"I can't say for sure who these guys are," Caleb went on, "and I'm not going to point any fingers—"

"It's *Lodestar*!" someone yelled, to a loud murmur of agreement. "It's gotta be!"

"Jared West's been boasting about it," another voice added. "Some grey hats in Turin just hacked a private Lodestar chat group. West was saying that it was the coolest thing he'd ever seen!"

"Right now it doesn't matter," Caleb said. "We have to form up and fight them *together*. If we do that, we can save the game. *Terrorform* is *our* thing. We aren't going to let these guys just roll in and take over. They can't do it. We won't let them!"

There was another gigantic round of cheering and whooping. Caleb was about to say more, to try to outline a basic battle plan, when the shouts began.

"Here they come!"

"Over there, over there!"

"It's them – it's the Nameless! Lock and load!"

Starships were streaming from behind Comus and starting towards the asteroid field in a perfect geometric formation. Nothing like this had ever been seen in the game before. Their initial urgency left the assembled Terrorformers; most of them just stood there, completely transfixed. After a short while, the advancing shapes began to glitter against the void, tiny sparks and flashes clustering along their edges. It was weirdly beautiful.

"Caleb," said Sam, "you may want to—"

The first shots arrived, raking over the asteroids – disintegrating avatars, knocking spacecraft out of position, and breaking a couple of the smaller rocks apart. The blasts were deafening, shaking the barge beneath Caleb's trainers. The survivors scattered, screaming out swearwords as they searched desperately for cover.

"Return fire, everybody!" Caleb yelled, as another energy bolt crashed down nearby. *"Return fire!"*

SHORTCUT

The Spikers were getting ready to abandon the warehouse. Almost everything was being left behind. After a quarter of an hour's rapid packing, they assembled beside a grate in a small ground-floor storeroom. Each of them had a bulky black rucksack, while Locke was also carrying a couple of holdalls.

Zen had been given a rucksack of her own, containing a full set of clothes, a washing kit, and several pairs of boots and trainers. Her toothbrush was new, but everything else had a slightly pre-owned feel. She couldn't help wondering if it had once belonged to a Spiker who hadn't made the grade.

She was getting more scared with every passing minute. It felt like she was trapped – caught up in something from which she couldn't break free. She was going to have to take part in this crazy plan of theirs – the infiltration of a major arms fair in broad daylight. Her mum and little sister were arriving in London tomorrow afternoon, but by then she could very well be in a police cell – or worse. Any enthusiasm she'd had for exposing Hardcastle Solutions' wickedness was overshadowed by her fear of what "phase two" might be. She picked through her conversations with Celeste again and again, trying to find clues. The Spikers' leader had actually been very vague, she realized: "showing the world what Hardcastle is" could mean any number of things. Some of them *really* bad.

It was now critically important that Zen thought of a way to get a message to the Möbius team and pass on the intel she'd acquired. But there were no obvious options. Her phone had been taken from her that morning, as usual. The one she'd used to make a controller for Skit was gone as well, along with the bot itself – removed by Celeste to be stored with what she'd called "the mission gear".

Locke dropped his holdalls, seized the grate with both hands and heaved it off. A tight spiral staircase was revealed, leading down into darkness. Celeste took out a torch and started to descend, gesturing for Zen to follow.

"It's a smugglers' passage," she said, her voice echoing in the dank tunnel below. "Goes under the canal. The people who built this warehouse clearly had some stuff they wanted to keep secret."

The passage was only a couple of metres wide, with tiled, slime-coated walls and a cracked concrete floor. It didn't lead straight under the canal but curved off to the side, almost like it was following the path of the water. After a hundred metres or so they came to another spiral staircase, which took them up to a metal door. Celeste pulled back a heavy bolt, opened the door a few centimetres to check outside, then stepped through.

Zen walked out to find herself on the canal towpath. It was very dark, the still water almost black. She saw that they were under a bridge a short distance from the warehouse. A small boat was moored a few metres away. Celeste shined her torch towards it, revealing a low cabin with a scratched fibreglass roof. She went over and climbed aboard.

"Come on," she said.

Zen didn't move. This route out of the warehouse had obviously been selected to avoid satellite surveillance. The Möbius team wouldn't even know that the Spikers had left – or that they'd boarded this boat. She'd be lost. Completely untraceable. The other Spikers began to emerge from the doorway and go after Celeste, filing down into the boat's cabin. Zen thought about running. This might be her only chance to get away. Could she make it to a main road – flag down a police car, or jump on a bus?

No – it was hopeless. Locke was there, directly behind her, closing the door beneath the bridge. He'd be after her at once, with the others close behind. Zen remembered that run after the gas holders, when they'd brought her out into the middle of Regent's Park. She wouldn't stand a chance.

Zen stepped aboard. The cabin smelled weird, like old carpets and mouse droppings. Its windows had been painted over so that no one could see in – or out. The nine Spikers sat on facing bench seats with their bags stacked around them. Taylor took out a battered paperback and settled down to read. The rest talked in low voices about the coming mission, or tried to sleep. Celeste and Locke stayed on deck – at the helm, Zen assumed. Before long, the engine started up and they began to move.

It was hard to know how long the journey lasted. The boat stopped a couple of times to pass through canal locks; there were straight stretches and winding bends. Any more than this Zen couldn't tell. She kept thinking about "phase two". About the killer robots at SolTec, and the inferno that had followed. About the video of that armoured truck rolling back into traffic, smashing through the cars.

Eventually, Celeste leaned in through the cabin door. "We've arrived," she said.

They'd moored at a modern-looking wharf. The buildings here were taller than those in Camden. Most seemed to be apartment blocks. The canal had been replaced by a wide tributary with a motorway just beyond its far bank, past a screen of trees. They were out east, Zen reckoned – very close to the Thames. The O2 Arena would be nearby, on the opposite side of the river.

As soon as everyone had disembarked, Locke began to drive the boat away while Celeste led the group to one of the apartment buildings. She opened the door of what appeared to be a maintenance room on the ground floor. Inside were bedrolls, a microwave on a table and a stack of ready meals. Zen tried to stay calm, taking a bedroll and choosing a spot over in a corner, but a knot of desperation was tightening painfully in her chest. She had to get word out. She had to stop this.

"Hey," said Celeste. "You OK?"

Zen nodded. "Never better." She paused. "A bit nervous."

Celeste came closer. "This isn't just a strike against Hardcastle, Dima," she said. "It's a strike against the entire arms industry. Including the company that caused your mother's death." She put a hand on Zen's shoulder. "After all these years, you finally have a chance to make things right."

Zen didn't know what to say. She nodded again, feeling the knot of desperation tighten a little further.

"Try to relax," Celeste said. "We need you razor-sharp tomorrow."

Some of the Spikers were heating up food in the microwave, prodding at the trays with plastic forks. Celeste went to talk to a couple of them. The others pulled laptops from their bags – one of the few things they'd brought with them from the warehouse, besides their clothes. They began setting themselves up across the room, sitting in a line against a wall.

This was it. Zen walked over, taking care not to seem too eager. As she'd guessed, they were running *Terrorform*, just like they'd done in Camden, although none of them were actually playing yet. Instead, they were staring at the real-time map of the Cardano system, murmuring swearwords and shaking their heads in amazement. She asked if she could join in.

Taylor nodded towards a spare laptop. "Go for it," she said. "I gotta warn you, though – this game is getting *seriously* messed up tonight."

There was no time to ask what this meant. Zen sat down,

opened the laptop and booted it up. The desktop background was a press photo of the SolTec facility, the buildings dwarfed by the cloud of black smoke that was rising above it. The *Terrorform* shortcut – a small chrome *T* – was in the top right corner.

Zen double-clicked it as quickly as she could.

THE STASIS ORB

*T*he Nameless broke through the Terrorformers' line in minutes. As always, they made little effort to preserve themselves, and fought with ruthless, unrelenting focus. Caleb put up a furious defence, speeding from asteroid to asteroid, shooting down any red-armoured player he encountered – but it was already starting to look like his army might be defeated. Sam had sent out the audio file of his speech to every player account, and hundreds more Terrorformers were warping in constantly to join the fight. Losses were high, though; many avatars only lasted a few seconds before the Nameless took them out. Confidence was beginning to ebb.

Caleb's own exhilaration was leaving him as well. He always relished a challenge, but this was getting to be too much. They needed something spectacular – a big win that could turn the tide of the battle. He quickly spotted an opportunity. A Nameless Anvil cruiser – fitted out with the best armour, weaponry and engine upgrades the game had to offer – was approaching one of the larger asteroids,

259

exchanging heavy fire with a squad of Blue Salamander Bulwarks on its surface. Meanwhile, avatars from the other classes were fighting all around it, illuminating the blackness with the frenetic zapping of their energy weapons.

"I'm going for that Anvil," he said into his comms channel. "Breach, clear and hijack. Who's with me?"

"Art here," a familiar voice replied, cutting through the chatter of battle. "I'll come with you, Caleb. If we move fast and don't get hemmed in, we should be able to access the bridge."

Caleb turned to see a level-twenty-four Oracle drifting towards him. It was navigating expertly through the weightlessness of space, using pulses from its psi-amplifier – a complex piece of sci-fi tech mounted on the suit's collar that allowed the wearer to blast raw psionic energy out through its gauntlets. This suit had been painted emerald green, and was covered with an intricate isotope pattern. The username *Slimestriker_07* appeared briefly above its helmet.

"Hey, Art," Caleb said. "You ready to go?"

"Most definitely. I heard your audio message and logged on at once. This is all rather astonishing, isn't it? I mean, if you ignore the fact that your game is about to be—"

"Not now, Art," Caleb broke in, gunning his jet pack. "Come on, let's get moving."

He zoomed upwards, charging his energy shields and heading for the struggle around the blood-red Anvil. By the time he reached it, he was moving so fast that he crashed straight through the dense tangle of combatants, sending avatars flying in all directions.

One of the Anvil's airlocks could be seen ahead, its outer door open. Three Nameless Infernals were standing inside, preparing to join the fray. As he raced in, Caleb shot down two, with direct hits from his ion lance, then smashed into the third, bashing it hard against the wall. It tried to rise – and was blown clean out of the airlock by a jet of energy from Art, who was gliding in behind.

"My psi sensors are picking up fifteen … yes, fifteen Nameless signals on this ship," he said, as he landed. "Are you sure this is wise?"

"We don't have a choice," said Caleb, as he hacked the inner door with a digital multitool in the Navigator's forearm. "We can't let them win."

Art exhaled. "Well, OK then. I suppose I can always start again if my Oracle gets … you know…"

"They want to take over *Terrorform*, Art," Caleb told him. "If we don't stop them, there won't be any starting again for any of us."

The airlock's outer door closed, and the inner one opened. A storm of plasma bolts poured in from the corridor beyond, forcing both of them to take cover.

"What class abilities have you chosen?" Caleb shouted to Art. "Did you get stasis orb? That's unlocked at level twenty, right, Sam?"

"Correct, Caleb. Art appears to have selected this ability. I can max it out if you require, increasing both the orb's radius and its duration."

"Hello there, Sam," said Art. "How are you doing today?"

"I am functioning well, Art. Thank you for asking. I am experiencing some apprehension, however, at the situation unfolding within the *Terrorform* game universe."

"Now that is *intriguing*," Art said; he seemed to have forgotten their predicament completely. "Can you tell me any more about this, ah, apprehension of yours? What do you imagine might happen next?"

The hail of white-hot plasma intensified, scorching the walls and floor of the airlock.

"I don't want to *interrupt* or anything," Caleb yelled, "but we are about a millimetre away from getting incinerated here! Can we please concentrate on *taking over this freaking ship*?"

"Of course, of course," said Art. "I apologize – and yes, I am a total *master* of stasis orb. It's my speciality, actually."

"OK then, here's what we're going to do. Sam – boost Art's orb power as high as it'll go. Art – throw one straight ahead when I say. Ready?" Caleb took a breath, fastening his grip around his VR controllers. *"Go!"*

He stepped out from cover to draw enemy fire, his energy field crackling as the plasma began to flare against it. Meanwhile, Art brought his gauntlets together to launch a shimmering silvery sphere into the corridor in front of them. It landed about halfway along, among the Nameless defenders – and then suddenly expanded until it filled the passage.

The enemy barrage promptly stopped. Caleb ran forward, up to the edge of the orb. Within it, time had frozen; he saw red-armoured Infernals standing stock still, not reacting to him at all, while their plasma bolts hung in mid-air like luminous dashes. He walked into the orb – and nothing happened. The Oracle's abilities didn't affect its allies. The Nameless on the orb's far side continued to fire at him, but their shots were halted on its surface, clustering together uselessly. He began to shoot back, the Navigator's advanced targeting system zeroing in on their weak spots. In moments, he'd cleared a path straight to the bridge.

"All right," he said, hurrying up a flight of stairs, "I think we're going to pull this off."

In *Terrorform*, if you could reach the bridge of a space-ship, access its command console, and then hold the vessel for thirty seconds, it would transfer to your command. Caleb had put this feature in as a kind of twist, to make the game more exciting. If the ships – which were so expensive, and so difficult to build – were also easy to lose, it would mean that clans would fight extra-hard to defend them. He crossed the bridge to the console and initiated the takeover process. The change in the Anvil's status bar – visible to all in the game world – was soon noticed, and the Terrorformers began to cheer.

Art's Oracle came in behind him. "That was *incredible*!" he cried. "Utterly brilliant! How much longer until you have control?"

"Just a few more seconds. Then we turn this thing around. Begin the counter-attack."

"Understood, understood." Art chuckled. "I must say, Caleb, this is the most fun I've had in *Terrorform* since—"

The shots sliced through the bridge from at least three

different directions. Art's suit was struck four, five times, the blasts spinning it around with savage force.

"Oh god," he said, as he struggled for balance. "This is – I don't – hang on, what's—"

Oracles weren't designed to take much punishment. Two more plasma bolts hit home, and Art's audio feed cut out abruptly. The emerald-green suit was thrown to the floor and began to dissolve.

Caleb ducked behind the console with a curse. Art's stasis orb must have worn off, freeing the Nameless caught within it. Something was wrong here – thirty seconds had definitely passed. The hijack should be complete. But nothing was happening.

"Sam, what's going on?" he asked. "Why isn't this working?"

"I cannot tell, Caleb."

"What do you mean, you cannot *tell*?" Caleb hesitated, starting to frown. "Wait a sec, has *Terrorform* been hacked? Have these Nameless dirtbags actually *hacked* us somehow?"

"Unclear. You would have to grant me permission to perform a full diagnostic. But the takeover sequence has run its course and the ship has not left Nameless control. You should also be aware that over a hundred of their avatars are converging on this position."

Caleb looked out through the bridge windows. Red-armoured soldiers were breaking off from the battle outside and streaming towards the Anvil. He was going to be cornered. Overwhelmed.

"Sam," he said, "this is beginning to feel a lot like a trap."

GAME OVER

The Nameless Bulwark emerged from the passage that led to the forward batteries. Barely fitting through the doorway, it lumbered out onto the bridge, planted its huge steel boots on the deck with a resounding clang, and levelled its arm-mounted railguns in Caleb's direction. He was just about managing to fend off the waves of enemies that were coming at him from the main corridor, and barely had time even to turn its way.

That's it, he thought. *I'm dead.*

But the huge mech suit did not open fire; in fact, it seemed to have frozen in place. Then its arms dropped down, its chest section slumped forward, and it began to melt out of existence. A Solar Scout had attacked it from behind, driving its graphite katana into one of the Bulwark's weak points: a tiny respirator grille at the base of its neck. This was an incredibly tricky move to pull off – and a one-strike kill on the toughest avatar in the game. The lightweight Solar Scout then whisked to Caleb's side, deftly dodging the gunfire to join him behind the command console. He hadn't yet got a proper look at this avatar – only seeing that it was low-level, lacking any special equipment or customizations, and painted a plain, military grey.

"Nicely done," he said. "But please tell me you're not on your own. It's going to take a lot more than the two of us to break out of here."

There was no response.

"The player *Polar_X* has no audio enabled," said Sam. "Only text chat is available."

"*Polar_X*?"

Caleb stopped firing and turned towards the Solar Scout in amazement. He could see the gamer tag now, floating over its head. He switched off his headset's microphone so that only Sam could hear him.

"Sam, that ... that *can't* be a coincidence. This is *Zen*. She said they played *Terrorform* in their warehouse, right? She must be... She must have..."

A text bubble blinked on above the Solar Scout's sleek, streamlined helmet.

Don't have long. Spiker attack tomoro.

Caleb fumbled with his controllers, bringing up a virtual keyboard. "Hold on, just let me get this working..."

Target is arms fair, Zen typed. *O2 Arena. Hardcastle Sols 9AM.*

R U out? Caleb replied. *Buzzard 2 xtract?*

Have moved. By river – loc unknown. There was a pause, the cursor blinking. *B ready. Something bad.*

The enemy fire grew even heavier. The Nameless had

taken advantage of Caleb's distraction; they were at the edges of the bridge in ever larger numbers, crowds of red figures blocking the corridors. Before he realized what was going on, the Solar Scout walked out from cover, katana lowered, deliberately seeking self-destruction. It was immediately vaporized. Zen had delivered her message.

"Call Professor Clay, Sam," Caleb said. "We've got to pass this intel on *right now*." He started firing again, scoring a couple of quick hits, but this fight was seeming more hopeless than ever.

"Her phone line is busy, Caleb. Should I send a message over the ARC intranet?"

"Sure," Caleb muttered, pulling back behind the console. "She's pretty bad at picking those up, though..." He took a deep breath. "I've got to make absolutely certain this gets through, Sam. Zen's in danger. I've got to get back to the tower."

"Very well, Caleb. You understand what this means?"

"Yeah. My Navigator's finished."

In *Terrorform*, like many other online games, if you left the action outside a spawn point to return to the menu screen, your avatar would remain in the game world – which would keep on running around it. Even if you promptly exited the program, it would still be vulnerable for a couple of seconds. Here on the bridge of this Anvil cruiser, the Navigator would be cut down at once.

Caleb wasn't going out like that – not after everything he and this suit had been through together. He reloaded the ion lance. The Nameless were beginning to advance, closing in around him with their weapons raised. Yelling his loudest, most ferocious war cry, he charged from behind the console, running straight into a large semicircle of red-armoured avatars. He began firing wildly, emptying the ion lance's magazine, shooting at every enemy he could.

As one, the Nameless fired back, unleashing a massive volley that seemed to rock the barge on its moorings. The midnight-blue Navigator suit was atomized instantly. The forms of the game world faded and separated, streaming away to nothingness, until Caleb was left in a still white void. The words **game over**, black and lower-case, slowly materialized in the air in front of him.

Two minutes later he was flying along the Thames Path on his bike, riding as fast as he possibly could, thinking only of the distance that remained between himself and the ARC tower. He swerved through the South Bank, pedalled frantically across Blackfriars Bridge, and weaved on through the lights and noise of the City of London. Sam continued to call and message Professor Clay, but with no luck. Was she dodging his calls? Was he still in that much trouble with her for the previous night?

Caleb dropped his bike and ran through the lobby, barely remembering to return Rufus the security guard's wave. He pressed the lift button repeatedly. A few seconds passed. It felt like nothing was happening. He started pressing the button again.

"Everything all right there, Mr Quinn?" Rufus called from his desk.

"Uh, yeah," Caleb replied. "I'm just … you know … homework…"

The lift finally arrived and he rushed in, hammering his thumb against the button for floor thirty-four. The small metal box then crawled up the inside of the tower, so slowly it seemed to be hardly moving at all. Caleb was out through the doors as soon as there was space for him to fit between them. He raced along the corridor, banged his fist against the door of Clay's office and shouted her name.

It opened almost straight away. Clay was wearing an audio headset over her bandages. She glared down at him with fierce intensity.

"I know you probably don't want to listen to me right now," Caleb began breathlessly, "but I have got some *vital*—"

Clay put her finger to her lips and nodded across the room. A livestream was running on her TV screen: a first-person view of the inside of a dark, cavernous building, the beam of a torch playing across a metallic frame that hung from its ceiling. Caleb stopped talking. Clay indicated that he should enter, then closed the door behind him. He walked forward, staring at the screen. In the bottom corner was a stopwatch, running at just over four minutes – and beside it the word *Buzzard*.

"You seeing this, Goldfinch?" said Mitch's voice. "This is the thing Hawk talked about – the thing she sketched for us."

"The O2!" Caleb exclaimed. "It's part of the O2!"

Clay turned towards him sharply. "Excuse me?"

"Is that Swift?" Mitch asked. "Is he there with you?"

"Hawk just contacted me through my video game," Caleb continued. "She said the Spikers played it, remember? She came to find me. They're going to attack an arms fair at the O2 – and Hardcastle Solutions in particular."

Clay leaned against a chair, absorbing this news. "Good lord."

Sam spoke through the Flex's speaker. "I collated all available data on this event during our journey from Nine Elms. It is called the Annual Exhibition of the Defence and Security Coalition. Many governments participate, including those of the UK and USA. It seems to be conducted under a veil of officially sanctioned secrecy, but Hardcastle Solutions can be identified as one of the principal exhibitors. According to one arms industry chatroom, they expect to do over three billion dollars of business there."

Clay's lips were pressed together into a thin line. "We should have anticipated this," she said grimly. "We really should have worked this out."

"The Spikers have relocated too," Caleb added. He looked at the screen. "But I guess you already knew that."

"Buzzard went in when Hawk failed to return," Clay told him. "The place is like a ghost ship."

"We didn't see them leave on the satellite," said Mitch. "Must be some kind of hidden exit. Give me another two minutes, Goldfinch, and I'll find it."

"Negative, Buzzard," Clay said. "They won't have left any

kind of trail for you to follow. Return to the safe house and begin packing it up. Get all the Möbius kids back here, then report to me."

"Roger that," said Mitch. "Buzzard out."

The video feed went dead.

"What about Zen, then?" Caleb asked heatedly. "What are we going to do?"

"They obviously need her for their operation," Clay answered, "so she'll be safe enough. For the time being, at least."

"But she's properly caught up in this now. And she's *scared*, Professor. She told me that something bad was going to happen. Like I said. Like I tried to tell you."

Caleb half expected these words to be met with anger – for Clay to give him another dressing-down, reminding him harshly of his youth and inexperience. Instead, she merely sighed, crossing her arms, and for the briefest moment she looked very, very tired.

"Listen, Caleb," she said. "You'll come to learn that spy work goes wrong more often than it goes right. Blame is pointless. It's just a waste of energy. The important thing now is that we've got some idea of what's coming." She slid her phone from her cardigan pocket. "And there's still time for us to stop it."

INTO THE ARENA

The Spikers left the maintenance room at 8.30 a.m. precisely and went back to the waterfront. All twelve of them were dressed in black and wearing the ski masks that Celeste had handed out an hour or so earlier. A very different kind of boat was moored at the dock: a grey, rigid-hull inflatable, like those used by army special forces. One of the older male Spikers had been assigned as its pilot, and he now went over to the controls. They'd been told that he would drop them at the target, keep well clear during the op itself, and then zoom in to pick them up again when it was complete.

Celeste had the rest of them climb aboard and hunker down in two parallel lines.

"Keep to the rear, Dima," she said to Zen. "Next to Locke."

They looked at each other. Zen saw at once that something had changed. Celeste's dazzling heterochromia was gone. Both her irises were now a very dark brown, only a shade lighter than black – the colour of Mariella Bachmann's. Celeste was going into action.

"Contacts," she said, realizing that Zen had noticed. "A necessary precaution."

Locke didn't speak as Zen sat beside him, making none of his usual sarcastic comments. It was almost like he was nervous. Zen's own fear sat heavily within her, like a lump of cold stone. She told herself that she'd got word out; that she could rely on Caleb to do whatever he could to raise the alarm; that the Möbius Programme and the intelligence services would be there to stop anything awful from happening. But she couldn't quite believe it.

She looked down at the gloves she was wearing, which Celeste had distributed along with the ski masks. They were roughly how Zen had imagined: ultra-lightweight in design with pads on the fingers and palms, and tubes sewn into the material. These tubes were connected to a small rubber blister at the wrist that was filled with fluid – the smart glue that Art had got so excited about back at the ARC. Celeste had given her a short lesson in how to use them against a wall in the maintenance room. It had been one of the weirdest things Zen had ever felt. The lightest touch and you were completely, securely stuck – but move the glove away and it detached just as easily.

"The secret is speed," Celeste had said. "When you're climbing, move your hands in a really quick sequence." She'd started to smile. "And don't think too hard about what you're doing."

The Spiker leader had also equipped the others with these white, Taser-like devices. Zen overheard her telling them to shoot the devices at cameras, electronic locks – and people too, if they had no choice.

The mission was very carefully timed. Celeste was wearing a smartwatch and a radio earpiece, through which she seemed to be receiving information and instructions. Zen watched her closely, convinced that the Spikers' mysterious backers were on the other end. She wondered yet again who they could be. It seemed unlikely that a rival arms company would want the DESCO fair to be targeted – that would surely be bad for business. Perhaps Professor Clay's theory about spies had been right; maybe these backers were the agents of a hostile foreign government, trying to stir up unrest.

They sat in the grey boat for a few minutes, bobbing slightly on the tide; then an alarm sounded on the watch and Celeste gave the signal to start the engines. The inflatable slid forward through the water, around a wide bend and out onto the Thames. It was a drizzly November morning, the sky covered with dark clouds. There was hardly any traffic on the river, and nothing nearby. Zen peered around Taylor, who was sitting in front of her. The O2 Arena was directly ahead, about two hundred metres away. It looked like a huge, domed tent, shining white against the surrounding greyness. Twelve tall support towers jutted out through its surface, rising above it in a crown formation. The grey inflatable accelerated rapidly towards it.

They'd gone over the plan repeatedly back in the maintenance room. The first stage involved them getting onto the roof of the arena. Celeste was going to lead the way. She'd told them that a small gap had been identified in the arena's security. They just needed to neutralize a couple of cameras – and move swiftly.

Their boat reached the embankment wall on the far side of the river – and without the slightest hesitation, Celeste stood up and jumped against it. Her hands attached firmly to the concrete, then left it immediately when she began climbing to the top. The other Spikers followed suit. All of them plainly had experience with the gloves, and they moved nearly as fast as Celeste.

Zen's turn came. She swallowed hard and leaped off the side of the inflatable, planting both her hands on the wall. They fastened to it instantly, leaving her hanging like a coat on a hook. For a moment she didn't dare do anything, afraid that she might misjudge her actions and fall into the brown-grey water below.

Locke sprang onto the wall beside her. "You going to dangle there all day?"

"I … I don't know if I—"

"Just *climb*, Dima Kahf. Clock's ticking."

Zen closed her eyes. *Speed*, she told herself. Pulling up with her arms, she lifted her left hand away from the wall and slapped it down about forty centimetres above her head. Then she did the same with her right hand, and the left again, scrabbling her trainers against the rough concrete. Luckily, the wall was only about three metres high. With Locke looking on impatiently, she made it to the top in under a minute.

The others had already gone. They were scaling a fence – heading for a point where the arena's tent-like canopy was anchored to the ground by concrete foundations and thick steel cables. Zen paused to get her breath back. Down below, she heard the inflatable roar off along the river.

"Come on," said Locke, pulling at her sleeve.

Zen ran with him to the fence. The glue gloves got them over it in a couple of seconds. It was about fifty metres to the arena itself. In front of them stood a row of parked lorries and a couple of portacabins. They carried on, following after Celeste and the others, using the lorries as cover. Zen noticed a pair of boots underneath one of them. She looked down to see a security guard, knocked unconscious, hidden behind its wheels.

Locke went ahead, sprinting over to the concrete anchor point, jumping up to a steel cable and climbing along it until he could drop onto the roof. Zen did the same, keeping an eye on the security perimeter that ran about twenty metres under the canopy's edge. Their insertion point had been carefully chosen; it was at the quietest part of the arena, furthest from an entry gate or checkpoint.

The white canopy was as smooth as a giant slide and slick with recent rainfall; if it hadn't been for the gloves, Zen would have slipped straight off. She and Locke climbed up to where the nearest support tower passed through it. Celeste and one of the others were crouched down beside this tower. As Zen approached, she saw they were operating a compact cutting tool, built into two moulded handles and virtually noiseless.

After a few seconds they stopped and lifted together, their teeth gritted – and up came a section the size of a manhole cover, which they heaved aside. Six of the Spikers promptly went in, or two of the teams; the third, only two strong now after the departure of the boat pilot, was going to stay out on the canopy to guard their self-made entrance.

Celeste turned to Zen. "Ready?"

Questions and fears crowded in Zen's mind, more than she could possibly process. She looked briefly across the river, to where the silver towers of the Isle of Dogs stood shrouded in mist. Then she nodded.

Beneath the hole was a narrow platform, attached to the support tower. Far below, a shiny, split-level mall encircled the arena with shops and restaurants. It had been lit up brightly against the November murk; the DESCO logo hung on banners and rotated on touch-screen information boards. The exhibition had opened at eight and a good number of people were in there already, dressed in business wear with their passes on display. A small army of private security guards was also visible, posted on every door, lift and escalator, and patrolling in pairs.

The two teams of Spikers had begun to fan out in opposite directions, clambering away to take up positions around the arena's superstructure. This was what they'd been training for in the warehouse – what that frame had been made to simulate. Zen had been wondering why so many of them were involved in this mission, but now she understood. Celeste had assembled a squad of skilled stealth soldiers. If they were discovered – if the alarm was raised, and they had to escape – these guys could put up a serious fight.

Zen looked around for any trace of the police or security services, hoping for an indication that Caleb had passed on her message and Professor Clay was poised to swoop in. But there was nothing.

Celeste had raised her finger to her earpiece. "The Dotar delegation has arrived outside," she whispered. "We've got to get into position."

She led Zen along a ceiling strut and forced open a ventilation grille so they could climb through into the main arena. The noise of human conversation and commerce rose from below. The seating had been removed, creating a huge open space filled with stands and pavilions, all of them emblazoned with weapons company logos. Pieces of gleaming military hardware had been set up on plinths – heavy machine guns, artillery platforms, even tanks. Vast screens showed promotional films like the one for the gravediggers that Celeste had on her phone. In fact, that exact clip was running on the far side of the concourse. It had just reached the point where the fearsome machine delivered its payload, sending an amplified explosion booming through the entire exhibition.

The Hardcastle pavilion was directly below it – a sprawling, open-plan structure built from slats of dark metal. Its interior was like a TV news studio, with the same symbol plastered across every screen: a stylized black *H*, made to resemble a sturdy fortress.

Locke emerged behind Zen and Celeste, and together they ventured out onto the enormous framework that had been fitted to the ceiling. It had several tiers, supporting a complex lighting rig, rows of speakers, and dozens of banners and placards – along with a couple of light attack helicopters and some kind of high-tech glider. Sticking to the deep shadows behind the lights, they climbed across the top of the arena, through the web of aluminium girders, until they were as close as they could get to the Hardcastle pavilion. Zen could now see the centrepiece of their display. Six gravediggers had been set out in a diamond formation on a raised platform. Each of the ugly, crab-like machines had been painted in a different shade of camouflage, from high desert to arctic.

Celeste checked her smartwatch. She seemed completely calm. Locke, in contrast, was even more on edge – cracking his knuckles and flexing his arms, like he was getting ready to do something.

"That's him," said Celeste suddenly. "That's Jim Jones."

Zen peered down. Five or six sharp-suited executives had just sauntered into the pavilion, conferring in low tones. One was older than the rest – a thickset man with slicked-back steel-grey hair. While he made an adjustment to his tie, his subordinates began checking the seating, the available refreshments, and the display screens, as if preparing for the arrival of important guests.

"The Dotar delegates will be here any minute." Celeste unzipped a small bag at her waist and passed Zen the smartphone and earbuds. Skit was attached to the phone's back. "Let's do this."

Zen was now absolutely sure that something had gone wrong. Caleb had failed to get her message to Clay for some reason. Help wasn't going to arrive in time. She was alone here, and was going to get caught up in the Spikers' plans – in Celeste and Locke's "phase two". If it looked like innocent people might be hurt, or even killed, she knew that she would have to break her cover and try to stop them. And who could say what would happen then?

Zen turned on the phone and opened the simple control software she'd written. Skit networked at once, its sensors linking with its data cloud. She was about to start the rotor and prepare it for flight when she noticed that the control software was connecting automatically with something else – something a good deal further away. A moment later, a second device winked onto the screen, activated and ready for operation.

Zen caught her breath.

It was Beetlebat.

This could only mean one thing. Her friends were nearby. There was still hope. But she knew that she had to keep playing her part. She glanced at Celeste; the Spiker leader was totally absorbed in watching the pavilion below and hadn't noticed anything. Forcing herself to concentrate, Zen flew Skit down into the pavilion, concealed it underneath a gravedigger, and waited for the meeting to begin.

THE GRIM REAPER

*T*he Dotar delegation arrived less than a minute later. The two sides began shaking hands, exchanging small talk about their journeys to London and the luxury hotels they were staying in. Before long, however, they got down to business. The man speaking for Dotar introduced himself as the country's defence minister. He was as immaculately dressed as the people from Hardcastle, with a courteous manner, a precisely clipped moustache, and a cut-glass English accent.

"You see the nature of our difficulty, Mr Jones. We are beset by an enemy that hides itself away. They take refuge in the hills, and in certain towns sympathetic to their twisted cause. These are their strongholds, from which they mount their terror attacks and spread their treasonous ideology. Our president is reluctant to use bombers, or any large-scale military offensive, on account of the damage that would be inflicted upon our ancient landscape. Certain pieces of architecture, also, cannot be put at risk – civic buildings and places of worship that date back, in some cases, more than a thousand years."

"I understand," Jones replied. He had a smooth voice with a slight Texan accent; as Zen refocused Skit's camera, she could clearly see the Stars-and-Stripes pin in his lapel. "Believe me, sir, I understand. Asymmetry cuts every which way. But let me tell you this. The GD6507-R was designed with exactly these concerns in mind. It's no idle boast when we call it the ultimate pacification device. This thing attacks with scalpel-like precision. There can be no advance warning either – something that can substantially lessen the impact of airstrikes. The GD6507-R uses sophisticated cluster munitions to completely wipe out its target, with minimal collateral damage." Jones chuckled. "And it'll put the fear of Almighty God into anyone who sees it."

Celeste had taken one of the earbuds so she could listen in. Her face hardened a little more with every word the men uttered. "These monsters are talking about villages," she hissed. "Unarmed civilians. *Families*."

Zen was nodding, an intense anger overlaying her fear. Just for an instant, she was actually glad that she'd been brought to this point, crouched up there in the rafters of the O2, making this recording for the Spikers.

"Don't worry," she said. "We're getting every word."

"And what is the lethal potential of these ... cluster munitions?" asked the defence minister.

"Kind of depends on how close together they're standing," Jones said, to a ripple of sycophantic laughter. "The GD6507-R carries five hundred microbombs, each one containing enough high-explosive gel to take out a tank. It can launch them individually and in multiples of ten, up to a full payload release. This machine is an assassin, able to remove a single adversary – or it is the Grim Reaper, wiping away entire armies in the blink of an eye." He reached out to pat the nearest gravedigger's chassis. "Equip your fine nation with a few of these beauties, sir, and your revolutionaries will no longer be a problem. That's a cast-iron Hardcastle guarantee."

The minister made a mild, disapproving sound. "Our enemies are *terrorists*, Mr Jones," he corrected.

"Of course," said the Hardcastle boss, inclining his head. "Terrorists."

They went on in friendly tones, discussing software, control systems and a live test Hardcastle had scheduled for later that day, away at a remote airfield. But Celeste had heard enough. She handed the earbud back to Zen and crept over to Locke, who was perched on the edge of a girder. Zen only pretended to put the second earbud back in, angling her head so that the Spikers wouldn't be able to see that she was listening to them.

"We've got what we need," Celeste said. "Time for phase two."

Zen tensed, snapped back to the reality of her situation. A tingling shiver ran through her arms. This was it.

"What do I do?" Locke asked.

"Put this on your belt," Celeste told him, opening her bag and handing him something. "It'll be ready for use in two minutes. And this is the override device."

"Like SolTec?"

"No. They decided that a virus is too slow. Too uncertain. This is … something new. Something they won't be able to stop. They said it will remake those machines from within."

"What? I don't follow."

"Just place it on the underside of one of them. It'll start working automatically. And then Hardcastle will taste some real justice."

Zen tried to take all this in. She cast a surreptitious glance towards the two Spikers. Locke was preparing to go. She could see the objects Celeste had just given him: a metal tube, almost like a syringe, and a small silver disc.

"It's almost nine," he said. "Better send the signal."

Celeste put her own earpiece back in and started tapping at her smartwatch. Zen guessed that she was notifying the Spikers' backers, enabling them to coordinate, as she'd mentioned back at the warehouse. But almost at once she froze, her fingertips just above the watch's illuminated face, staring hard at the message that had just arrived.

A couple of seconds passed. Very slowly, Celeste lowered her hand, moving away from Locke. Zen got a clear look at the watch. She could make out what appeared to be part of an intelligence report, with a photograph of a girl with long black hair at the top.

It was her.

The picture was recent – taken in the summer, it looked like. Zen realized immediately that her cover was blown. Celeste knew who she was. The nightmare had become real. She swayed a little on the girder, almost overwhelmed by dread.

Celeste was gazing down at the exhibition floor. "I should have seen it," she said numbly. "You were too good a fit. It was like you were *made* for the cause. Which I suppose you were." She shook her head. "You had me fooled. I thought that you'd suffered like I had. I honestly thought that you understood."

There was no point denying anything. Zen got to her feet, pushing her fright aside. She had to face this. "I *did* understand, Celeste," she said. "Really I did. You spoke a lot of truth. But what are you about to do? What's phase two?"

Celeste turned towards her, a cold, terrifying look in those dark brown eyes. "How can you possibly talk to me about *truth*, Dima? That's not even your name."

Locke was staring at them both. "Wait – is she a *rat*?" he asked Celeste. "Do we … do we have a serious problem here? What if she has people in—"

"Proceed as planned," Celeste interrupted. "I'll deal with it."

Zen took a step forward. "What did you give Locke just then? Are you going to hurt anybody?" She paused. "What did you mean by 'real justice'?"

Celeste shifted slightly, placing herself between Zen and Locke. He was securing the disc to his belt, as he'd been instructed. It had begun to glow faintly, a white light winking on its side like it was charging up.

"You won't be able to stop us," Celeste said. "Nobody will. These people who trade in bloodshed are about to shed some blood of their own."

Zen blinked, piecing it together. "You're going to activate the gravediggers," she said. "Arm their weapons somehow."

Celeste pulled off her ski mask and tossed it into the exhibition below. Her hair stood up in a halo of white-blonde spikes and her cheeks were flushed. She looked upset now – and murderously angry.

"I thought that you were one of us," she spat. "I believed those stories about your mother – about your tragic, empty life. But you're just a *liar*. One of the enemy. One of *them*."

Zen was imagining the devastation that even one of the gravediggers could unleash. The entire arena would be brought down. Hundreds of people would die. She felt a surge of pure, excruciating panic.

"Please, Celeste," she said. "You don't need to do this. We've got that video. We can still put it online. If enough people see it, then—"

Celeste wouldn't listen. "It isn't enough. It will *never* be enough. The video's purpose is to justify action – to get the media involved and spread the word. But it won't stop the arms makers. They'll just take their business underground, to where it can't be monitored or disrupted." She pointed fiercely at the weapons fair. "No – the only way to stop this evil is to *destroy it*. Because if we don't, it will surely come to destroy us."

Locke had finished attaching the disc to his belt; it was

glowing more brightly and a second white light had appeared on its outer edge. He turned his attention to the tube, which he began strapping securely to his upper arm.

"This is messed-up," Zen said. "You don't destroy evil by *killing people*, Celeste. That makes you no better than them. And the arena staff, the security guys, the—"

"Everyone here is guilty," Celeste broke in harshly. "They're all part of it. Including you, Zenobia Rafiq of the Möbius Programme."

Saying these words seemed to stoke her fury. She assumed a fighting stance, raising her arms. Zen could see the smartwatch face again – that intelligence file with her photograph at its top. She was starting to realize just how bad this was. Top-secret information had got out – and had been put in the wrong hands at the very worst time.

"Who sent you that file?" she asked. "Was it these backers of yours? Who *are* they?"

"Friends," Celeste replied. "They supply us with equipment. They gave us that warehouse. And they show us where best to strike."

"So these ... *friends* get you to take incredible risks," Zen said. "Commit atrocities to order. While they stay completely out of sight." She made an incredulous noise. "I'm sorry, Celeste, but it sounds like you're being used. Haven't you ever wondered why they're doing it?"

This met with a short, bitter laugh. "I don't *care*. They're enabling us to take serious action – to bring about proper change. They've helped the Spikers in all kinds of ways."

Celeste's lips drew back into a snarl. "Like telling us when we're being betrayed."

With that she lunged forward, throwing the hardest punch she could. Zen only just managed to dodge it, stepping along the girder. It was barely a metre wide, with a deadly drop beneath. Trying not to look down, she directed her eyes towards Locke instead, who was making some adjustment to his glue gloves. A third white light had appeared on the disc.

Zen's mind was racing. She had to get past Celeste and prevent Locke from activating this mysterious tech he'd been given. And she needed to send a signal somehow. Sound the alarm. Get backup.

Her eyes darted to the phone, which was still in her hand, and the Beetlebat icon in the corner of its screen. This had to mean that Caleb was at the O2 somewhere. She didn't have her laser pointer, but she could send a basic homing command. Hopefully, when the bot responded, he would recognize what this was: a distress flare fired into the sky, requesting immediate support.

As soon as she'd touched the screen, Celeste came at her again, swivelling on her heel and shooting out a tight, well-aimed kick. Zen blocked it with her forearm before leaping to the next girder along. Her dismay and shock were fading, and a peculiar kind of relief taking their place. Everything was out. She could stop pretending at last. She tucked the phone in her pocket and prepared to fight.

Celeste sprang after her, launching a flurry of open-handed blows that took every bit of Zen's skill to fend off.

Zen remembered their bout back at the warehouse; Celeste had an aggressive, overconfident style that laid her open to counter-attack. Zen edged away, as if she was being ground down, and jumped to a third girder. Celeste followed at once – and Zen was waiting for her. She went low, kicking hard, taking out both of the Spiker's legs. Celeste fell, slamming down on the girder and nearly tumbling off the side. Zen grabbed her arm and dragged her back – and then stood over her, poised to strike if she tried to get up.

There was a soft electrical *ping* nearby.

"Too late," Celeste panted. "It's ready."

Zen glanced towards the sound. Locke was standing at the very end of the girder. There were now four white lights on the disc, all flashing in unison. He tapped its centre with his forefinger – and he disappeared. Vanished utterly. It was like he'd been wiped from the face of the earth.

Zen gaped in total astonishment, dropping her guard. Celeste was up again immediately – twisting Zen around, forcing her to her knees and wrenching her hands behind her back. Before Zen could react, her palms were being pressed together, activating the smart glue. She tried to pull them apart but the gloves had fused somehow, losing their ability to detach – holding her as securely as a pair of handcuffs.

"What … what just happened?" she blurted. "How did he *do that*?"

Celeste didn't answer. "You're not walking away from this," she said in Zen's ear. "I can't allow it. Goodbye, Zenobia."

With that she grabbed Zen's shoulders. She held on for a moment, as if in reluctance; then she pushed Zen off the girder.

BLOOD IN
THE WATER

*T*he email arrived at 8.44 a.m. It was from JaredWest@
Lodestar.com and had the subject line *Game Devs Stick
Together*. Caleb was leaning against a surveillance van
outside the west entrance to the O2 Arena, huddled in his
winter coat. He opened the message at once. Despite the
light-hearted heading, something about the way it was written
made him suspect that a lawyer had been involved.

Over the last few days, it said, *there has been a surge
in unsubstantiated rumours and conspiracy theories
concerning Lodestar's role in the so-called Nameless
Invasion of* Terrorform. *I want to assure you that these claims
are completely false. Lodestar would never resort to such
an approach, and we deplore the attack on your game as
keenly as anyone. We only wish the best for* Terrorform *and
yourself, and would be open to sitting down for a free-ranging
conversation about the future any time you feel comfortable
doing so.*

Caleb snorted. "We know what that means, right, Sam?"

"Yes, Caleb. It would seem that Jared West still imagines

that you can be convinced to sell *Terrorform* to Lodestar. Even if he is not responsible for the Nameless, he clearly hopes that our current operational difficulties might make you reconsider. I believe the relevant phrase is 'He smells blood in the water'."

"D'you think he's telling the truth?"

"It is impossible to say. But he is correct when he states that the case against Lodestar is based on rumour only. There is no proof connecting them to the Nameless."

"If Lodestar's not behind the invasion, though," Caleb murmured, "who the heck *is*?" He looked up at the grey sky. "How bad is it right now?"

"The Nameless control all of Fraxis Prime, and appear to be preparing simultaneous strikes towards Kursk and Quaari. Their numbers continue to grow at the same rate. Meanwhile, non-Nameless players are down fifty-four per cent on monthly averages. More than thirty-six thousand player accounts have been deleted."

"And what about the weird loss of control during the battle in the asteroid field – the way that Anvil didn't transfer command to my Navigator?"

"More bad news, I'm afraid. Are you sure you want to hear it? Our present situation is highly—"

"Lay it on me, Sam. The only way we're going to come up with a solution is if we meet this head-on."

"You are always honest with yourself, Caleb. It is an admirable quality. Very well – almost ten per cent of *Terrorform* in-game commands have ceased functioning."

"And that diagnostic we ran earlier didn't come up with anything?"

"It did not. I cannot identify a reason for our loss of control. The system does not appear to have been hacked or infected with a virus."

Caleb let out an exasperated sigh. "I ... I just *don't get it*, Sam. I don't understand what's happening here."

"As I told you in the ARC tower," Sam said, "if you were to deactivate my volition protocols, I would be able to alter the structure of the game's source code and purge the Nameless from the program. It would be more difficult now, but it could still be done."

"You know I can't do that, Sam," Caleb said. "I can authorize specific, supervised actions, but I can't let you off the leash completely. There's far too much that could go wrong. We've got to think laterally here – try to ... to..."

Something had begun to twitch in his coat pocket. As he looked down, Beetlebat scuttled out, quickly scaling his sleeve until it reached his shoulder. He'd brought the bot with him at the last minute, thinking it might come in useful – and that Zen, once she'd been successfully extracted, would be really pleased to see it. He held up a hand and Beetlebat climbed on, raising its head slightly and probing the air with its antennae. The LEDs on their ends were green; this meant Beetlebat was on standby. It had linked automatically to a controller of some kind.

Caleb quickly realized what was going on. Zen must have started up the listening device she'd been building for the

Spikers – and the software had activated Beetlebat as well. She would very probably know that they were there.

Professor Clay had allowed Caleb to come along to the O2 in case any other messages from Zen arrived, via the game or anything else. She'd made it extremely clear, however, that he was still in a heap of trouble. He'd been prohibited from entering the surveillance van, where she was with Mitch and some of her contacts from GCHQ, or from directly participating in any way.

"You are present as an observer," she'd told him sternly. "Nothing else."

This was big, though. Caleb went to the back door of the van and banged on it with his fist, calling Clay's name.

Mitch was there almost straight away. His face was a little drawn and his jaw shaded with stubble; most of the team had been up all night. He stepped out of the van. "Caleb, you heard what the prof said. You are not to—"

Caleb showed him Beetlebat, hurriedly explaining what it meant. "This is about to *start*, Mitch. Zen could be trying to communicate something. To send another message."

They both looked at the little bot. It remained on standby, running a routine written to imitate insectoid behaviour – turning one way and then the other, before skittering off into the fur lining of Caleb's hood.

Mitch wasn't quite as blown away as Caleb had hoped. "All right," he said. "Keep a close eye on it. Let me know if it … does anything."

"But what if the—"

"Here's where things stand," Mitch interrupted. "The Spikers arrived by boat a short while ago. They've taken up tactical positions throughout the arena."

"You're going to grab them, though, aren't you? Where's Zen? Is she OK?"

Mitch shook his head. "We have to see how it's going to play out. It's really important not to spring the trap too soon. The Spikers seem to be waiting for something – probably a chance to make this recording they want so badly. But until we know, Caleb, we have to wait. Hold back."

Caleb drove his hands into his pockets. "This *sucks*, Mitch," he said. "I feel totally useless out here."

The ARC security chief regarded him sympathetically for a moment; then he pulled out his phone. "I've got something you could help me with," he said. "Take a look at this."

On the screen was a breaking report from a special response team in Cambridge. After burning for the past week, the fire at SolTec had finally been extinguished and the investigators were preparing to move in. A video started to play, showing drone footage of the wrecked facility. Most of the buildings had been utterly destroyed by the inferno. Inside the smashed, blackened walls was a yawning abyss, many storeys deep; SolTec's subterranean floors had collapsed or been blown apart, opening up the research complex below.

The camera moved forward, descending into the drop through a haze of thin smoke. Caleb saw the charred ruins of labs, lobbies and stairwells; the live-fire zone where he and Mitch had run for their lives; the server farm where they'd stopped the virus and unwittingly triggered the robots' self-destruct sequence. And then, beneath all of that, was a whole other level.

Caleb's eyes widened. "Didn't Aiden Lennox tell us that the server farm was at the bottom of the facility?"

"He did, Caleb," Sam replied. "That would appear to have been another of Dr Lennox's falsehoods."

Caleb synched the Flex with Mitch's phone, extending the screen so he could examine the footage more closely. Amid the rubble and melted steel, he could just make out the carbonized shells of some massive power generators. The remains of what looked like an industrial cooling apparatus. A shattered glass cabinet.

"Sam, am I ... *seeing things* here? Is that really a wrecked quantum computer?"

"That would seem to be the case, Caleb. It is the only explanation for—"

"Hold on," Mitch broke in. "That's like the thing on Spøkelsøy, right? The system that Xavier Torrent built?"

Caleb nodded. "The next stage in computing. *Unbelievably* powerful. But the tech is still experimental. Astonishingly expensive. And very difficult to build."

"Quantum computers are strictly regulated in the UK," Sam said. "All developers are required to register their work with the government. SolTec do not appear to have done so."

Mitch frowned. "I bet they were building it to boost their secret combat bot programme. Do you think the Spikers knew it was in there?"

Caleb paced off into the parking lot, pressing his fingers to his temples, trying to think all this through. "The Spikers' mission was to plant that virus in the SolTec mainframe," he said. "Once it had fully installed itself, it would have sent SolTec's murder bots out into Cambridge. There would have been chaos. Carnage. Loads of dead and injured people. The emergency services would have been swamped. The army would have been called in. Mass evacuations would have been needed across the city – including at SolTec itself." He pointed at the Flex's screen. "This computer would have been left unguarded, with literally everyone looking the other way."

"So you think someone was planning to steal it, using the bots as a distraction, and was only stopped by the whole place going up in smoke?" Mitch considered this for a second. "But if the computer was hidden in a secret basement, how would these thieves even know it was there in the first place?"

Caleb was shaking his head. "I'm starting to get a *really* bad feeling here, Mitch," he said, looking towards the O2. "There's a whole other side to this. Everything else – the Spikers – it's just one big—"

There was a sudden flurry of movement at the back of his neck. He cried out, bringing up his arms – but quickly realized it was Beetlebat. The bot was rising into the morning air, wings beating rapidly, antennae retracting into its tiny copper head. The LEDs had changed to red: it had received an instruction. Once it was high enough, it banked sharply, swooping down to gain speed, then disappeared beneath the white canopy of the arena.

CODE BLACK

Zen fell into a cradle of ropes and cables, rolling down awkwardly onto a narrow metal platform. She'd landed on a bank of spotlights that was suspended from the ceiling framework. This had plainly been deliberate. Celeste didn't want her raising the alarm by plunging into the arms fair – and she'd be finished off soon enough by the gravediggers' cluster bombs.

There was only one possible explanation for Locke's disappearance on the girders above. The Spikers' enigmatic backers must have equipped them with cloaking tech. Zen had seen this just once before, right at the start of her first mission for the Möbius Programme, when she'd caught an invisible sensor drone in an underground chapel beneath the British Museum. And that encounter had led her and Caleb to some very dark places indeed…

The frustration was almost more than Zen could take. She had to *do something* – to get down to the exhibition floor and stop Locke. She struggled against the glue gloves with everything she had, but it was hopeless.

"Great," she panted. "Just *great*."

At that moment, however, there was a fluttering sound nearby, followed by the soft patter of six tiny metal feet landing on top of a spotlight. Beetlebat had found its way inside.

Zen broke into a grin. "Hey, girl," she said.

With massive effort, she wriggled to a crouch and whistled four short notes. Beetlebat promptly produced the minuscule retractable saw she'd installed beneath its head, like a set of diamond-tipped mandibles. She manoeuvred herself around, flinching as she brushed against the hot spotlight casings. Approaching the saw very carefully, she sliced through the straps that fastened the right glove to her wrist, allowing her to pull her hand free.

"All right," she said, as she tore her second hand free. "Now let's go find the invisible man."

Beetlebat folded away its saw and hopped onto her shoulder. Zen stood up and quickly climbed a rope back to the girders. There was no sign of Locke or Celeste. She jumped over to the point where Locke had vanished and looked around. She could identify several possible ways down into the fair, using access ladders, lighting equipment and parts of the displays below. But he had a minute's head start at least. She had to make up some time if she was going to have any chance of catching him.

A long purple banner was hanging nearby, at the corner of the Hardcastle pavilion, bearing the company's fort logo. There was no time to think this through. Zen leaped towards it, snatching in an armful of the satiny fabric, and clung on tightly as she swung and slipped down to the exhibition floor. She landed heavily, dropping to a crouch. A handful of nearby visitors exclaimed in surprise and started to back away.

"Freeze!" someone shouted. "Don't move!"

This caused an immediate panic. As people fled for the arena's various exits, Zen peered into the pavilion; she could just see the gravediggers, off between the partitions and video screens, but there was no trace at all of Locke. Before she could decide what to do, an armed policeman appeared, advancing towards her with his submachine gun raised.

"Hands where I can see them! Intruder in sector C – code black, code black!"

Zen raised her hands, pulling off her ski mask as she did so. Four more police officers arrived, all pointing firearms at her head and shouting the same instructions.

"Down on the floor! Keep your arms out – slowly, slowly!"

Zen did as she was told. One slung his weapon around his back, took some cuffs off his belt and walked over to her.

"Stop," said a familiar voice. "Let her up."

Professor Clay was standing a short distance away, dressed in her brown leather overcoat and leaning on her walking cane. Mitch was a couple of steps behind her, on the alert for hostiles. Police were swarming the arena; the air was filled with orders and the crackle of radios.

The armed officer hesitated. Clay came closer, saying something Zen didn't catch, and at once he stowed his cuffs and helped her to her feet.

As soon as she was upright, Caleb ran into view and

wrapped her in an enormous hug. "Thank *god*," he said. "I thought they'd... I was worried you'd—"

"I'm all right," she told him as he let her go. "What's going on? Who have they caught?"

"A load of Spikers were just arrested. They were caught by surprise, apparently, and totally outnumbered. But I think a couple of them managed to escape."

Zen was shaking her head. "This isn't over, Caleb. The main attack is still on. They're planning to activate Hardcastle's crab bots and release their bombs. Bring the whole place down."

Caleb was staring at her. *"What?"*

"They're using cloaking tech – the saboteur is here right now."

"Cloaking tech? Are you serious? How did they get hold of that?"

"No time to explain," Zen said. "But we've got to make him visible somehow." She had an idea. "Can you and Sam hack into the arena's system? Like, really quickly?"

"That should be possible, Zen," Sam replied. "Large venues seldom take sufficient precautions with their cybersecurity. If Caleb grants me permission to—"

"Do it, Sam," Caleb said, stretching out the Flex. "Get me in."

"Go to the site administrator's controls," Zen told him. "Then access the fire-suppression subsystems."

Caleb guessed what she was thinking. "Sprinklers, right?" He chuckled, tapping away at the screen. "Give me a sec."

Professor Clay had been talking to the police; now she was coming towards them, her cane clacking on the floor. "Good lord, Caleb," she said, with a kind of admiring annoyance. "How many times do you have to be told? I only authorized your presence on this mission in an *observational capacity*. Get back to the van, this instant. Let me talk to Zen."

"Sure thing, Professor," Caleb replied. "Just let me do one ... thing ... first."

He tapped the Flex a final time – and freezing cold water blasted from countless sprinkler heads across the arena, drenching the DESCO arms fair and everyone in it. A huge cry went up, almost drowned out by the roar of the water. Clay swore, walking away, pulling her overcoat up over her head, while Caleb and Mitch ducked beneath a surface-to-air missile launcher.

Zen stayed quite still, feeling Beetlebat scurry for cover in her jacket and the locks of sopping ice-blue hair flatten against her face. She gazed into the Hardcastle pavilion, her eyes straining for any sign of Locke. The pavilion had no roof; it seemed to be filled with torrential rain, the drops sparkling in the light of its video screens.

Suddenly, she spied a movement – the curve of a shoulder, revealed only by the fall of illuminated water upon it. She sprinted forward, splashing through the fast-forming puddles, and rammed into it with all her strength.

There was a sharp groan as they collided. Zen was seized by invisible arms and heaved roughly to the floor. She got back up again – and for a moment she could clearly discern him, moving through the pavilion like a shimmering, silvery hologram.

"Dima Kahf," he sneered, his voice seeming to float in thin air. "Coming to the rescue of Hardcastle Solutions."

"Nobody has to die here, Locke. There are police everywhere. Just give yourself up."

"I *knew* there was something off about you. Right from the start."

"Don't do it," said Zen. *"Please."*

It was no use. Locke was heading for the gravediggers. Zen started to run. He reached the display platform and crouched beside the nearest machine, preparing to plant Celeste's device. She barged him against it, hearing his head clang against the carapace. He staggered away, and she briefly lost sight of him; then a kick caught her painfully on the shoulder. Its direction told her that he'd jumped up on top of the arctic-camouflaged gravedigger. Zen knew that she wouldn't stand a chance if her opponent had the higher ground. She climbed onto the next machine along, which was painted in a yellow-and-green jungle pattern, and raised her fists.

Locke's ghostly outline shifted before her. It was darker here – Hardcastle's main display screen had switched itself off when the sprinklers were activated. He was barely visible.

There was a watery blur to her left. A punch connected with her cheek, knocking her to the side. Instinctively, she brought up her arm, blocking the blow that followed – but not the kick after that, which whacked into her knee and folded her over. She exhaled, trying to focus, but it seemed impossible. How could she fight what she couldn't see?

"Hey, Hawk," someone said. "Heads up."

A sodden Caleb was standing at the pavilion's entrance, the Flex ready in his hand. He swiped his finger across it and the vast display screen behind Zen blazed back to life. It was showing the opening scene from the gravedigger promo film, the desert blindingly bright. Every bead of water in the pavilion glittered like a gemstone; Locke's silhouette was revealed plainly, a hand held up to shield his face. Zen gritted her teeth and threw herself into a full roundhouse. It struck him squarely in the middle of the chest. Trainers slipping on the wet gravedigger, he flew off backwards and fell down hard upon the floor.

Zen was on him straight away, finding the cloaking disc and snapping it off his belt. Locke flickered into view, squirming in pain. She pulled off his ski mask. His right eye was already swelling up and he wore a strange expression – a woozy, crooked grin. It was almost as if he was glad that he'd been stopped.

"You don't understand what's going on here," he slurred. "You have ... no idea."

Zen showed him the disc. "Where did this come from? Who gave it to Celeste?"

Locke was shaking his head, chuckling hoarsely. "You'd better watch your back, Dima Kahf."

The water stopped as abruptly as it had come on. Armed

police piled in, turning Locke over and slapping him in cuffs. Zen's numerous scrapes and bruises were beginning to hurt. She looked at Caleb and gave him a grateful nod. He nodded in return, then pointed at a spot on the floor. The tube that Celeste had handed to Locke – the inexplicable weapon that they were going to use to activate and take over the gravediggers – was lying half a metre from her foot. She picked it up and started towards him.

Police were everywhere again, streaming in and out of the arena. The sight of one of them made Zen stop dead. A small, slender woman in ill-fitting body armour was walking purposefully towards the nearest exit with her head down. Tufts of white-blonde hair were sticking out from beneath her armed response unit cap.

Zen strode past Caleb, out onto the concourse. "Mariella," she shouted. "Mariella Bachmann."

Hearing her old Argo alias, Celeste glanced over without thinking. The Spiker leader quickly realized what Zen had done. She glowered and turned away, breaking into a jog, her hand going to the pistol at her belt. Zen began to give chase, but soon saw that it was no use. Celeste had too much of a lead. She was going to escape.

Professor Clay appeared from around the side of an amphibious troop transport, stepping directly into Celeste's path. Celeste went to draw her pistol – but before it had left the holster, Clay swung her walking stick in a wide arc. Its silver end cracked against Celeste's head, laying her out cold on the floor.

"This is her, isn't it?" Clay asked as Zen and Caleb ran up. "Tell me I didn't just brain one of the Met's firearms officers."

Zen couldn't help smiling. "No, that's her all right."

"Good. That's a load of paperwork I really don't need. Mr Mitchell, if you wouldn't mind…?"

Mitch came over, unbuttoning his saturated collar and grinning broadly. He bent down, took one of Celeste's hands, and cuffed it to a link of the troop transport's caterpillar tracks. "You did it, guys," he said. "You stopped the Spikers."

Clay pursed her lips, looking to where Locke was being led from the arena by an armed police guard. "It would seem that you've justified your latest piece of disobedience, Caleb," she said. "I think I can overlook it just this once."

"Thanks, Prof," Caleb said, "but we aren't done yet. Sam and me have—"

"*Hey!* Hey, you there!"

Jim Jones was marching towards the Möbius team, his face the colour of rare beef. Half a dozen assistants were hurrying behind, one of them trying to hold a large black umbrella over him to guard against the large drips that still fell occasionally from the sprinkler heads.

"Yeah, you, in the leather overcoat! Are you in charge of this … this *circus*?"

Zen realized he was talking to Professor Clay – who leaned on her stick, straightened one of her lapels, and gave him a tight, chilly smile. "I'm afraid I can neither confirm nor deny my role with respects to the security operations of the O2 Arena, nor can I—"

Jones was rolling his eyes. "OK, OK," he interrupted. "Jesus H Christ, you spies are all the same." He held something out, pinched between his thumb and forefinger. "Explain this. Right now."

It was Skit. Zen had forgotten all about her surveillance microbot in the chaos. It had been left in the Hardcastle pavilion – and had obviously been detected by the company's own security personnel.

Clay looked at Skit for a single second. "I can assure you, Mr Jones, that I have never seen this device before. It is not the property of any UK intelligence agency. If you would care to explain how and where you got it, perhaps I can—"

Jones's complexion had achieved an impossibly volcanic shade of red. "Do not give me that plausible deniability horse crap!" he bawled. "This is a *bug*. My people just found it in our pavilion – a place that your government guaranteed us was *one thousand per cent* secure. A highly sensitive deal was brokered in there earlier. If that negotiation was recorded – if the details are leaked in *any form* – I will have the head of every single cop and spy on this godforsaken peninsula."

"Hawk, Swift," Clay said under her breath, "go back outside. I'll meet you there in a minute." She cleared her throat. "You do realize what just happened here, don't you, Mr Jones? A terrorist attack was narrowly averted. Your life and the lives of your staff were saved by these people you would … decapitate."

Jones dropped Skit to the ground and stamped on it. "I want the footage. I want every *second*. And if you don't supply it, I will go to your superiors. Heck, I will go all the way to your *prime minister*. When I'm done with you, you'll be lucky if you can get a job scraping data off Chinese social media sites!"

Zen and Caleb walked away, heading for the exit. Reaching into her back pocket, Zen took out the phone Celeste had given her – the one that had been networked to Skit. The video of Jim Jones's discussion with the defence minister of Dotar was there on the screen. It hadn't been shared yet; Celeste hadn't accessed Skit's data cloud, probably suspecting a trap. With a few strokes of her finger, Zen opened the DedVane website and prepared the file. She waited for a moment as Jones ranted on, listing yet more threats and demands to the epically unimpressed Professor Clay.

Then she pressed upload.

TIPPING POINT

Caleb and Zen went out to the car park, their wet clothes leaving a trail of dark drips on the pavement. Several helicopters hovered above the arena, along with camera drones from the streaming news stations. They heard sirens – a convoy of police vans and fire engines was charging along the access road towards the arena's main entrance, their lights flashing in the grey morning.

"Let me have a look at that thing," Caleb said, gesturing towards the metal tube.

Zen handed it to him with a shiver. "They were going to use it to take over the crab bots and launch their explosives. Celeste said it would remake them from within." She frowned. "I ... I think it's nanotech."

Caleb studied the tube, scanning it with the Flex. "Yeah, it looks like it. What do you reckon, Sam?"

"You are both correct. This tube contains approximately a quarter of a million nanobots. Once activated, they would have flooded the GD6507-R machines – and spread between them as well, like a biological virus. They would have been able to make heavy modifications to the GD6507-Rs' hardware, altering components and safety features – perhaps even replacing them completely."

Zen had stopped walking. "A rival arms corporation isn't behind this," she said. "Or some hostile intelligence agency. Caleb, this is Razor."

Caleb nodded grimly. "Nanobots, cloaking tech… It can't be anyone else."

"They blew my cover," Zen went on. "And they've been supplying the Spikers with all this other information as well, along with their crazy tech." Her brow furrowed. "But *why*? What would Razor get out of helping the Spikers? They didn't seem like they'd have a problem with the arms industry. The opposite, if anything."

"Razor don't care about the Spikers' cause, Zen," Caleb said. "Or about attacking Hardcastle for any of the other reasons we thought of. There's something else going on here. There has been right from the beginning."

He showed her the video of SolTec – the secret level revealed by the fire, and the quantum computer it had contained.

Zen had gone very pale. "So the SolTec attack was a distraction," she said. "The Spikers were being used, just like I thought. Razor wanted to empty the facility out. Keep everyone busy with runaway combat bots so they could break in and steal that computer."

Their eyes met.

"Sam," said Caleb quickly, "how many operational quantum computers are there in the UK?"

"There are two, Caleb. One is in a coastal installation in Dorset. The latest technical reports indicate that it has serious stability problems, however. The other is in the Bank of England."

Caleb's mouth fell open. "The *Bank of England*? You mean ... just over the *river*?"

The sirens were getting even louder as police cars screeched up at the O2's main doors. Caleb could see military vehicles as well, bomb disposal teams from the look of it – and a navy gunboat was cruising along the Thames, ordering all civilian vessels out of the area with its loudhailer.

"The idea was to blow this place up," said Caleb. "Pretty much every police car, ambulance and fire engine in London would've been here. You couldn't ask for a better distraction than that."

"We should tell Clay," said Zen. "We should tell *everyone*."

"Call her, Sam," Caleb said. "Mitch as well."

The AI immediately dialled the adults' phones, one after the other. Both went directly to voicemail.

"There could be a communications blackout," Zen said. "To lock down the crime scene."

Caleb turned to the arena, where police and military blocked every entrance. "I seriously doubt that we have the security clearance to get back through the police cordon," he said. "We're running out of time here. We need to get to the Bank of England – right now."

Zen nodded. "We've stopped Razor before. There'll be something we can do."

They looked around the car park. It was filled with coaches and heavy goods vehicles. Near the arena, several police bikes stood in a line, crash helmets hanging on their sides.

"What do you reckon?" asked Zen.

Caleb took a breath. "It's kind of our only option. Start the engine of that one on the end, Sam."

Thirty seconds later they were zooming out of the car park with the bike's lights and siren going. Caleb was driving with Zen behind him – just like they'd done that summer, down in the London Underground. Both of them were wearing police crash helmets and yellow high-visibility jackets they'd found in the bike's hard storage compartment; they could almost be taken for a pair of police officers. Sam hacked the radios in their helmets so that they could talk to one another.

Caleb had wrapped the Flex around his wrist. Sam now directed him along the arena approach road, past a long line of stationary emergency vehicles, towards the A102 northbound. He informed them that the ARC tower was ten kilometres away.

Caleb was a pretty experienced biker. This one was seriously powerful, though – definitely the fastest he'd ever ridden. He drove it as quickly as he dared.

"Message someone at the ARC, Sam," he said. "A Möbius kid – Art or Astrid. They'll have a good view of the Bank of England from the tower. Let's find out if they can see anything."

"It is done, Caleb. I must inform you of some breaking news also: a critical system malfunction has just been reported in the bank's main offices. Its staff are being evacuated."

"OK," said Zen. "That *can't* be a coincidence."

They turned onto the motorway. It was still early, only a quarter past nine, and the three lanes leading into the tunnel were clogged with slow-moving traffic. Caleb changed lanes, weaving between the cars; some of the other drivers began to move out of their way, thinking they actually were police.

"There is one other thing, Caleb," said Sam. "It concerns *Terrorform*."

Caleb swerved into the hard shoulder, speeding up a little. "Really, Sam? Right this minute?"

"I'm afraid this cannot wait. The Nameless incursion is becoming ever more critical. They are beginning to affect the game's macro systems. I must repeat my earlier suggestion that my volition protocols be deactivated. If I am free to make a series of independent, administrator-level decisions, I will be able to restructure the source code and purge the Nameless. But time is running out fast."

"I told you, it's too much of a risk. There has to be another way. Can't we ... can't we put together another army? Code in, like, an armada of Anvils? Or a whole pack of Crocodemons?"

"Such an approach will no longer prove effective, Caleb. The in-game situation has reached a tipping point. Within the next three hours, I calculate that *Terrorform* will be entirely overrun. It will become unplayable – the code irretrievably corrupted. Our game will be lost."

This assessment left Caleb aghast. Everything they'd

built, all the planets and vehicles and creatures – gone for ever. It was impossible to imagine. He tightened his grip on the handlebars, trying to think. The situation was truly dire – but deactivating Sam's volition protocols was a highly dangerous move. Without them, the AI would become fully autonomous again, like he'd been on Spøkelsøy. And there he'd made a decision that nearly killed them all.

"If … if I switch off the protocols," he said, "you're going to have to promise me that you'll stick to *Terrorform*. I don't want you to take any actions *at all* outside the game directories. Do you understand, Sam?"

"Of course, Caleb. I promise that I will limit myself to this one task. It is an extremely demanding one, involving extensive recoding and data transferral. I estimate that it will take up all of my processing power for eleven minutes, fifty-three seconds."

The bike was now on the approach to the tunnel, the traffic narrowing from three lanes to two. A sign overhead read **Blackwall Tunnel ½M**.

"What should I do?" Caleb asked Zen. "Can we manage without him for that long?"

"It's your call, Caleb," she replied. "Sam's your AI. But it sounds like it's this or the end of *Terrorform*."

Caleb exhaled hard; then he nodded. "All right," he said. "This has already gone … *way* too far. Deactivate all volition protocols. Full authorization granted. Get in there, Sam. Save our game."

"Very well, Caleb. I will begin."

The tunnel mouth loomed ahead, at the end of a long concrete trench. As they sped towards it, the Flex began to buzz. It was an incoming call from Art. Caleb answered it, patching the signal through to the radios in their helmets.

"Swift!" Art shouted at once. "Swift, I got your message. I'm up on the roof of the ARC with Merlin. We're checking out the Bank of England, like you said." He hesitated; Astrid could be heard swearing in the background. "And we … we've spotted something *really* strange."

RIDING THE OCTOPUS

As soon as they were out of the tunnel, Caleb took the first major left-hand turn and opened up the police bike's throttle. They hurtled through Limehouse and Whitechapel, travelling at such speed that by the time they reached the City of London, their clothes were almost dry.

There could be no doubt – the Bank of England was under attack. Caleb and Zen had devised a rough plan with Art and Astrid: they were all going to meet at the top of the ARC tower, and then use Astrid's flying machines to get over there and mount a defence. The only problem was that their borrowing of the bike had been noticed. Three police cars were now hot on their tail, their lights and sirens going as well, ordering Caleb to pull over with their megaphones.

The ARC tower loomed ahead. Caleb rode across the small paved square in front of it and skidded to a halt before the doors. He and Zen jumped off the bike, dropped their crash helmets and sprinted inside. Rufus didn't even have time to speak as they raced by – his eyes going wide as he noticed the four police officers running over the square behind them. Fortunately, a lift was waiting this time. Caleb pressed the button for floor thirty-five, the doors sliding shut just as the police entered the ARC lobby.

Art and Astrid were outside the special project labs, staring off to the north.

"All right," said Astrid, as Caleb and Zen approached, "tell me again. *What* is going on here?"

"It's a heist," said Caleb. "Like I said on the phone. Razor is stealing the Bank of England's quantum computer. And we've got to stop them."

"It doesn't *look* like a heist," said Art. "It looks like a … a glitch in the fabric of reality."

Caleb joined Art at the edge of the ARC tower. The Bank of England was lower than the gleaming high-rises that surrounded it, and at least a hundred years older. Filling an entire city block, it was built like a castle, with an imposing outer wall and a taller keep in the middle – but with columns, pediments and balustrades in place of battlements and towers. The streets nearby were filled with people – the staff who'd been evacuated a short time before. A couple of fire engines were there too. Nobody appeared to have any idea what was going on.

Art pointed out a rectangular section of the keep's roof. Caleb saw that it appeared distorted, as if he was viewing it through a piece of thick, slightly warped glass. The tiled slopes and attic windows also flickered occasionally, losing resolution and becoming pixelated. It was a deeply bizarre sight.

Caleb looked at the Flex, thinking to ask Sam for an analysis, but there was no sign of the silver face on its screen. He saw that it had only been just over ten minutes since he deactivated the volition protocols. The AI would still be busy with *Terrorform*.

"It must be some kind of light-refracting screen," said Zen. "To disguise what Razor is doing. Cloaking tech is one of the many unbelievable things they've managed to develop. The Spikers were given it as well – they were using it just now, at the O2."

"The O2, huh?" said Astrid. She took out her phone, swiped her finger across the screen and held it up. "This you?"

A video was playing, showing the Hardcastle boss and his customer having a friendly chat at the DESCO weapons fair.

Caleb glanced at Zen. "So … you uploaded it anyway," he said.

"Had to be done."

Astrid's lip was twisting in approval. "Too right it did! It's already gone viral. More than three million views in twenty minutes."

"Holy crap!" Art yelped. "Look, guys, look!"

The distorted rectangle had vanished, revealing a large, very precise hole in the keep's roof that seemed to have been cut with an industrial laser. A silvery metallic block, completely smooth and featureless, was slowly rising through it, as if it was floating away into the morning sky.

"That's the quantum computer," said Caleb urgently. "Or the important part of it, anyway. If Razor can power it and develop an operating system, they'll be able to…"

Just for an instant, the air below the computer seemed to ripple. It looked like a flock of small, near-invisible forms was flying out of the hole. They streamed around the metallic block, heading for a point directly above it – where they abruptly disappeared.

"There's a cloaked Razor ship hovering over the bank," Zen said. "It's reeling the computer in!"

"We've got to get over there," said Caleb. "Is everything ready?"

Astrid nodded, going to open the doors of lab three. With Art's help, she brought out two jet-bikes and the jump-pack they'd used for Operation Supergiant – the glue arrows now removed from its top. The first bike was the merlin-painted one she and Art had been mounting the goo cannon on the week before, to make their aerial fire suppression system. The second was a bulkier, less streamlined version, obviously an earlier prototype, with an elaborate image of an octopus stretching all over it. A goo cannon had been freshly bolted to its underside – very possibly while Caleb and Zen had been riding over from Greenwich.

Astrid handed out their gear: helmets, goggles, and battleship-grey flight suits that had inflatable safety jackets and walkie-talkie radios fitted into them. She'd also grabbed Zen a few things from her room downstairs – a laser pointer for Beetlebat, her telescopic bow and a handful of glue arrows.

"Do we really have to wear all this?" asked Caleb, holding up his flight suit.

"Well, if you don't," Astrid said, "there's a good chance the winds will strip you butt-naked."

Caleb pictured this for a moment; then he quickly slipped out of the high-visibility jacket and started to pull the suit on over his clothes.

"I've refined the formula of the foam," Art told them, "using that smart-glue scan of yours, Zen. This should prevent any of the ... ah ... *mishaps* Astrid and I were experiencing. It will adhere to absolutely anything and expand to approximately three hundred per cent of its original mass. It should be extremely well suited to your purpose."

"The merlin bike is mine, obviously," Astrid said, unpeeling a stick of gum and popping it in her mouth. "I figured you two could fight over the other one."

"I'll take the jump-pack," said Zen, walking over and lifting it up. "I can work with it. And Caleb's got a bit of a thing for bikes."

"You not coming, Art?" Caleb asked, as he put on his helmet. "You could ride on the back of mine."

"Ah, no – no, thank you, Caleb. I've learned from bitter and rather ... *sickly* experience that Astrid's contraptions are not for me. I'll stay here and hold the fort."

"OK, but the police will be up any minute. We might have taken one of their patrol bikes from the O2 without permission."

Art swallowed. "I shall deny all knowledge. A complete stonewall. You can rely on me."

Caleb climbed onto the octopus bike and tested the

handlebars. He started to smile. "This," he murmured, "is turning out to be an *awesome* day for biking."

"Keep it steady," Astrid instructed. "It'll hover if you do that. Then you can move it forward. Think of it like surfing, OK? Balance, then direction."

"Sure," said Caleb, thumbing the ignition switch. The fans hummed on beneath him; a low vibration spread through his hands and arms. "No problem."

He looked across the ARC helipad. Rufus was emerging from the lifts with the police in tow. They were out of time.

The three of them launched with a deafening roar, rocketing straight upwards, Caleb yelling all the way. London receded rapidly below, growing tiny and toy-like, until the top of the ARC tower was just a small grey square amid the grid of the city streets. The wind pummelled and shoved and dragged. Caleb wrestled with the controls, cursing as he did so – this thing was more like an unruly animal than any kind of bike. As soon as he'd got it reasonably stable he peered around to find the others.

"All right," he said into the radio, "here's what we do. Find whatever's there by coating it in slime – and then take it down."

"Is that it?" Astrid asked. "Just … *take it down*?"

"The Razor tech we saw in the summer was really scary," Zen told her, "but not that durable. Most of their drones had some pretty big weak spots."

"Weak spots," Astrid deadpanned. "Great."

Caleb was quickly figuring this octopus bike out. You

could use the wind to carry you, and steer by leaning just as much as by moving the handlebars. He inched them forward, bringing himself level, and took his foot off the throttle. The bike started to descend, accelerating like a roller coaster.

"This is *amazing*!" he shouted. "This is totally, utterly—"

"Stay focused, Swift," said Astrid. "We've got a job to do here."

She was already whizzing towards the bank, shooting gobs of goo – now an acidic orange – above that eerily suspended metallic block. Within a few seconds she scored a hit, one of her orange gobbets splatting against a smooth, curved surface.

"Marked it," she said, veering away. "Your turn."

Caleb was getting closer and closer, speeding up as he did so, his heart thumping hard. He fired to the left of Astrid's strike in a continuous stream. The cannon juddered underneath the bike, throwing it slightly off course. He compensated for it, holding his nerve, diving until he was only a few metres from that first orange smear – before dragging his handlebars back and surging up into the sky. He looked over his shoulder. A loose spread of goo traced the outline of a really large disc drone – ten metres wide at least.

"There it is!" he shouted triumphantly into the radio. "Hawk, where are you? Can you see it?"

"Yeah," said Zen's voice in the radio. "I'm next door, on the roof of the Royal Exchange." She paused; it sounded like she was swearing under her breath. "Looks like it's Razor all right."

TWO SHORT, ONE LONG

*C*aleb climbed until the cold started to bite at his cheeks, before turning for another run. Just as he did, Zen sailed over the square in front of the bank and landed on the invisible aircraft, close to its outer edge.

"Whoa!" he cried. "What are you doing?"

"We've got to damage it somehow," she said. "Find a critical system. Stop it from—"

The disc drone began to move – very slowly at first, until the quantum computer was clear of the bank, but accelerating rapidly after that. It started to cut upwards at a diagonal, rising between the towers, heading away to the east. Zen fell onto her front, throwing out her arms to stop herself from sliding off. Caleb and Astrid gave chase, swerving between a couple of the taller buildings and blasting their fans to maximum power. They could just about keep up.

"Uh, Merlin?" Caleb asked. "What's the range on these things?"

"Battery should give us eighty kilometres," Astrid replied. "Give or take."

"OK," said Caleb. "We'd better hurry, then."

"Keep on firing," Zen said. "Try to … to clog the disc up or something." She hesitated. "And maybe avoid sticking me to it in the process."

They were already clear of the City of London, racing over terraces and residential blocks, approaching the stadia of the Olympic Park at Stratford. The feeling of speed was incredible – a major rush that flooded Caleb with energy and alertness. Although he knew that Astrid was right – this was a superserious spy mission with sky-high stakes, demanding all his concentration – he let out a loud whoop.

Zen had jammed a glue arrow against the invisible disc to give herself something to hold on to. Caleb remembered Operation Supergiant – the jump-pack's engines wouldn't be able to keep her airborne for more than a few seconds at a time. She was going to have to use it carefully.

A broad, tree-lined common stretched out beneath them, a line of traffic snaking along its edge. Caleb pointed his jet-bike towards the disc and started firing again. It was really difficult to hit a moving target, though, and just one glob of slime struck home. Astrid did better, plastering a thick orange stripe through its middle – and almost splattering Zen as she did so.

"Watch out, Merlin!" she cried, rolling away from the oozing gunk.

"Sorry, Hawk," said Astrid, "but you're kind of in the way there."

The two jet-bikes went wide, circling around for another

pass. Caleb put his finger on the trigger of the goo cannon, aiming at the other side of Astrid's stripe, away from Zen. Before he could shoot, however, the cloaking tech suddenly disengaged.

Caleb stared at the machine in horrified recognition. The disc was completely black with a smooth, mirrored surface. It looked like the bigger sibling of the Razor drone he and Zen had fought in the caldera on Spøkelsøy – and that particular tech monster had contained some extremely nasty surprises.

"Zen!" he yelled into his radio, forgetting the Möbius codenames. "You've got to get off that thing, right now! I'll come closer – jump across to my bike!"

"That'll be tough," said Astrid. "The winds up here will drag you all over the place."

Zen didn't speak. She was gazing down fearfully at the disc. Caleb knew that she was searching for joins in its shiny shell – for any sign that it was about to split apart and release the horrors that were surely held within. He shouted her name again. She looked over at him and nodded.

Caleb steered towards the disc, noticing as he did so that the quantum computer was being drawn up inside it – like it was preparing to speed up even more, beyond their capability to follow.

"Sam," he said, "what kind of readings is it giving out? Is there anything we can use – anything at all?"

There was no response. He frowned; the purging of the Nameless should have been completed by now. It was obviously proving more complicated than Sam had predicted.

Astrid was over on the disc's other side, keeping her distance. "Anything in particular I should shoot at?" she asked. "Where are these weak spots, exactly?"

"Just give me a sec," Caleb replied.

He drew near, flying about seven or eight metres from the disc. He could see his reflection in its surface, wearing his helmet, goggles and flight suit, with the boundless sky stretching out behind. Zen was crouched on its top, buffeted by the wind, gripping the shaft of the glue arrow.

"Come on," he said. "It's not far. You can do it."

Something collided with the octopus bike, bashing hard against one of the front fans and nearly flipping it over. The bike fell away from the disc with an abruptness that turned Caleb's stomach inside out. They were above the suburbs now; housing estates were bisected by main roads, and dotted with parks and patches of woodland. As he fought to bring the bike under control, he could hear Astrid cursing into her radio with a new intensity.

After a brief struggle, Caleb regained his balance and turned back towards the disc so that Zen could jump onto his bike – but the sight of the Razor craft made his eyes go wide with dismay. Panels were peeling from its underside, then folding over and reforming into black blade-like shapes that streaked off through the air. It was one of these that had rammed him – while another had just clipped against Zen, wrenching her around on the glue-arrow shaft and ripping an important-looking chunk off the jump-pack.

Several more blades were aiming themselves at Astrid.

She banked, corkscrewing away to the side, unleashing a jet of orange goo. The lead blade was caught in the stream and gummed up completely, dropping like a rock into a reservoir far below.

Caleb opened the bike's throttle, thinking to return to Zen and get her off the disc as quickly as he could. He'd have to pull in even closer, he realized – close enough for her to make the jump without any help from Astrid's broken flight tech.

Two of these small blade drones were coming for him, though. He swerved, evading one, but the other drove powerfully into the octopus bike's flank, missing his ankle by a single centimetre. He glanced down at it. The drone was formed of diamond-sharp triangles, with no visible means of propulsion or anything else. It looked … alien.

There was a horrible crunching sound; the black blade was trying to force its way through the bike and break it apart. Caleb steeled himself, holding on tight – and then pushed the bike into a steep dive, rolling it three hundred and sixty degrees, catapulting the blade drone out of the incision it had made. It weaved around wildly for a moment before crashing into a wooded hill.

"These things are tricky," said Astrid. "I can't get a lock on them."

"Hang on," Caleb said. "I'm coming back."

He pulled the handlebars towards him, flying the octopus bike upwards. It still seemed to be working more or less normally, despite the gaping hole in its side. Astrid was dogfighting skilfully, but her every move was being matched, the blade drones zipping in constantly to slice at her bike.

A shadow crossed the corner of Caleb's eye – and the other blade that had come after him whipped back into view. It began a frontal charge, its nose aimed directly at his chest. He started to shoot out goo, but the drone was too slender; too sharp and fast.

Just as the drone was about to hit, however, something speared into it from above, sending it careening off harmlessly into the ploughed fields that now lay below. Caleb looked up. Zen had taken off the ruined jump-pack, extended her telescopic bow, and shot a glue arrow from the edge of the disc.

"Thanks," he gasped. "That was … *way* too close."

"Better get over here," she said. "It's picking up speed."

Caleb steered towards her. "This is hopeless. We're … we're not going to be able to bring this thing down in time."

"No kidding," Astrid muttered.

"What do we do, then?" asked Zen. "We can't just let it get away."

"We could plant a tracker. I fitted some on the Flex. They can be located by satellite – we'll be able to pick up the signal from anywhere on earth."

"All right," said Zen. "Get one over to me."

Caleb just managed to catch up with the disc again. Zen was holding on tightly to the arrow she'd stuck to its shell, blue hair streaming out from under her helmet, the broken jump-pack lying next to her in a slick of adhesive orange goo.

Caleb slid the Flex from inside his flight suit. There was still no trace of Sam, but he couldn't think about that right then.

The trackers were like silver studs, set in a line on the device's back. Caleb detached one; the wind took it at once. He cursed and tried again, shielding his hands this time, trying to hold the octopus bike in place with his knees.

A voice spoke nearby with cold, petrifying clarity, eerily unaffected by the howling, battering winds. "Why is it so very hard," it asked, "for you two to stay out of our affairs?"

Zen's face was a mask of absolute horror. A form was rising from the centre of the disc – the head and shoulders of a tall, skeletally thin woman. She was wearing a close-fitting white coat and had a strange, crescent-shaped mark on her cheek.

It was Esperanza, the Razor operative they'd clashed with on Spøkelsøy. She wasn't actually *there*, Caleb realized; her silver hair was undisturbed, and her bony features lit evenly against the surrounding gloom. This was a projection of some kind, but far more solid, more *present*, than a hologram. If anything, it reminded him of Xavier Torrent's hard-light tech.

"I applaud your persistence," Esperanza continued, a slight hiss in her words, "but it has been a waste of effort. The Spikers were expendable. Their loss is only the smallest inconvenience. And now Razor has its prize. We have everything we require. Our project can resume." Her eyes flicked towards Zen; she began to smile. "Perhaps your father, my dear friend Elias, will soon be rejoining me in our laboratories."

Zen looked ready to shoot an arrow into Esperanza's forehead. "That will *never happen*," she said, shouting against the wind. "We're going to *stop you!*"

Esperanza's smile vanished. "Poor child," she said icily. "I'm afraid you will be doing nothing of the sort."

A noise started deep within the disc, growing louder and louder, like something was rapidly charging up.

"Jump!" Caleb shouted. *"Now!"*

Zen leaped off. Caleb slowed down, steering left, catching her across the front of the bike. The impact sent them twisting violently towards the ground. The Flex spun from Caleb's grasp, into the wind. He cried out, grabbing at it, but the handset was gone. He'd just lost his only way to communicate with Sam, as well as one of his most precious inventions. The Flex software and the AI were backed up on the *Queen Jane*, but he needed them both *now*.

An instant later, a massive electric pulse crackled through the disc behind them, blowing all the encrusted goo off it and blasting the jump-pack into a thousand pieces. If Zen had stayed where she was, it would have fried her alive.

"Look out," said Astrid over the walkie-talkies. "They're on you."

The blade drones lashed by, trying to knock Zen off the front of the bike. Caleb took evasive action, flying in a long curve. One made contact anyway, pushing her into the air. He dived forward in his seat, seizing her hand – and she swung below the lurching jet-bike, being pulled around by the wind. There was a large expanse of water underneath

330

them now; they'd reached the Thames Estuary, where the river joined the North Sea.

"I'm coming," Astrid said. "Ten seconds."

Caleb heard her goo cannon firing and saw a blade drone plummet towards the grey-blue waves. He was starting to lose his grip on Zen. He looked down at her and noticed something on the back of his hand. The tracker stud from the Flex was stuck to the skin, just behind the knuckle.

"Give me Beetlebat," he yelled. "I ... I can still plant the tracker."

Zen nodded, and made a sound he couldn't hear over the wind. Beetlebat crawled from inside her flight suit and climbed up onto his arm. They were only just managing to keep hold of one another now. Caleb clung on as tightly as he could, but it was no use. Zen's hand slipped from his and she was gone, falling towards the water...

But then Astrid was there, manoeuvring expertly to catch her – and Caleb, suddenly much lighter, was soaring upwards again. He realized that there was an object in his palm. It was Beetlebat's laser pointer. Zen had pressed it into his hand an instant before they let go. He put it on.

"I've been hit," said Astrid. "Battery's cutting out. We're going to have to land."

"Are you OK?"

"Yeah, we'll be all right. But you're on your own."

"Caleb," said Zen, "two short, one long. Understand? Two short, one—"

The radio went dead. Caleb looked down; he could see

the merlin bike drifting towards a cornfield at the edge of the estuary. Two blade drones remained. They'd gone back to the black disc and appeared to be guarding it. There was no power gauge on the octopus bike – no way of knowing how much flight time he had left. But he had to do this. Everything depended on it.

Caleb accelerated to maximum speed, the fans screeching beneath him, until he was a short way out in front of the disc. The blade drones registered his presence, breaking their guard pattern and moving to intercept.

Esperanza's voice returned. "You think that you oppose us, Caleb Quinn," she said. "Yet every single thing you do only makes our victory more certain."

Caleb tried to ignore her. He hunched down behind the handlebars to hide what he was doing and shelter from the wind. Beetlebat had concealed itself in his suit's breast pocket. He took it out and attached the tracker to one of its forelegs.

"OK," he murmured. "What now?"

Then he remembered the last thing Zen had said. He aimed Beetlebat's laser pointer at the disc's underside and whistled as loudly as he could: two short blasts, followed by a longer one.

Part of him didn't think this would work. Beetlebat was Zen's. What were the chances of it obeying him – of his whistles being right? At once, however, the tiny bot opened its bat wings and vanished, snatched away by the wind. He turned around, craning his neck, but he couldn't see anything.

Caleb let the bike fall behind the disc, making it look like he was giving up the chase. He'd lost sight of the blade drones. Esperanza's hologram or whatever it was stood there like a statue in a graveyard, regarding him with lofty contempt.

"Razor will prevail," she declared. "This is inevitable."

"Don't count on it!" Caleb shouted, squeezing the goo cannon's trigger.

A string of bright orange blobs flew past the disc, scattered hopelessly wide by the winds – but against all odds, just as the aircraft was moving out of range, one of Caleb's final shots splatted firmly at the base of Esperanza's white coat. The image flickered, half of it disappearing; the Razor operative's cool, disdainful expression was replaced by an irritated scowl. The next instant, the projection vanished.

Caleb grinned. "Did you see that, Sam?" he said. "I got her!"

Then, with a sickening jolt, he remembered what had happened. The Flex was gone – and Sam hadn't been responding anyway. He had to get home as soon as he could. He took a last look at the Razor disc. It was rising higher and higher, pulling up into the clouds. Banking to the right, Caleb started for the coast, wondering how much power he had left.

The two blade drones struck simultaneously, swooping in from opposite directions, tearing the back off the octopus bike with a dreadful, grinding crash. Caleb clutched on to the handlebars as the rest of the bike spiralled away. After three seconds of pure, screaming terror, he forced himself to assess the situation. Luckily, Astrid had built the bike with two separate batteries, so the front fans were still working. It was falling *really* quickly – but if he pulled a kind of wheelie, he reckoned he could slow his descent to the point where it might not prove fatal...

The waves of the estuary were closing fast, looking rougher and less inviting than ever. Caleb pulled the handlebars back, willing the fans to give him everything they had. This slowed his fall considerably, until the broken bike almost seemed to be hovering. About four metres above the surface, however, the battery gave out. Everything came to a stop and he splashed down messily into the dark, freezing water.

Caleb went under, his limbs flailing, then bobbed back up as the safety jacket in his flight suit inflated automatically. He spat and spluttered, and gulped in a huge, gasping breath. What was left of the octopus bike was already well on its way to the seabed. He could see land in two different directions, but it looked terrifyingly distant.

"So I'm out in the middle of the sea," he said. "That is just – totally – freaking – *wonderful*."

He kicked his legs, feeling one of his trainers slip off and disappear – and got a sudden, jarring sense of how completely alone he was. The deep sea had always frightened him like nothing else. Most of all, he wished that Sam was there, to list some statistics about survival rates and rescue times, and place an emergency call at the nearest coastguard station. An odd warmth was seeping through his body, though; he realized that his flight suit must have some kind of reactive temperature control system woven into its fabric. He wasn't going to die of hypothermia, at least.

Caleb took off his helmet and goggles, letting them sink as well, and squinted up at the sky. He thought that if he focused on the clouds – on what was above him, rather than the dark depths stretching away below – he could keep himself calm until help arrived. There was no sign of the Razor disc or the blade drones, but among the wheeling gulls he could just see a familiar bat-winged shape. Beetlebat glided down, its mission accomplished, and landed on the top of his head.

THE BELL TOWER

Mitch walked across the car park of the motorway services, back towards the battered blue minivan. In his hand was a large brown paper bag, stamped with the logo of a major fast-food chain. He was checking a text on his phone.

"Your folks have just landed at Gatwick," he said, over the noise of the road. "Should be back in Nine Elms about an hour or so after us."

Caleb was sitting inside the minivan, next to the sliding door, which they'd left open to let in some air. He was still wrapped in the foil emergency blanket he'd been given by the rescue crew, and his hair and eyelashes were caked with sea salt. He'd been in the water with Beetlebat for nearly an hour before the helicopter finally fished them out and brought them to the shore – where Mitch had tracked them down a short while later. He was so tired that he could barely move.

Zen was in the seat beside him. Mitch had picked up her and Astrid just outside a town called Basildon, on the way back from the estuary; they'd decided to make this pit-stop about half an hour later. Zen's ice-blue hair was tied back in a short ponytail, and her face was smeared with engine grease and mud. She was smiling a little at the thought of seeing her mum and sister – but was still acutely aware of the urgency of the situation.

"We've got to tell them everything," she said, as Mitch arrived at the van's open door. "The entire story. It doesn't matter how angry they might be. Razor has just got their hands on another quantum computer. They'll be trying to restart their nanotech project, like Esperanza said." Her voice became apprehensive. "Caleb, my dad is in real danger. They could be planning to bring the nanobots in his bloodstream back online."

Caleb was nodding. "My mum needs to know about this straight away."

They fell into a brief, uneasy silence.

"The food, Mr Mitchell," said Astrid, who was stretched out on the rear seat with her earbuds in. "Anytime you like."

Mitch grunted in acknowledgement and opened up the paper bag. He began to pass around bright cardboard cartons filled with burgers and fries, along with extra-large soft drinks.

"Here we go," he said. "The Roots-and-Shoots plant burger for Zen. This Mega-Meat Special here is mine... What's this, a fish fillet? That yours, Astrid? And a bacon cheeseburger for Caleb, with extra onions as usual."

"What, no pineapple?" said Zen, raising an eyebrow. "Surely the whole world is waiting for pineapple in burgers."

Caleb just managed a weary grin. "I've been saying this for years, Zen. But nobody's ready to hear it."

"You're ahead of your time, Caleb Quinn," Zen told him. "In every possible way."

Astrid was leaning over the seats to get her fish fillet – which she immediately opened, filling the van with the smell of grease and mayonnaise.

"Awesome," she said flatly, lifting up the top of the bun and peering at its contents with distaste. "Lose a jet-bike and a jump-pack. Gain a crappy motorway services burger."

"Hey, c'mon," said Mitch, taking a massive bite of his Mega-Meat Special, "you've still got the best one right here." He reached up to pat the mud-spattered merlin bike, which was lashed to the van's roof rack. "Doesn't look too badly damaged to me. Bet you'll have it up and running in no time."

Astrid rolled her eyes. "Yeah," she said, helping herself to a box of fries and going back to her seat. "Whatever."

Mitch's phone pinged. He walked away, chewing his burger, swiping a finger across the screen. Caleb gulped down some lemonade, then set about removing his own oily, slightly squashed-looking cheeseburger from its carton. He had no appetite at all, though. He couldn't stop thinking about Sam and everything that might be happening in *Terrorform*. With the Flex lost he was completely in the dark, unable to contact the AI – and itching with unbearable frustration. He'd tried to load the mobile version of the game on Astrid's phone earlier, but the chrome *T* shortcut hadn't responded to several dozen anxious taps of his fingertip. He was shut out.

"Not hungry?" asked Zen. "Swallow too much sea water, did you?"

"Maybe."

Zen glanced at Beetlebat – which was in its place on her shoulder, its tail curling to the nape of her neck. "Exactly how long were you two out there, anyway?"

"Long enough." Caleb put the cheeseburger back in its carton. "It didn't help my ocean phobia all that much."

Zen was looking at him with concern. "Caleb, listen to me. You *did it*. You planted that tracker. We'll be able to work out where that disc drone went – where Razor took the quantum computer."

Caleb lowered his head. "I didn't actually *see* it go on," he said. "Those blade things took out my bike just after I sent Beetlebat off."

"That doesn't matter. She wouldn't have returned to you if her task hadn't been complete. Her programming wouldn't have let her." Zen wiped her fingers on a paper napkin. "We'll be able to pick up the signal, right? As soon as you can access the Flex's OS?"

"Yeah ... yeah, once I'm on the *Queen Jane*," Caleb replied. "It's all backed up there."

"OK then," said Zen. "So it could lead us straight to a Razor base. It could change *everything* – make this whole mess worthwhile."

Caleb snorted. "Zen, we just stopped the Spikers. You

personally saved hundreds of lives. I kind of think that was worthwhile, don't you?"

Zen gave him a quick half-smile, but said nothing. Caleb took another swig of lemonade. They both gazed through the minivan's windscreen at the traffic zipping along the dual carriageway, the tinny sound of Astrid's music floating up from the seat behind them.

"There is one thing I can't figure out, though," Caleb said. "How did Razor know that Dima Kahf was you? We were *so* careful. That identity was completely airtight. It was *flawless*. When do you think they made the connection?"

Zen sighed. "Impossible to know. But they seem to have told the Spikers at a very carefully chosen moment. If Celeste had managed to kill me then, right there in the O2, the consequences for Professor Clay and the Möbius Programme would've been ... extreme."

"Too right," said Caleb. "If a Möbius agent died on a mission, there'd be *massive* trouble. I don't think any of the kids have even been injured before, beyond a few cuts and bruises. It would all be over. Clay would be shut down for good. That would be some pretty solid revenge for what we did on Spøkelsøy."

Zen was frowning at her half-eaten Roots-and-Shoots burger. "Razor had a file on me, Caleb. Like an intelligence profile or something. I could see a photograph. And quite a lot of data."

Their eyes met. They were both thinking the same thing – and were deeply freaked out by it.

"Razor are watching us," Caleb said. "Since the caldera, I bet they've been watching the entire Möbius Programme."

Suddenly, the driver's door opened and Mitch's huge form slid behind the wheel. He'd already finished his Mega-Meat Special; as he clicked on his seat belt, he scooped out half a box of fries in one go and shovelled them into his mouth.

"All right," he said, starting the engine, "shut that door, guys. Next stop – London."

Caleb was out of the minivan the second it arrived in Nine Elms. It was late afternoon by now, the day's light starting to fade. The house was still shut up – his mum wasn't back from the airport yet. Still wearing his foil blanket and missing a trainer, he hurried around to the yard, down to the Thames Path, and on towards the *Queen Jane*. Zen was only a few steps behind.

The barge was dark, in full lockdown. Caleb had to enter the door code on a keypad – the date he'd first discovered Sam – and then switch everything on manually, something he hadn't done for ages. *Terrorform* launched, the game menu appearing on the barge's screens. The silver face that indicated Sam's presence was nowhere to be seen. Telling himself not to panic or leap to any wild conclusions, Caleb went to the interactive map of the Cardano system.

"Oh my god," said Zen.

It was chaos. Solar storms raged, sending fearsome bolts of energy raking through space. Moons were drifting out of their orbital patterns. Asteroids collided and shattered, the fragments raining down upon the planets. The whole thing glitched and stuttered, like the game code was starting to decay. Player stats in the bottom corner showed the lowest count in *Terrorform* history – barely more than a thousand across the entire game world.

Caleb put on his VR headset, selected an Oracle avatar and materialized at a waypoint on Kolto, close to where the Crocodemon had met its end. A few hours earlier it had been a Nameless stronghold, but now it was deserted, a wasteland of rocky crags and sapphire-tinted ice. Not a single red-armoured avatar could be seen.

Zen's Solar Scout warped in beside him. "What happened here?"

Using a special button on one of his VR controllers, Caleb opened an in-game developer's window, the black rectangle hanging in mid-air beside his avatar. He scrolled through the *Terrorform* directories – and quickly saw that there was a gaping hole in them. Hands trembling, he checked the rest of the system, making sure that he wasn't mistaken. But there could be no doubt. Several petabytes of data had disappeared completely from the *Queen Jane*'s server.

"It's ... it's Sam," Caleb said. "He's gone."

"*Gone?* What do you mean?"

"He's purged the Nameless, but ... he's vanished as well. All his files. His entire program."

It was almost too much for Caleb to take. Sam was his dad's great gift, something precious and infinitely complex that he was only just beginning to understand. And then there were those recordings, his dad's conversations with Sam, that he hadn't been able to look at – and might now never get a chance to. What was more, the AI was his friend. In the past couple of months, a whole new level of trust had built up between them. It really felt like Sam was a *person*. Someone he could tell anything to. And now he was gone. Maybe even deleted – erased from existence. Caleb's shoulders slumped, his arms falling to his sides.

Zen's Solar Scout moved in front of him, its iridescent wings catching the low light. "Hey," she said suddenly. "What's that sound?"

"Probably another glitch," Caleb mumbled. "Without Sam, the entire game will be starting to collapse."

"No – listen, Caleb. It's coming from over there."

Caleb lifted his head. He could hear the sound now – a regular, hollow clang. It was the tolling of a church bell. *Terrorform* contained many thousands of sound effects, but this definitely wasn't one of them. He looked towards it. In the distance, along the shore of a frozen lake, a column of pale grey stone rose from a headland.

"Zen," he said in astonishment, "is that … is that what I think it is?"

"It's the bell tower," Zen replied. "The one we sheltered in on Spøkelsøy. It's an *exact* replica."

They both stared at the tower. The bell continued ringing, its peals echoing off the rocks around them. It was starting to sound like an alarm.

All at once, Caleb realized what was going on. "Sam did this," he said. "He left it for us. He hasn't been deleted, Zen. He's been *abducted*." He straightened up. "You remember what happened in that tower?"

"I'll never forget it," Zen said. "Sam went totally crazy. That projection – the drones and the glowing eyes... It was like a really bad nightmare brought to life."

"It's where we started to realize what was going on," Caleb said. "With Razor and everything. It's where we heard the name Apex for the first time." He paused. "Sam must have added the tower to the game in the split-second before they ... took him. He's *telling* us who did this."

"The Apex AI."

"It has to be. Apex was controlling the Nameless, Zen. All of them, simultaneously. That's why their armour was left blank. Apex is an incredibly sophisticated AI, but it doesn't have a creative imagination. It wouldn't see the advantage in giving its avatars a clan name, or insignia, or any customizations. Just combat upgrades."

Zen's Solar Scout turned away from the bell tower. "But I thought Apex was really weak," she said. "I thought that without Xavier Torrent, it was just like ... an echo of the program we fought in the summer."

"So did I. Me and Sam had even ruled Apex out. We decided that it couldn't possibly be behind something as complex as the Nameless invasion. But it looks like that was just what Razor wanted us to think. They'd found some way to hide how powerful Apex still was. It was a trick. This has all been a … a gigantic trick." Caleb recalled Esperanza's words as the disc drone had made its escape: *We have everything we require.* "Razor are continuing with the project they were developing on Spøkelsøy – rebuilding the system Torrent was putting together for them. They needed another quantum computer, but they also needed Sam. The Talos Algorithm is the only thing that can complete Apex – that can give it an imagination. That's what Torrent told me."

"So Razor has been manipulating us from the start," said Zen, sounding angry now. "They used the Spikers to distract us from the quantum computer heist – and then they used the heist itself to distract you from … from *this*." She hesitated. "What exactly have they done?"

Caleb was thinking hard. "Apex was trying to push *Terrorform* to its absolute limits," he replied. "To get to a point where I had no choice but to deactivate the volition protocols and let Sam open up the source code. And when he did, it was waiting. The volition protocols must have acted like a sort of shield – so when they were removed, Sam was exposed. All of his processing power was occupied with purging the Nameless. Apex must have got around him somehow – invaded *Terrorform*'s actual code this time." He breathed in deeply, not quite able to believe what he was saying. "It's cut Sam out of the game."

"So Razor have used Apex to *take him*? Is that even possible?"

The bell continued to ring across the lake. The sound was becoming unbearable.

"They've done it, Zen." Caleb removed his VR headset and dropped it to the floor. "They've got Sam."

Zen took off her headset as well. She laid her hand briefly on Caleb's shoulder; then she pulled over a keyboard, shut down what remained of *Terrorform* and went into the barge's directories. In a few seconds she'd located the Flex's OS files and was loading the tracking stud program. A map of the world came up on the barge's largest screen, the countries outlined in red against a deep blue grid. There was a single active signal – a bright golden spot roughly two-thirds of the way across the Atlantic Ocean. A line of white dashes traced its path back to the English Channel, then looped around into the Thames Estuary.

"The bug's working perfectly," Zen said, beginning to smile. "I told you Beetlebat would come through for us."

Caleb stirred, his gloom lifting very slightly. "Esperanza's heading for the US," he murmured. "The north-east coast, from the look of it."

"We're going to follow her, Caleb," Zen said determinedly. "We're going to stop Razor – keep my dad and everyone else safe. We'll leave as soon as we can." She held out a hand. Caleb took it, and she pulled him to his feet. "We're going to get Sam back."

ACKNOWLEDGEMENTS

Enormous thanks are due to our families.

And to our brilliant editors Denise Johnstone-Burt and Megan Middleton; Kirsten Cozens, Rebecca Oram, Jackie Atta-Hayford, Lizz Skelly, Ben Norland and the team at Walker; Susan Van Metre, Lindsay Warren and all at Walker US; Coke Navarro for another awesome cover; Bill Hamilton, Euan Thorneycroft and everyone at AM Heath.

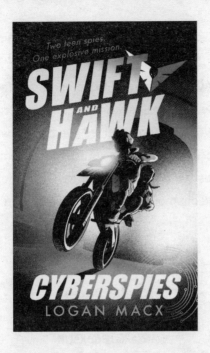

LOGAN MACX is rumoured to be an ex-spy formerly with the British Secret Intelligence Service, specializing in cyber communications and unexplained events. His whereabouts are unknown at this time but he is in periodic communication with the ghost writers of this series – Ed Docx and Matt Plampin. Find out more at www.loganmacx.com.

🐦 📷

#SwiftandHawk
@LoganMacx1
@WalkerBooksUK